From the Heart
The Sweetbriar Mountain Series

Nora Everly

To Piper,
I finished this book because of your encouragement.

To my readers,
Thank you for being here!

Chapter 1
Violet

"I don't have enough coffee or middle fingers for today."

Everything that could possibly go wrong in a day had already gone wrong and the clock had yet to strike eight a.m. I woke up confused and cranky well after my alarm had gone off and after finally making it outside to leave for work, I was greeted by a flat tire. It only spiraled further down the crapper from there.

Currently, I was back at home sitting in my car with my head pounding from what was sure to become a migraine. I was also covered in almost dry, sticky foam courtesy of my hell-bent-on-betrayal espresso machine and some unruly steamed milk. But I had known something was about to go extra-horrid-change-your-life-wrong the second I had approached my driveway and saw my husband's latest Porsche still parked in the driveway—with his secretary's little red Honda parked next to it. Apparently, my coffee shop's espresso machine wasn't the only thing in the mood to stab me in the back this morning.

1

I pulled in behind the Honda, shut off the engine and stormed out of my car. All I wanted was a shower, some fricking Advil, and maybe a damn nap. It looked like I was going to get a whole lot more than that. I was about to see something horrible. I could feel it.

How do you know when a marriage is over?

Several times over the years, I'd tried to recall the moment—or even a ballpark time period—when my marriage went from happy to . . . less happy. From shaky to in serious trouble. But I could never do it. Tom and I had loved each other once; that was a fact. But somewhere along the way, we'd grown apart. Hence why I'd made the choice to soon file for divorce. I had decided that February 1 would be the day to tell our sons. I didn't want to taint the holiday season for them.

A wave of nausea hit me as I approached the porch and the *snick* of my key in the lock made me flinch, but I persevered and stepped into the foyer anyway. After deciding to head up the back stairs, I tossed my keys on the kitchen island and tried to mentally prepare for whatever I was about to discover.

Choking back bile, I started up the stairs. I didn't want to catch him in the act, yet I couldn't force myself to turn around and leave. The car in the driveway was my first clue —of today, at least. The knock-off Louis Vuitton bag I spied sitting on the stairs was the second.

I continued down the hall to our bedroom. Tom and I had moved into this house almost twelve years ago. The same year our twin boys started kindergarten and I opened my coffee shop in town. My pregnancy had been a surprise, but Tom had insisted it was meant to be. After we got married, I left college to have the boys and found a job as an educational assistant. Tom had been in his junior year and gone on to graduate, then worked his way up to owning his own real estate agency right here in Sweetbriar, Oregon. He was ambitious and determined to make a good life for us, and he did it. But he had developed expensive taste over the years and the more money he made, the more his sweet disposition had disappeared. Sadly, he replaced it with a big-ass ego, an air of condescension, and an overabundance of concern about what other people thought of him. Keeping up with the Joneses was not good enough for Tom. He preferred to lord his success over everyone we knew. He wanted to be the only Jones in town.

A finite number of happy family smiles greeted me as I passed the portraits and school pictures lining the hallway. I ended up standing in front of our wedding photo, hung in an inset arch, right next to our bedroom door.

Who was that girl?

Hope shone in her eyes while two baby boys grew in her belly. Tom had worn a rented tuxedo and an adorable, sweet smile that I hadn't seen in far too many years to count.

"Tom! Tom! Tommy!" a woman moaned. It sounded like his secretary. I kept forgetting her name. Or maybe I had just subconsciously refused to remember it. It had been clear upon meeting her that her goal was to end up right here—beneath my snake-in-the-grass husband.

"Bethany, baby—" he grunted.

Bethany. That's it.

Through the partially open door, I could hear the rhythmic squeak of the box spring and the slap of his hips against hers.

Cheating on me in my own damn house.

As if in a trance, I pushed the door all the way open to see them, naked, right in the middle of the bed. They faced the mirror over the dresser, too wrapped up in the obscene show they were putting on for themselves to notice they had an audience.

"Tommy. Please. Please. Please," she begged as she writhed beneath him.

He collapsed forward onto her back, kissed her neck, and said, "I love you, babydoll."

My stomach twisted into a knot as time stood still. I let out a gasp, and suddenly trying to recall the precise day things started to change between us didn't matter anymore. My marriage was now officially over.

February could eff right off. No one cheats on me.

He rose to his knees when he heard me gasp. "Violet! Shit!"

We locked eyes for one brief moment until he scrambled for his robe at the foot of the bed and put it on. Almost eighteen years of marriage and all he had to say was *"Violet! Shit!"*?

"What are you doing here?" He looked annoyed.

"Excuse me?" I wasn't the one banging someone else in our freaking marital bed on my brand-new sheets. "Uh, I live here, and I have a headache." Maybe I should leave. But I still couldn't make myself move. My marriage had gone up in flames. But here I stood, allowing myself to feel the burn.

"Another headache? Really?" he scoffed.

"Oops," Bethany chimed in with a satisfied smirk on her face. She rose to her knees next to Tom, then snatched his T-shirt from the edge of the bed to put on. "Maybe I'll let you two talk for a few minutes. Do you need to talk to her, honey?" *Yuck*, baby talk. And, who in the heck does this girl think she is?

"Yes. I do." He nodded as his eyes darted swiftly between the two of us. Caught between past and present. Wife and mistress.

She kissed his neck and smirked at me when he sucked in a breath. "Don't forget who you belong to now," she whispered as she got up to saunter into my bathroom.

Would fire be enough to get skank off my towels?

Despite all my instincts telling me to get the hell out of there, I stood still with my temper simmering beneath the surface. It pushed all other feelings to the back burner, and I was grateful for it.

After a nervous sigh, he finally addressed me. "Violet, have you checked your email today? You always check it first thing in the morning. Don't let your *headaches* start affecting how you run your business—"

"What? Email? No. My morning has been a total disaster." Each word he said fueled my anger but, like usual, something held me back from expressing it. Later, I was sure there would be other feelings—humiliation, grief for the loss of the family I had fought so hard to keep, possibly nostalgia, and maybe worry for my boys and our future. But for now, rage was working for me. It kept me on my feet, and I needed to stay upright so I could leave with my dignity intact.

He drove a hand into his hair and let out a huff. "I explained everything in the email. You shouldn't be here right now. I didn't intend for you to see this. But now that you've just seen me with Bethany you should know that we're in love, Vi. And this isn't just an affair, or a fling. I want a divorce so I can marry her. I thought maybe you could pack your stuff this weekend—"

"Are you crazy?" He'd gone crazy. Absolutely, totally insane. "*You* pack your stuff this weekend. I'm not leaving my house," I argued, because what the hell? We had sons together. This was our *family's* house.

"We wouldn't have this house if it weren't for me. You

can't afford to keep this place on your own, and you know it. The boys can stay with me until you find your own place."

I was not about to leave my boys with him and his new *girlfriend*. I panicked and swiftly changed course. My sons were more important to me than staying in this house. "I guess you've got it all figured out. Fine, I'll leave. But I'm taking the boys with me. And this argument isn't over."

"Obviously, it's not over. We'll need to file for divorce," he huffed indignantly. "Fine, great. You're right, they should be with you. I'm taking Bethany up the mountain to ski for the weekend anyway—which I also told you about in the email—so you can pack up your stuff and a few things for the boys while I'm gone."

"Skiing? I thought you had a real-estate conference in Portland." My face fell. *I am so stupid.*

He shook his head. "I really didn't want you to find out like this . . ." The statement hung in the air as if there were nothing else to say.

"So you sent an email? A freaking email—*Gah!* You are unbelievable. I know we were having problems, but to end it this way? After all these years together? Cheating on me? And a fucking email? You couldn't have just sat down and talked to me and asked for a divorce like a decent person?"

His head dropped. "Vi, I don't know what to say."

"Oh, I don't know—you could try *I'm sorry?*"

Motherfucker.

Morbid curiosity kept me asking questions I didn't really want the answers to. "How long has this been going on?" I demanded.

His eyes darted to the bathroom door. "Physically? A little over six months."

Physically.

"Six months," I repeated on a breath. It had been almost

a year since we had been intimate. Plus, two years of marriage counseling that clearly didn't take. Too much time and money had been spent on dates and dinners with my husband that, according to our marriage counselor, would put the fire back into our marriage. But I had been wasting my time trying to rekindle what had already been a pile of ash.

I looked to the floor with thoughts of STDs and tiny little Toms running around Sweetbriar darting through my mind. "Are there more? I mean, other than Bethany?" The fact that I hadn't lost my shit yet was astonishing. Either I was stronger than I thought, or it would all come out later in some kind of epic lady-tantrum. Hopefully, I would be alone whenever it occurred.

Earnest eyes met mine for a brief second and I recognized the man I used to know. "No! Just her. I swear, Vi. It's only ever been Bethany." I studied his face with narrowed eyes. I believed him. But I would make a doctor's appointment anyway, just in case. I'd obviously been wrong about him before.

I needed to get out of here. After spinning on my heel, I crossed the hallway to the stairs to leave.

Sudden realization halted my progress, and I froze at the top of the stairs with a bitter laugh. All my plans revolved around stupid, freaking February 1. My sister Rose had just gotten married on New Year's Eve and I'd been planning to buy her house and move in with my boys. But not yet, dammit! I needed more time to figure out what to say to them, and she needed to finish moving her stuff out. *Crap!*

My bed was tainted. I could never sleep in it again. This whole house was dirty with betrayal and filled up with lies. The filth would be impossible to scrub away. There was no way I could stay here even if he had agreed to be the one to leave. Tears clouded my vision as I rushed down the stairs, stopping in the kitchen to grab some Advil and a glass of water. My hands shook with frustrated rage as I filled a glass at the sink.

Had *she* been in my kitchen?

Drank from my glasses?

Eaten off the plates we'd picked out together?

I slammed the glass down to the countertop, onto the lovely grey granite we'd chosen together five years ago when we'd remodeled the kitchen. We were happy five years ago. *Weren't we?*

Was anything real? And why was I so upset when I had planned to leave him anyway?

Oh yeah.

The humiliation.

The younger, blonder, boobier, secretarial cheating situation that had made my life into a cliché.

I was about to be gossiped about *so hard*.

My heart pounded in my ears as my breath grew shallow. Forget Advil—I needed my migraine prescription and a dark room. But the pills were upstairs in the bathroom currently occupied by my husband's secretary-slash-mistress.

And my bedroom? *Ew*.

I had to get out of here. But I had *nowhere to go*.

I had tolerated the little digs about my coffee shop, my body, my*self* that he'd dished my way over the last few years. I did it for my boys, to keep our family together. I'd put up with it until I couldn't do it anymore. But this was *beyond too much*.

I choked on a sob and swiped my hand under my eyes to catch the tears, wincing as the overhead light caught on my rings. A gold wedding band, the tiny speck of a diamond engagement ring Tom had proposed with, and on top, the three huge diamonds he had insisted I wear when he felt he'd finally made it. I used to enjoy seeing them sitting pretty on my hand, a little reminder of the family we had created together and how far we had come when no one thought we would last. I extended my hand out to look one last time before slipping them off and placing them on the counter. All the while memories—happy, sad, and everything in between—swirled around me as my eyes darted over the house. This was like a death. My life as I had known it was over, and it was flashing before my eyes.

I slammed my eyes shut and collapsed on one of the bar stools at the island to rest my cheek against the cool granite, just for a minute. I needed to get the pounding in my head to stop before I left. My heart raced and grew burdened with sudden stress as it sank inside my body.

I had been planning my exit.

I wanted a divorce.

What in the frick was wrong with me?

"Oh, honey. Don't become a cliché. A sad, scorned little woman." Bethany grinned at me as she swanned down the stairs. Clearly, she thought she had won a great prize in Tom. Sure, he had oodles of money, a nice car, and this huge house in town. He had all the necessary requirements one looks for whilst digging for gold. But she had missed one pertinent fact: she was destined to become *me*, and *he* would eventually find somebody to replace *her*. The circle of life for cheating assholes.

I ignored her. Nothing I could say would get rid of that smug, smackable look on her face, and I wasn't willing to expend the effort on a catfight. He wasn't worth it, and I was beginning to wonder if he ever had been. I stood up and grabbed my purse.

"Bye now," she said with the bitchy smirk she always gave me whenever I saw her in Tom's office or my coffee shop.

I muttered under my breath as I left, "Just wait until he cheats on you, dumbass."

I had some of my headache prescription in my office. I could hide out in there until I decided where to go for the night, or until school let out and I had to tell the boys. Their relationship with their dad was already on shaky ground; this would make the bottom drop out from underneath it. My boys weren't completely oblivious to what went on in this house, no matter how hard I had tried to cover it up or brush it away with jokes and deflection. Our family therapist was making a fortune off my guilt and inability to just freaking leave.

Without sparing her another look, I found my keys on the table and headed to the front door. If she wanted him, she could have him. How long would it take until he started running her down like he'd been doing to me over the last few years? I almost felt sorry for her, but her motivations had been clear since the moment I'd met her, so I was okay with letting her reap what she had oh so carefully sewn.

I was done with him. Finally.

D-O-N-E. Done.

I slammed the door behind me as I left and immediately regretted it when my head started pounding again. Startled, I looked up and saw a car pull up to the curb with a squeal a split second before a large man jumped out.

Jake.

Headed my way with a face like thunder, storming up

the front walkway as I drifted down. "Violet, I have to tell you something and this isn't going to be easy to hear—"

"Not now. I have to get out of here." I tried to step to the side to go around him, but he blocked my path with his tall, broad frame, and angry energy.

His eyes softened as they met mine and I quickly looked away. Sympathy would only make me start crying again. "This is important, and it's about Tom. I don't know how to tell you this—"

"What? That he's been cheating on me with Bethany for the last six months?"

He inhaled a sharp breath. "Six months? That long? Shit."

"Is that what you wanted to tell me?" I crossed my arms and stared up at him.

"Yes. I've been one step behind you all morning. I saw them together about an hour ago. Kissing in the parking lot of—"

"It doesn't even matter. I saw them myself, Jake. Right in my bed. But—" I looked up, seeing his soft blue eyes gleaming with sympathy and care as I met them with mine. "Thank you. I mean, you're his best friend. I appreciate that you were going to tell me and not try to cover for him."

He snorted. "I don't give a shit about Tom. *You're* my friend. Don't you know that by now? Tom can go to hell."

We both jumped as the front door opened. Tom and Bethany stepped out onto the porch, dressed for the workday and bearing Tom's bags packed for their ski trip. "Moretti! Hey, buddy," Tom called, sounding like it was just a normal day.

"Hey?" Jake's face showed his incredulity as he threw his arms out to the side. "That's it? Are you crazy, doing this so publicly? I saw you kissing her in front of your office.

And I wasn't the only one. Don't you have any respect for your family?" My jaw dropped. I had yet to contemplate which side our friends would each land on when the news got out. I was happy Jake chose mine. He was a good man and the boys had always adored him.

"I sent her an email—"

Jake huffed out a hostile laugh. "An email? Are you fucking serio—"

"I have to go." I darted around him, trying to ignore their angry words. I hopped in my vehicle and started it but slammed to a stop halfway out of the driveway when I saw Tom attempt to shove Jake off the porch. Jake shook him off and turned around. He strode angrily to my car, tapping on my window when he arrived. I rolled it down, then rested my hand on the frame as I turned in my seat.

"I want you to call me if you or the boys need anything. Any time, day or night, you can call me. Do you hear me, Violet?" His anger melted away as he spoke. His smile grew gentle as he studied my face.

"Yes, Jake," I murmured, still shaken from their confrontation on the porch.

His eyebrows knitted with concern. "I mean it. I'm going to call you tonight to check on you and the boys, and you'd better answer."

"Okay. I'll answer." I breathed.

He echoed my *"Okay"* with a soft whisper, then covered my hand briefly with his before taking it away. "You drive carefully. Is Holly still going to be at the shop when you get there?"

I nodded.

"That's good. You shouldn't be alone today. I'll talk to you tonight—in fact, I'll swing by and drop off dinner for you and the boys. Will you be here at the house or—?"

"I'll be here. I have to pack."

Storm clouds filled his eyes again. "That bastard . . . We'll talk more later." He pressed the pocket square from his suit jacket into my palm. "Just in case you need it on the way. Bye, sweetheart."

"Goodbye, Jake." I managed to say. I watched as he got into his car and drove away. Then I got out of there.

What the hell was that?

Chapter 2
Violet

"Coffee is a hug in a mug."

By the time I left the house, the early morning traffic had died down. I slowed to a crawl anyway. Being in my car was like sitting in a bubble of denial. I was alone and on the move. A vision of turning onto the highway and driving the heck out of dodge for a few days flittered across my mind before I rejected it.

My thoughts wandered as I drove through the almost empty streets toward my shop. Main Street in Sweetbriar ran the entire distance of town. It was lined with pine trees, evergreen shrubs, and turn-offs to neighborhood streets and entrances to small shopping centers and offices. The city buildings sat in the center of town surrounding a lushly landscaped courtyard, while my shop sat across the street in a shopping center designed to look like a row of mountain houses. Sweetbriar had been my home since birth and my shop had been *the* spot to get your coffee for practically a decade. It was only a matter of time before everyone knew what Tom had done to me. Then the humiliation would ensue as the town gossips spread the news. I was about to be in the middle of the coffee shop talk . . . only I owned the shop, so I couldn't escape it.

Ugh! Why couldn't Tom have kept it in his pants until stupid February first? Cheating was the one thing I would never, ever tolerate. I had put up with a lot of shit from Tom over the last few years for the sake of keeping my family together, but he had crossed the line this morning. My heart ached for my poor boys—nothing like a small-town cheating scandal and divorce to make the last two years of high school memorable. And we were barely into the new year! The holiday season would always have the stink of betrayal on it. *Damn it.*

I could have called my mother or any one of my seven siblings to take care of my boys so I could hide out for a while and they'd do it in a heartbeat. Alas, I was not one to run from my problems. So here I was, sitting in my parking spot near the dumpsters behind the adorable strip-mall where my shop sat, staring at the back door. I'd driven up to this place, parked right here, and gone to work almost every day for over a decade. I looked over the top of my *"Reserved for Violet"* sign and vowed (a.k.a. lied to myself) that today would be no different than any other. So what if people found out my husband was not only an asshole, but a cheater too? Would that make my coffee less awesome? No freaking way.

This was *my* place. My coffee fueled haven of delicious smells, yummy treats, and happy customers. It was warm, cozy, and always welcoming. I named it *Violet's* because everything inside expressed what was inside of me. I poured my energy—I poured *myself*—into my business to create something I could be proud of, no matter what stupid Tom had said about it over the years.

I shut my eyes against the sudden deluge of memories. Tom had never wanted me to open my own business. Once he'd started making money in real estate, he wanted me to stay home with the boys and be a perfect little *wifey*. He needed a woman who would sit around and wait for him, but that woman was not me and this coffee shop was the only thing I had ever refused to compromise with him on. I mean, we had a housekeeper, a gardener, and a pool service. Once the boys started school, what would I have done all day?

At least I would have family back-up today. My little sister Holly would be working for me while she was home. She was a travel journalist and blogger but was taking an extended break for reasons she hadn't informed me, or anyone else in our family, about. I wasn't pushing her to spill her secrets. Unlike with my other two sisters, pushing would drive this one away. She was a carbon copy of our mother. Tall, blue-eyed, and blonde, though Mom's hair was mostly silver now. They were both blessed with effortless elegance and kind hearts, and I was overjoyed that Holly was finally home. My mission was to give her a reason to stay, not badger into telling me why she was here. "Violet, is that you?" she called out after I slammed the shop's back door closed behind me and locked it.

Despite my determination to face everything head on, I again grew tempted to turn around, get back into my car, and check into a hotel or perhaps retire to a fishing boat in Alaska. I did not want to deal with the cheating bombshell today—or ever. Why couldn't I just end my marriage and move on without having to talk about it?

"Yeah, it's me . . ."

She popped her head through the swinging doors and waved me over.

"Are you okay? Jake was here earlier looking for you. He was all smoldery and intense and—uh, he was worried about you. Is something going on?" she whisper-hissed. Jake had been an object of fascination to my younger sisters ever since I'd first brought him and Tom home for a visit during spring break my freshman year of college. It was no secret to anybody that Jake had put himself through college and law school by modeling on the side. In fact, he was on a few of my romance-novelist-mother's bestselling book covers, and had graced the pages of catalogues from sporting goods stores to high fashion. But his biggest claim to fame—and big break into making serious money—were the undie campaigns that had ended up in fashion magazines and on billboards in several big cities around the world. He hadn't modeled in years, but his face was still on ads for a popular perfume at cosmetic counters across the country, a fact he occasionally bemoaned with good-hearted humor. Jake was tall, dark, and gorgeous, with a jawline that could cut glass, sexy, deep blue eyes, full lips, and lately he'd been sporting a lumberjack-sexy dark beard with hints of silver. I enjoyed a good laugh at his expense every time he came into my shop—he was a head turner. He was also one of the best friends I'd ever had in my life and I, along with my boys, adored him.

Holly and I jumped when we heard the bell on the front door of the shop jingle like crazy followed by the slamming of said door. "Darling! Violet, my baby! Where are you?"

My mother.

Freakin' great.

I'd hoped to disappear, or at least lock myself in my office for a few hours—alone. To have some time to sort my feelings, place them into appropriate perspective, then dump them into boxes to bury in my subconscious as needed to maintain my sanity. That, and it was way too early to have a glass of wine and unwind in a bubble bath, or partake in one of my other favorite stress relievers: a shot of tequila and a soak in my hot tub. *Frick!* There would be no more hot tub after tonight. I had to move out of my house, and I doubted I could fit the hot tub in the back of my Range Rover and move it to Rose's place. I blew out a frustrated raspberry and rolled my eyes at Holly, who scrunched up her face in sympathy.

My mother had a lot of opinions on just about everything, but the one that came between us off and on throughout the years was her dislike of Tom. She would never admit to it, but I knew she didn't approve of him. I also knew there was no way my mother would ever allow anyone to treat her the way I had allowed my husband to treat me over the last few years. It had driven a one-sided wedge of shame between us. She would never judge me— she would only ever help me—but I knew she was aware of it. My entire family knew. They kept quiet out of respect or fear of driving me away, or maybe both. It was the kind of silence that was deafening, because I knew with one word from me against Tom, the silence would change to a cacophony of supportive outrage that would force me to deal with all sorts of feelings that I would never be in the mood to sort through.

"Is it busy out front?" I asked after a longing look at my office door.

"No worries. The shop is full, but the line is gone. How's your headache?" she asked, after a side-eyed head-tilt at my mother making her way to the back of the shop.

"It's growing. I'm going to my office to take my migraine medicine, stare at the wall, and *not* think about anything. I'll tell you what happened later, but feel free to assume it's all about Tom. You can send Mom back if she starts getting all *Mom* on you, okay?"

"You got it." Her smile was sweet and understanding but I didn't need that now. Sympathy almost always made me cry and I was on the edge of a mental breakdown. Tears? Existential dread? That lady-temper tantrum that was roiling beneath the surface? Who knew which way I'd crack? It was too soon for even me to tell. "I'll get back out front. Get some rest, Vi."

"Thanks, Holly." I closed the door behind myself, popped my migraine medicine, and plopped onto my sofa, stuffing a pillow behind my head and propping my feet over the arm. I should have thought ahead and bought a bigger couch. Or a pullout. At five-foot-eight, I was too tall for this one. I threw my arm over my eyes with a sigh. An odd sense of freedom filled me at the thought of not seeing Tom tonight. Against my will, I surprised myself and grinned as I turned to my side.

"Honey! I'm here for you." My mother burst into the room with her hands full of my take-out coffee cups. She was perfectly put together as always, stylish from top to toe in designer jeans, high heeled boots, statement necklace, and a tweed blazer. Her long silver hair shimmered over one shoulder while her heavy black framed glasses perched on her delicate nose *just so.* "Drink this and we can talk. I have news and I'm not sure—"

With a graceless heave, I sat up and reached my hand out for her offering. It was a fact that coffee made everything better. Especially my coffee. She passed it to me, then perched on the couch. Her eyes were expectant and full of that same sympathetic gleam I had seen in Jake's expression at the house.

She knew. Somehow the news had already started spreading through town. "You know? About Tom? Freaking *already?*"

Her beautiful face crumpled. "Oh, my poor baby. You've heard for yourself? I wanted to be the one to tell you. I wanted to be here to cushion the blow for you somehow. I'm so sorry."

"It's not your fault. And I didn't hear it, I saw it. I caught the live show in my bed."

Half of the oxygen in the room disappeared as she inhaled her outrage. "Noooooooo!" she all but growled. "That duplicitous piece of trash! With his secretary? Bethany? Yes?" Her eyes were huge, her expression shifted to her pissed off mama bear setting, and suddenly I was glad she was here. I could use a dose of her righteous indignation and strength. Hopefully some of it would rub off on me.

"Yeah, Bethany. He was banging her in my freshly washed sheets. Then she stole his T-shirt and took herself into my bathroom with my brand-new towels, like she had every right to be in there. He told me to move out while he's up the mountain skiing with her all weekend. Naturally, I get the boys." I sneered my disdain. "One can't have teenage boys underfoot when you want to screw your secretary all over the damn house, am I right? But apparently, he sent me an email this morning explaining it all. That makes it A-OK in his deranged mind."

She slammed her coffee on my desk with a thud and stood up. "The two of them are utterly contemptible. He has become a narcissistic piece of trash over the years. Where is their decency?" With a pivot, she pointed at me. "You listen to me, Violet. You will take him for everything he has! Or at least your half. You deserve it, honey. He'd be nowhere without you. You supported him while he finished college and you were pregnant with twins. That scum-dwelling swamp goblin! That back-stabbing, liar! Ooooh!" Her head darted side to side until she lurched and grabbed her purse from where she had just tossed it on the couch. "I'm going to his office. He's going to get a piece of my mind. She will too, if she's there. That tramp-faced, lying little hussy! She knew full-well he was married man. She's met you. She knows the boys. She buys coffee in *this very shop*. For shame!"

"No. Please, don't! Stay here and help me figure out where to take the boys tonight. I can't stay at the house if I want to erase what I saw. Unfortunately, eye bleach is not a real thing and it's too early to move into Rose's place. I just want to forget I was ever married. I had plans, and he ruined everything! February first, Mother! It was all supposed to wait until then and now I have nowhere to go, damn it! I only have a few hours to think of what to say to the boys and—of course. Of. Course. That jerk left town, leaving me to do all the heavy work with Finn and Nick! Are we going to break the divorce news together? Nooooooo—"

She drew her head back on her neck. "February first? I —you were going to leave him?" She shook her head in confusion. "Never mind, we can talk about that later. First things first, you will all come home with me. *Of course.*"

"If I do that, it can only be for a night or two. I need to get the boys to a new normal as soon as possible. Maybe Rose will finish clearing out her stuff this weekend." It was starting to hit me that I had a lot to do in a very short period of time.

She sat down and pulled me into her side. "Honey, even if Rose's place were available, you can't create a new home for yourself and the boys in a night or two. Furthermore, your feelings matter too. You need time to process all of this. You can have your old bedroom back. The boys can stay in your brothers' old rooms. I'll make your favorite pancakes for breakfast and get the boys off to school for you." She paused and smirked at me. "And since you'll be home, no more ditching the family Sunday dinners." My mother was a stickler about us going to her house every Sunday for dinner. I had been avoiding it for one made up, bull-crap reason or another for months. It had been getting harder and harder to hide my marriage issues from my family.

I heaved out a sigh. "I didn't want to bring Tom on Sundays anymore, okay? And fine. I can't resist your apple cinnamon pancakes. There's nowhere else to go anyway."

"Well, thanks a lot," she joked.

"I didn't mean it that way," I wrapped my arm around her waist and snuggled into her side. She was immaculate and smelled like a meadow while I was still sticky from my steamed milk incident earlier.

"I understand about Tom on Sundays, but"—she waggled her finger at me—"now you have no excuse! Ha! I'll call my attorney when I get home. Take the day off and rest before you tell the boys. I'm here for you, however you need me to be." She patted my knee, the gesture full of love and sympathy. "Honey, I know you don't like talking about your marriage. I promise not to push. I just want to be there for you, okay? Your father will too, once he gets home from skiing with your brothers."

No pushing? Wow. "Sounds good. But I'm going to finish my day here. My pills are kicking in. And I'll get my own attorney. I had planned on asking Jake to give me a recommendation."

"Good idea, darling. Talk to that gorgeous Jake and tell him all about it over dinner. Wear something pretty and make it very clear you're getting a divorce. Get your ducks in a row right from the start."

"Mother!" I sat up to glare at her. Talk about inappropriate timing. "Jake will not be one of my ducks to line up. He's my friend who happens to be an attorney in town. That's it."

She stood up with a grin. "I'm only teasing you—sort of. It's too soon for that kind of talk. But he's always been interested in you, sweet pea. Aside from those intense blue eyes and astonishing physique, he's a good man with a solid moral compass. I mean, I've worked with him on several charities over the years, and this year's Winter Gala will raise money for the charity he's starting in his mother's name. I think this could end up perfect for both of you. Later, of course. Uh, much, much later, well after your divorce is final and you've settled into your new life. Okay!" Shaking her head, she shimmied and clapped her hands together, then shouldered her purse. "I'll see you tonight. Bye!"

She was smart to dash out of my office before I could reply. But was I smart to let her go before giving her a piece of my mind about Jake? Probably not. She had ideas flashing in her eyeballs and once she started, it was hard to make her stop. The matchmaking impulse was strong in her. *No pushing . . .* Sure, she said no pushing me into talking about Tom. I couldn't help but notice there were no promises not to push about Jake.

Whatever. I had other—too many—things to deal with and no time to care about who might be interested in me or not, let alone time to start worrying where my ducks would end up.

Chapter 3
Jake

"But first, coffee."

My feelings for Violet had always been complicated. Something about her had caught my attention and had snuck into my heart and burrowed inside to stay. Tom wasn't the only fool where she was concerned; I had let him steal my chance with her back in college and the ache of regret had been a constant companion ever since. Over time, I had forced myself to accept Violet's role in my life as the wife of my best friend, who had herself become one of my closest friends. She had become so important to me that I quit allowing myself to think of her in any other way. I killed the fantasy before it ever had a chance to develop into yearning. Lust had no place in my brain when it came to Violet. I rarely allowed it because I adored her so much it hurt.

I had been living on a razor's edge since I first met her. Seeing Tom kissing Bethany cut me up inside. I knew there was no stopping the hurt Violet would undoubtedly feel, but the possibility of a chance at having *more* with her bled into my heart and drowned out all the reasons why she was forbidden. The thought of Tom being out of the picture filled me with nothing but want, like I had time traveled back to college and was falling for my best friend's girl all over again.

Maybe this was finally my chance with her.

Or maybe I should keep my feelings to myself and ensure the friendship we'd built over the years remained intact. The thought of losing her even as a friend after all this time was unfathomable.

"Uncle Jake."

Startled, I spun in my chair. I had been spending a lot more time in my Sweetbriar office lately. I was employed by a large law firm in Portland and had recently made partner, gaining me enough clout to open Lyla's Place, named after my mother. It was to be a safe place for abused women, as my mother had been. It would operate as a shelter and legal aid center, teach self-defense, and offer therapy both in groups and by referral for one-on-one sessions. I'd finally earned enough money and respect in this area to make the dream into a reality. I could finally do something tangible in her name like I'd always promised myself I would. "Harper, hey." My assistant/niece bustled into my office, takeout bag in hand.

"I brought breakfast burritos and bad news." She studied my face with expectation as she sat down.

"If this is about Violet and Tom, I already know."

She let out a sigh. "Well, I saw it for myself right before I dropped Bella off at school. I know Tom is your friend, but I feel like I can finally admit that I never liked him. What a douchebag."

Involuntarily, I barked out a laugh. "I haven't liked him in years." *Douchebag*—that was putting it kindly. He was an idiot. An absolute fucking fool. Violet was perfection. The ideal woman. She was everything I could never find, no matter how many women I had dated over the years while trying to shove her out of my heart.

Harper grinned. "I had my suspicions. And it does fit in with the stories floating around town." Harper is my older sister's only child, but that didn't stop her from disowning Harper after she got pregnant during her senior year of high school. I let Harper move into the other half of my duplex here in Sweetbriar and she's been my tenant/neighbor ever since. Her daughter, Bella, is as cute as could be and now a kindergartner. A few months ago, Harper earned an office management certificate from the local junior college and had finally accepted my offer to come work for me.

"Of course you did. What stories?" I played dumb about the recurring rumor that I only remained friendly with Tom to keep my friendship with Violet because I was a lovesick chump. Was it true? That was a question I had been avoiding since my college days. It was a question that'd had no place in my life as long as there had been no hope.

"Did you tell Violet about Tom?"

"I was going to. But I didn't get to her in time." There was no way I ever would have allowed Violet to play the fool, and I wished I could have spared her the sight. Tom and I grew up together in Portland. He'd been my best friend all through school and into college, where we met Violet. However, he'd changed so much over the years I'd long stopped thinking of him as my friend. Tom and I grew up poor, but only one of us seemed to remember where we had come from.

"Poor Violet. Jude said she left Holly in charge of the shop to go pack up her and the boys. She doesn't want them to have to deal with moving out of the house. Jude said she won't let any of the family help either. She wants to be alone. I just can't imagine." Jude was one of Violet's younger brothers and Harper's best friend.

"What? Back up a second. I thought she was going back to the shop for the day."

She shrugged. "That's what he told me. Mrs. Barrett is picking the boys up from school when it lets out and taking them home with her." I stood. Harper smiled knowingly. "Are you going to head over there?"

"I—yeah, I think I will. I'll try to help her pack. Maybe she'll listen to me."

"Oh, she'll listen to you, all right. Everybody knows—"

"Nobody knows anything," I insisted.

Her eyebrows raised as she smiled at me. "Yeah, they do. Everyone knows you secretly—"

I sighed; I was long since tired of the rumor that reared its head over the years about my feelings for Violet. Even though almost everything I'd ever heard had been somewhat true at one point or another, it was no one's business but mine—and I denied it every time. Usually by finding a girlfriend. Serial monogamy was the best deflection. It also kept me from getting too lonely over the years. "No, they don't. I'm not secretly anything, Harper." I smiled to soften my denial. "Vi has been my friend for years. I care about her and the boys, and that's the end of it."

"Okay, fine," she huffed. "You know you can talk to me. I dump everything on you all the time. I'm a grown up now, Uncle Jake. You can tell me stuff too."

"You're sweet, Harper. But that's not going to happen."

"Yeah, I guess it would be weird to talk about your love life. You're more on the dad side of the line than the uncle side of it anyway. And come to think of it, it would be weird for an uncle too." Touched, I turned back and grinned at her. "Maybe I'll have Bella start calling you grandpa or pop instead of Uncle Jake," she added.

"Ha ha, very funny. I just turned forty. That isn't old enough to be a grandfather, is it?"

She shrugged with a grin. "I have no idea. I'm not friends with math. Will I see you later?"

"Probably. But lock up if I'm still gone when you get off. There's a lasagna in my freezer if I'm not home in time for dinner."

"You do too much for me," she protested, as usual.

I grinned and shot back my usual answer. "Family helps family. Would you help me if I needed you?"

"Okay, yeah, you know I would," she conceded. "But that isn't the point, and you know it."

"I'm older, just like a dad—you said it yourself. Listen to my wisdom and eat the lasagna." I flicked two fingers out in a wave as I left, shutting the door and getting the last word.

* * *

I pulled into the driveway next to Violet's SUV, but my knock on the front door went unheeded. The idea that she was in that big house packing up her memories alone didn't set well with me. She wanted to be by herself and I respected that, but I also felt compelled to help. I pressed the doorbell and stepped back to peek in the adjacent window for any movement.

"*Ugh!* I'm out back!" The shout came from the back-yard. "You guys never give up, do you? Quit blowing up my phone and quit offering to help. At least for now, anyway. And if it's you, Tom? Go screw yourself, I'm packing."

With a grin, I stepped off the porch, rounded the house and let myself through the side gate. I heard the jets and saw the steam floating over the crisp winter air before I rounded the corner to the backyard proper. She was in the hot tub at the edge of the massive rectangular built-in pool.

"Oh, Jake, it's you! I decided to enjoy my hot tub one last time before I pack. And don't you worry, the pool service was here today performing a cleansing with chlorine. All the cheater cooties are gone. Buh-bye spray tan! *Hasta la vista* lube, or whatever the heck else they probably left in here." She cackled to herself as she sat back in the water. Holding up her glass, she beckoned me closer. "Want some? This is expensive tequila. You know how Tom is about high-quality booze." She flopped her other hand around, giggling when she splashed herself. "I decided to have a drink and toast the end of my marriage. Grab a glass and join me. It'll be less pathetic if I have someone to toast with."

"Sure. Why not?" She didn't appear to be drunk and the bottle was almost full. But I'd never seen her in a mood like this. Her beautiful hazel eyes shone with humor, but the tightly bound tremor in her voice told me she was about to let loose and cry. Or perhaps throw something, or maybe scream. For once, I couldn't read her, and I was intrigued. I grabbed a glass from the outdoor kitchen and turned around to slide a chair from the table to the edge of the in-ground hot tub.

"You should get in with me. It's warm in here." She sat back against the curved side with a sigh, letting her head drop forward when the jet activated against the nape of her neck. "I don't know what I'll miss more when I leave. This hot tub, or all the years I wasted here on that jerk-faced weasel I married. What do you think?" Her head popped up and she pushed the bottle of tequila toward me with a brittle smile.

I took it and poured a healthy shot. "Thanks. But I wouldn't call those years a waste, Vi. You got two great boys out of it."

"I could have had them without getting married," she harrumphed. "Tom wasn't even there when I gave birth. You and my mother were. Remember?" I had been at their apartment helping Tom put the boy's cribs together, but he'd left halfway through the project. Her labor had hit fast and hard. She'd taken my hand and hadn't let go; even as I'd driven her to the hospital to meet her mother, she'd held on.

With a grin, I threw back the shot. "How could I forget? I'm lucky I still have my hand. You almost squeezed it off when Nick finally came out."

"I'd felt crappy all day, but Tom left to play golf and suck up to his boss anyway. Who leaves their cell phone in the car when their wife is about to give birth to twins? That should have been my very first wake-up call. And now, everyone will know he cheated on me once they start seeing him around town with her. Cheating with his secretary." She lets out an incredulous groan. "The ultimate cliché. He'll end up moving her in here—into *my* house. Could this be any more humiliating for me and the boys?" She blinked rapidly, her eyes shimmering in the sunlight, before she threw her glass into the pool and turned her back to me. She choked out, "I need to be alone," just as her shoulders started to shake.

I stood, rounded the hot tub and sat cross-legged next to her on the tile. "Vi, no one will ever think less of you because of Tom's actions. You've made your own reputation in town, separate from him."

"Everyone who comes into my shop will know. Then I'll get *the look*. That little smiley head tilt, complete with soft, sympathetic eyes—you know what I'm talking about—

and I don't want that pity look, Jake. I prefer to be the one to *give* the pity look. Then I usually offer a free muffin or a cookie or something. I don't want to be the one *getting* that look. I mean, there are only so many sympathy cookies I can eat!"

"Your customers love you, Violet, and a lot of them have been where you are. The divorce rate in Sweetbriar is high, just like everywhere else." I stated facts, hoping it would offer some perspective.

"I guess so," she sniffled. A wisp of a smile crossed her face as I brushed a tear from her cheek with my thumb. "Thanks, Jake."

"Any time. I mean that." This time her smile was real, albeit tremulous.

"I'm supposed to be packing. But I couldn't bring myself to go inside. Not after this morning."

"I could help you. Or I could hire some movers and take you out to lunch instead."

"We're going to stay at my mother's house. I guess I should start with clothes for the next few days—"

The gate squeaked open, and our heads swiveled to the side. "Eff that. You should clear out the entire house then set up a camera to film Tom's reaction when he gets home and finds it empty." Rose strolled through with an evil smile on her face. Following closely behind were Lily and Holly. It was clear Violet's sisters were not about to let her pack alone.

"Don't be mad. I have Luke's truck out front," Lily announced. She sheepishly added, "I also brought Luke. He's waiting and ready to go with an entire crap-ton of boxes and packing tape. Please let us help you. Also, I never stop having to pee. Can I go inside? Please?" Lily moved back to Sweetbriar over the summer, then married her first love Luke after a long separation. She was currently expecting twins.

"Go ahead, Lil. The patio door is open," Violet said.

Holly brought up the rear. "I called Piper to watch the shop. She'll close for you. Jude and Levi are out front with Levi's truck. Ash and Cade are skiing with Dad." Violet's huge, loving family always fascinated me; she was one of eight siblings, while I grew up in a small family with my mother, older brother, older sister, and a semi-absent, always-asshole father. Violet was second in line and the oldest daughter—Ash was the oldest, followed by Violet, Cade, identical twins Lily and Rose, Holly, and then fraternal twins Jude and Levi. Piper has been Violet's best friend since elementary school.

"You guys don't listen worth a crap, do you?" Violet shook her head.

"We really don't," Rose replied with a grin. "You know the saying, 'Many hands make light work'?" Violet nodded. "Good, because we have a lot of hands here right now and we want to do this for you. You shouldn't have to deal with moving on top of . . ." She waved her hand around and winced. "But, if you really do need to be alone to do some weird ceremonial goodbye ritual or light Tom's shit on fire in the driveway, we'll leave. I mean, if you're going the second route, no witnesses would be better anyway."

"No, please stay. I'd thought I wanted to do this by myself. Kind of like saying goodbye and good riddance to my former life. But it's too much for me right now—"

With a nervous sigh, Rose continued. "We will absolutely help you. Trevor is at my place with his truck loading up some of the stuff I've already packed. But first, to back up, none of us are here to say a word about Tom unless you want to talk about it. No talking, no discussing anything, and no opinions allowed. You tell us what you want to keep, and we will load it up. Now here's where Trev comes in—I'm not fully packed, but we can take your stuff to my place . . ." She paused to grin at me. "I mean, *your* new place, early. That is, if you don't mind some of my things still being there while you settle in."

Violet sat forward with a splash. "Heck yes, I would love to move in early! And I don't care what you have left there, I'll finish packing it up. Uh, will you tell mom that I won't be staying with her?"

Rose laughed. "Yes, I'll tell her. So, it's settled. We'll pack the boys' stuff and your office. And all your clothes and jewelry. Pictures of the boys off the walls? Their little keepsake chest in your room?"

"That would be perfect. I don't know what to say. Rose, you've fixed everything—everything fixable, anyway. I'll feel so much better if I only have to move once."

"You don't have to say a word. We have this handled. Text if you think of anything else we should pack."

"Thank you," Violet whispered.

"We love you," Holly answered, and led the way into the house.

When we were alone again, I caught her eye. "Get dressed. I'll take you to Riverview Grille. There's a Reuben with your name written all over it."

"My favorite. But you don't have to—"

"And yet, it's already a plan." I grinned at her.

"Fine. Take me to a nice lunch and get me out of this dump." She raised her chin, letting the twinkle in her eyes chase the sad away. At least for the moment.

"Come on, beautiful, let's get you out of here." I stood and held out my hands. She took them and treated me to a small smile. I hauled her to her feet.

Due to years of practice, I had perfected the ability to prevent myself from checking out her body every time I saw her. But something about seeing Tom kissing his secretary this morning had loosened the leash I had been keeping on my eyeballs, and I did a full top-to-toe perusal over her gorgeous form. She was clad in a black one-piece bathing suit cut low in a V at the chest and high on her hips with a swath of white tied in a bow around her little waist. She was shiny slick from the water and steam shimmered in the air around her as she rose. Feeling disoriented, I sucked in a huge breath to regain my senses. I had been sucker-punched in the gut by long legs and plentiful curves. Looking at her had been a bad idea.

What I had forced myself over the years to see in black and white was now in vivid color and *right there* in front of me, close enough to touch. Hazel eyes flecked with gold and russet, tiny brown freckles on her nose, rosy cheeks, and dark brown waves with hints of auburn piled up high on her head in a haphazard bun. Her alabaster skin was tinted pink from the water and warm to the touch as I slid one hand up her forearm to steady her as she stepped out of the hot tub. My breath hitched and I had to look away. "Get changed and I'll call for a table on the deck."

"You really don't have to—"

"I'm hungry," it came out as a low growl. Her grip on my other hand tightened as her eyelids fluttered shut. Suddenly I pictured her holding my hand in several *very* different scenarios. My heart pounded itself straight back to the past as even more long buried feelings began to unearth themselves.

She bit her lower lip. "Well, then let's get you fed. I'll just go and get dressed."

"I'll wait here."

"Okay, I'll hurry." Instead of heading for the house to change, she stood looking up at me with a bemused expression before her nose crinkled and she laughed.

"What is it?"

"Can I have my hand back, Jake?" She tugged lightly. I ducked my head and let her go. All the things about her I had spent years convincing myself were merely cute—her heart-shaped face, her crinkle-nosed laugh, her wide, toothy smile—had blown past cute today and morphed back into irresistible. My body burned with the desire to throw her over my shoulder and run away with her caveman style.

I forced my lowered gaze away from the curve of her cleavage and back to her face. "I'm sorry. Must be low blood sugar." I joked to cover my discomfiture. No woman had ever caught me off my game like Violet just had.

"Happens to the best of us. I'll be right back." Her lips pressed together, and she let out a nervous breath. "Don't go anywhere."

"I'm not leaving without you."

She gestured to the house with her thumb. "One fully dressed Violet, coming right up," she joked before crossing the patio toward the back door. As I watched her long legs eat up the distance with her hips swaying and just the perfect amount of wiggle in her walk, I realized, just like all those years ago, I was about to fall under her spell again— and I couldn't let it happen. It was way too early for such things. She was still married to my so-called best friend, for fuck's sake.

Chapter 4
Violet

"May your coffee kick in before reality does."

What was I doing?

My eyes darted side to side on the lookout for my siblings as I stood shivering on the hard wood of the family room floor. I left my robe and work clothes in the pool house. I couldn't go back outside where I just flirted with Jake.

Jeez. It had been so long I'd forgotten what flirting felt like. My eyelashes had definitely fluttered a few times, and I could swear that I'd bit my lip and maybe even teased him a little bit.

"Vi?" Rose popped her head out of my downstairs office. "Hey, are you doing okay?"

"I'm fine. I need to get dressed for lunch."

"And yet, there you are, staring at the wall behind my head. Where's your towel?"

"I . . ."

"Need to dry off and get dressed? Go out to lunch with Hot Jake?" Her lips quirked up in amusement. "Everyone is

36

upstairs packing up the boys' stuff. Your room is empty for now. Go for it."

"Yeah, I have to do all of that. But, Rose . . . I think I just flirted with him. But I'm not really sure."

She rolled her eyes. "Of course you did. You flirt with everyone. You don't have anything to worry about."

I jerked my head back. "I do not."

"You so do. You have innocent flirty charisma, and you can't help yourself. You flirt with men, women, senior citizens, babies, your espresso machine, puppies—it's why everyone loves you. Oh wait . . . that means that if you recognized that you flirted with Jake it must *not* have been innocent! Go for it, Violet. I approve. Move on from that butthead Tom in style."

"Don't be crazy. I'm still married, for goodness' sake. And I have the boys to think of."

"Sure, but not for long, right? February first is out the window. You've always said cheating is your deal breaker, so your time is now." She spread her hands wide and smiled. "The era of Violet begins. No more crying over Tom. No more of his rude little comments and definitely no more of him making you feel like crap all the time. You never, ever deserved to be treated the way he treated you. I mean, he would have met the lord in person a long time ago if he were married to me. That man crossed way too many lines before he ever cheated on you." She winced. "Damn it, I wasn't supposed to bring him up, I'm sorr—"

"No, it's *you*, so it's okay." Out of my entire family, Rose was the only one I was ever willing to talk about my marriage with. In fact, she was the only one who'd known of my secret February first plan. She was always there to listen, she always supported me, never judged, and ninety-nine percent of the time she kept her opinions about Tom to herself. It was only recently that she had been encouraging me to leave him if he didn't start treating me better.

"Really? Well, then I recommend you find something pretty to wear and let your hair down. Have a nice lunch and try to relax. Let a man besides Dad or our brothers be nice to you for a change. Or maybe go to my place and get brainless with a bag of Doritos in front of the TV? I'm fully stocked with Diet Coke, and there is a brand-new Hershey's variety bag in my coffee table." I smiled as she dangled our favorite treats in front of me with a grin.

My grin faded as I shook myself out of the trance I had stumbled into this morning and took a step forward. Being in this house again was stirring up memories both happy and sad. "No thank you. I think I need a hug—a big one. And some coffee. I've only had one cup today."

"Oh, Vi. Only one cup? How are you still alive?"

Tears filled my eyes, only sheer force of will kept them from falling. "I don't know. Mom brought coffee back to my office at the shop and it's still sitting on my desk. I didn't even drink it." My lower lip trembled, and it was then I knew whatever grip I'd had on my composure was about to slip away. "Rosy Posy, I'm having a really, really bad day."

"Aw, come here." She spread her arms wide and flapped her hands as she ran across the family room to me. Rose was barely five foot two and built like a waif with boobs. I was at least six inches taller, and her trying to hold me bordered on ridiculous, but I was way past caring. I rested my cheek against the top of her soft red hair and let out a massive sigh. "We need to sit down. This isn't working," she mumbled into my cleavage.

"'Kay." I let her lead me to the couch where she wrapped me up in one of Gram's afghans I kept draped across the back.

"Curse my shortness," she grumbled as she yanked me into her chest and wrapped her arms around my shoulders to stroke my hair. I huddled against her like a giant toddler as big sloppy tears formed in my eyes.

"Violet?" Jake popped his head in through the patio sliders.

I muttered, "Oh god . . ." in response and yanked the blanket over my face.

Rose answered for me. "Can you make some coffee? Poor thing has been trying to function all morning on only one cup."

"Of course." The deep rumble of his voice filled the room, but I didn't dare peek until I heard his footsteps move across the hardwood floor toward the kitchen.

"I'll never live any of this down," I mumbled from beneath the blanket.

"You have nothing to live down. You're entitled to fall apart. There's not one person on this earth who doesn't lose their shit sometimes. You've earned it, Vi. Let it out."

"I can't lose my shit. I need my shit to be bound up real tight—totally constipated—so I don't freak the boys out tonight. They saw me crying over *This is Us* a few weeks ago and they couldn't take it. I had to quit that show. They can't see me like *this*." Determined words were one thing, but feelings were another. Tears continued to stream down my face. It seemed I could deny them all I wanted, but they would fall no matter what I said. "Damn it. Please don't let him screw up the coffee. I need it real bad."

She laughed. "I'll make more if he does," she soothed. Rose flicked my scrunchie out of my hair and smoothed it back with her palm. I glanced at the clock above the fireplace. I had a good three hours before school was out and I had to see the boys. There would be plenty of time to fix my face and depuff my eyes. I settled into Rose for the long haul.

"Coffee is ready," Jake announced.

"You're awesome." The smile in Rose's voice was audible. I peeped through the wide weave of Gram's afghan and saw him step through the arched entrance bearing my silver coffee service. It smelled heavenly.

"We'll skip lunch together today. But I will take a raincheck." He grinned, then bent to place the tray on the coffee table.

"'Kay," I agreed and sat up. As I looked around more tears fell. "You know, I never loved this house," I sobbed. "It's way too big and fancy. When the boys were little, I was always afraid I would lose one of them in here."

The sofa depressed next to me as Jake sat down. "You did lose Finn once, remember? During hide and seek at their sixth birthday party. He fell asleep right there, behind that coat rack you used to have next to the stairs." Rose leaned across me and smacked Jake on the leg.

"I remember that!" she cried. "Finn used to be such a sneaky little booger."

I choked on a laugh, the sound coming through my tears making me sound unhinged. "He really was. He kinda still is." I watched wide-eyed as Jake leaned forward to pour coffee into my favorite mug. He added a scant half teaspoon of sugar and a perfectly sized splash of cream. After stirring it *only* once, he handed it to me.

"Do you still take it like this?"

"Yeah, this is exactly how I like it. Thanks," I whispered. Rose nudged the crap out of my side. I elbowed her back and shot her a glare.

Twinkling eyes met mine when I turned back to Jake. "You're so picky I don't think I'll ever forget," he said.

"You're a good friend, Jake." I smiled as I sank back into the cushions and sipped the coffee. "This is perfect."

"You deserve nothing less, Vi. Don't forget that. I'd better get back to the office." He stood. "I'll be in Sweetbriar indefinitely for work, so don't hesitate to call me. That goes for the boys, too."

"What would I do without you?" I murmured, suddenly struck with the crazy thought that I would miss Jake more than Tom if he ever left my life. *It's just gratitude and nostalgia mixing in with the anger—that's all it is.*

"Sweetheart." His smile hit me someplace I'd never felt him before, and I shivered. "You'll never have to find out. Take care of our girl, Rose."

"I will." She grinned at him and I laughed as I flashed back to twelve-year-old Rose's awe-filled grin the first time she met Jake all those years ago. He flicked two fingers out in a wave, then turned to leave. "You're not going to have a choice in this," she whispered. "You're gonna end up in love with him someday whether you like it or not. Shoot, I'm halfway in love with him and I just married the love of my life, dream-come-true Trevor. And you should hear the way Mom talks about him every time she works with him on a charity in town. He's one of the good guys, Vi."

"I know he is. But let's not get carried away." She was totally going to get carried away. I could already sense it happening; they all would. No one in this family knew how to mind their own business. The Barrett family was nosy and it started right at the top with my mother.

"I won't, I promise." She smiled and crossed her heart, laughing when I rolled my eyes. "I'm serious. No one will meddle. I won't let them. This is a different situation than Lily's and mine were. You're getting a divorce, which makes it way more complicated, and you have kids to consider. Are you okay for now? I'm going to finish loading up your office."

"Yeah, I'm okay." I held up my mug. "I have coffee now." She got up and left, kissing the top of my head on the way out.

Heavy footsteps pounded down the stairs as Levi entered the room. "I've already taken the remote control batteries and added vegetable oil to all the shampoo and body washes. You weren't planning on a showering here, were you? Because I'd advise against it."

"Uh, thanks? I'm surprised you haven't found Tom and punched him in the face. That's more your style."

"Tom is lucky you guys have kids together. Finn and Nick are his eternal protection against this fist in his face." He held his fist out toward me and I bumped it in return, grinning.

"I respect your restraint, Levi."

"It's all about tiny revenge today. I just finished repro-gramming the security system, temperature control, and exterior lighting. Plus, I fucked with a bunch of shit I don't even understand. He'll soon know the downside to having a smart house when this one loses some IQ points. I also short-sheeted your bed and loosened all the toilet seats—low tech, but annoying. Maybe I'll head into to the kitchen and take one bite out of each slice of cheese in the fridge before I leave. Who knows?"

"Don't be surprised if all the toilet paper ends up at Rose's tonight, along with his toothpaste and deodorant." Holly shrugged from the arched family room entrance.

"Now, that's what I'm talking about." Levi's laugh boomed through the family room, making me smile. "Let's get back to work. Don't forget to take the lightbulb out of the fridge. And the coffee creamer."

I sighed. "You guys are totally crazy, and I love you. I'm going upstairs to change." After making it to my room, I shut the door and quickly donned the everymom's yoga pants, T-shirt, and hoodie combo, then headed into the adjoining bathroom to brush out my hair and stare at my face in the mirror. I decided to allow myself a moment to contemplate my life, this stupid day, my lying, cheating, butthead husband, and the end of my marriage.

I would get through this, just like I had everything else in my life—by making the best interest of my boys my top priority. Anything else simply did not matter.

Chapter 5
Jake

*"How do I take my coffee? Seriously, very
seriously."*

I should have hung around and helped pack up. Or
taken her out to lunch anyway. I probably could have
cheered her up. "I have time for all of that later," I
mumbled to myself.

"Time for what?" A laughing voice answered, startling
me.

I spun my chair around and grinned. "Uh, nothing," I
answered as Liam Snyder from McCabe Contracting, the
business located across the hall from my office, entered
through the slightly opened door after I waved him in. Liam
worked with Luke McCabe, Violet's brother-in-law. I had
worked for Luke's father as his attorney until his death a
couple of years ago, and was now much happier to have
Luke as a client. His father had been an asshole of the Tom
variety, full of self-importance and arrogant disdain for
those he considered beneath him, which was just about
everyone in town. Sadly, that had included his own son.

He placed a manila folder on my desk. "The plans for the athletic and recreation portion of the center are done. But there was something else I wanted to talk to you about."

"Of course. Have a seat. I'm all ears." I gestured to one of the two chairs on the opposite side of my desk.

"Luke mentioned you need volunteers to teach the self-defense class. I can teach Brazilian jiu-jitsu, karate, basic self-defense, and I am a certified personal trainer. Also, and I don't mean to get too personal, but I'm pretty sure we have common motivations when it comes to this sort of thing." My eyebrows raised as I regarded him. I knew a little about his background—as anyone with access to the internet would—and mine was no secret either. We'd both come from abusive households.

"That would be great. In fact, both Luke and Dahlia suggested I invite you to join my advisory board."

A slight smile crossed his face. "I'm honored, and I accept." After a flick of his wrist to check his watch, he stood to head to the door. "But I have a meeting in ten minutes. Let me know what you decide about the classes and we can iron out the details for everything later."

"I will. As soon as we come up with a schedule for the center, we'll discuss it. Later, Liam."

"Yep." A knock at the door turned him around.

"Go ahead and let them in," I answered.

"Liam, sweetheart, I'll see you for dinner later." Dahlia Barrett, Violet's mother, kissed his cheek as she passed him to enter my office. "Hello, Jake, darling," she said as she swept into my office and sat in the chair across from my desk. "I have bad news. Ben was off skiing with Asher and Cade, as you may have already heard. They just called to let me know that he's broken his ankle. They're on their way home right now. He's already in a cast. They waited to call me about it, and I am unhappy to say the least. I should have been there. But that's not the problem. Our problem is that I can't possibly plan your mother's charity gala with you. I'll have a husband in a cast at home, and it will take all my attention and spare time to make him adhere to the doctor's orders. You know how Ben is—getting that man to rest will be near impossible. Plus, I'm on deadline for my latest book. I'll go through my contacts later tonight and find a replacement to help you—oh!" She stood suddenly as a huge smile crossed her face. "I have the perfect person. I'll call you later. Did Liam volunteer for the self-defense classes?"

"Yes, he did." I smiled at her.

"Perfect! Violet and the rest are still packing. I'll be at home soon. If you need me, I'm just a phone call away." With a cat-who-ate-the-canary grin, she stood and left my office almost as fast as she had entered it. Holly Barrett had also volunteered her services for the self-defense class earlier this morning while I'd been at Violet's shop. Knowing Dahlia, it was no coincidence. She had been pushing people together like chess pieces all over Sweetbriar for years, and usually with great success.

I wondered who she was going to push my way to help me plan the gala. A slow grin crossed my face as I recalled the fact that Violet often worked with her mother on charities in town and I found myself hoping she would replace Dahlia almost as much as I needed it to not be her. Along with those thoughts came visions of us working together over dinner, or here in my office, or in my bed the morning after—

Stop it.

Violet has always been pure temptation. I had grown used to being around her in small doses and with Tom around. But today was different, and I struggled with how to wrap my head around the changes. Ultimately, I had to conclude that now was not the time to let my heart run free when it came to her, for way too many reasons to count. But that wouldn't stop me from dropping dinner off for her and the boys later—which would only serve in proving to myself, once and for all, that I would never be able to stay away from her, no matter how much it hurt.

Chapter 6
Violet

"Drink some coffee and pretend to know what you're doing."

T revor smiled at me from Rose's porch as I pulled my Range Rover up to the curb to park. With his arms full of boxes, he crossed the lawn to his truck in the driveway. "Hey, Violet! I've almost got Rose's bedroom cleared out for you," he yelled.

"Thank you so much, Trev. You have no idea what this means to me," I called back as I exited my SUV to stand on the sidewalk and take in the sight of what would be my new home.

"It's no problem. The dryer is full of clean sheets—you know how Rose is about laundry—and the second bedroom is empty and ready for the boys' beds." He chuckled as he deposited the boxes in his truck. I laughed. Rose and house-work were not friends.

With a sigh, I headed up the walkway. Rose's house—*my* house—was small. Two bedrooms and one bathroom to share between me and my sons. Still, it felt spacious for its size. A furnished living room, eat-in kitchen, and screened back porch were the only other rooms in the house. My boys were used to having their own rooms and a lot more space than this place had to offer. I hoped they would be okay with sharing a room. The fact of the matter was, Rose was giving me a deal and a huge break. Houses weren't cheap in Sweetbriar and I was lucky to have an affordable place to go and be on my own with my boys. My shop did great business, but Tom was right; there was zero chance of me being able to afford to keep our house by myself.

Once I made it up the three steps to the covered front porch, I sat on Rose's bench swing and allowed my gaze to wander over the tree-lined street. Sunlight filtered through the breaks in the clouds to peek through the treetops. A small smile crossed my face as I relaxed and took in the quiet downtown neighborhood. If the weather was nice, I could walk to my shop. It seemed strange that such a simple thought could bring a smile to my face, especially since I had yet to break the bad news to my boys about Tom, but I couldn't help myself. I was feeling better by the second.

"You doing okay?" Trevor took a seat across the porch in one of the white wicker chairs situated on either side of a matching table. The table was topped with an overflowing planter stuffed full of trailing ivy and purple pansies that added charm to the cozy space.

"I think I'm going to be fine. Is that weird? Especially considering what I walked in on this morning."

"No. Sometimes divorce is just the inevitable end to a huge heap of bullshit you've been putting up with. You feel liberated instead of brokenhearted. Is that it?"

"Yeah, that's exactly it." I felt like I'd just lost two-hundred-twenty pounds of jerk-ass attitude and blind ambition, but I was not about to say that out loud in front of anyone.

"I know what it's like." And he did. His late wife was a piece of work. Except she'd been more of the criminal variety, unlike Tom, who kept his destructive behavior to vows and promises and not the law.

I sat forward and looked up at him. He was handsome, with dark brown hair and empathetic brown eyes. "I feel like I could be happy here," I confessed. His eyes crinkled at the corner as he grinned at me. My sister was a lucky woman. Trevor was a sweetheart and a hottie; if he remained faithful to her, she would have the elusive husband letter L trifecta: looks, loyalty, and love. Could a girl really expect it to have it all these days?

"You've got this, Violet. It might not be my place to say it, but you deserve better than Tom."

"Thank you, Trevor. For helping with the move and being so nice about everything."

He chuckled. "We're family now. I'll always be here for you and the boys."

"Mom!" My head snapped to the driveway to find Finn and Nick exiting their vehicle with haste.

"Where's your grandmother? She was supposed to pick you up from school and take you home. Wait, no, you're early. School isn't out yet!" I rushed off the porch to meet them on the walkway. "What are you doing here? Is everything okay?"

Finn answered first. "We heard what happened with Dad, so we left. We've been trying to find you for the last hour. Why aren't you answering your phone?"

Frantically, I patted my pockets. I must have left my phone in the pool house. "It must be at the house. Trev, can you call Rose and ask her to check the pool house, please?

Gah! Can you also call my mother and let her know I have the boys?"

He nodded as he headed to his truck. "No problem. Let me know if you need anything." He addressed the boys. "That goes for you too, guys."

"Thanks, Uncle Trev," Finn answered before entering the house.

"Let's go inside, Nick. We can talk there."

"Are you getting a divorce now?" he demanded. "Please, Mom, tell us we don't have to go back home. I don't want to ever see his face again."

I had always tried to keep any sort of conflict away from the boys by covering Tom's insulting remarks toward me with jokes or pretending that it didn't bother me. I should have known better than to think they were oblivious to it. More and more, my February first plan seemed like a foolish idea, and I was horrified as I contemplated the hurt I had likely caused my sons by staying with Tom for too long. Our family therapist pulled me aside after our last session and said as much, but I had still been clinging to my stupid February first plan.

"We're going to stay right here. Trevor was clearing out some of Aunt Rose's things, so we'll have room to move in. But, Nicky, let's go inside. Please? We'll talk it all through, yeah?"

"Okay. Fine." He spun on his heel to precede me to the porch while surreptitiously wiping beneath his eyes.

Finn was already on the huge sectional couch digging through the coffee table drawers where Rose kept all her good snacks. A small smile crossed his face as he unearthed the bag of Hershey's mini chocolate bars she'd told me about earlier today. "Can I eat these?"

"Yeah, go ahead. I'm not quite sure where to start. Sit

down Nicky, please?" I glanced at him pacing in front of the huge built-in entertainment set across from the couch.

"Bathroom," he mumbled and turned his pacing into the hallway.

Through a mouthful of chocolate, Finn informed me, "He's embarrassed. Brianna and her mother live in Sweetbriar Court across from Bethany and they saw Dad leaving her apartment late last night. He kissed her in the doorway. Bri told Nick about it at lunch today." He studied my face with narrowed eyes as he spoke. "But you already know everything, don't you?" Brianna is Nick's girlfriend, or he was dating her, at least. All I know was that she was at the house the other day making out with him on the couch.

I sat at the end of the sectional, wishing it wasn't too early to just go to bed and forget this entire day had ever happened. "I found out this morning. I have to confess something to you both. I was planning to leave your dad. I wanted to do it on February first so we could have one last holiday season together as a family. I didn't want to give you boys bad memories by filing for a divorce in the middle of it all. I guess that was stupid—"

"It wasn't stupid. It was nice. You're always nice, Mom. Too nice," Nick said as he reentered the room to join us on the sectional couch and reached for the bag of candy. "But you shouldn't have let Dad be such a dick to you all this time. Why did you do that?" His eyes met mine with determination. We had never talked about this before, or even acknowledged there were issues between Tom and me. I took them to a therapist because on some level I recognized our home life was causing damage . . . but it meant I could avoid talking about the actual problem with them directly. I could admit now it had not been my brightest idea.

Finn looked away while I inhaled a sharp breath. "I, uh .

. . well, at first, I didn't want you guys to lose your family and I hoped he would stop, and we could be normal again—"

Nick interrupted, "But he never stopped. He got worse. He was so mean to you, but you would make jokes about it or ignore it, and we—"

"We hated how he talked to you, Mom, and we didn't know what to do about it," Finn finished for Nick.

"Families shouldn't treat each other that way," Nick whispered. "And husbands should love their wives, or at least respect them enough to—"

Ouch. "You're right. Of course, you are. I just—"

"It couldn't have been easy," Finn added softly before a look of hard defiance eclipsed his sympathetic expression and pinned me in place waiting to see what he was about to say next. "Especially since he wasn't always such an asshole. I'm done with him. I don't care what anyone says about it."

"Okay. I mean, you're entitled to your feelings, Finn, and I accept that, as well as part of the blame for—"

"No! Fuck that, Mom," he thundered back. "You're not taking any of the blame for what a piece of shit he turned into." Normally I would say something about his language, but I knew it was important to let them get their feelings out.

"None of this is your fault," Nick agreed. "It's all on him. All of it."

"Okay. All right. Let's try to just—can we all settle down, just a bit? I don't want you to hate your father. I understand why you're angry with him and you have a right to be. But I'm going to make it all better, I promise. I'm going to buy this house from Aunt Rose. I know this place is not what you're used to, and you'll have to share a room—"

Nick and Finn exchanged a glance. Nick shrugged and

Finn let out a breath, the harsh glint in his eyes easing as he sat back in the cushions. "I don't get why he gets to stay at home when he's the one who fucked around on you," Nick finally stated.

"I can't afford to keep the house by myself—"

"This is total bullshit. So, he gets to have everything?" Anger reentered Finn's eyes as he shouted. "He gets to treat you like shit, cheat on you, and kick you out of your own house? I fucking hate him." He stood up and stalked to the front window to stare blindly outside.

"It's completely unfair," Nick concurred. "But it won't be so bad to share. That bedroom is pretty big. Right, Finn?"

"Yeah. I'm not mad about staying here. That isn't it, okay?" he ground out.

"I understand, Finny. I get it. It isn't right, not at all. But for now, I'm thankful we have this place, and I'm going to make it work for all of us—"

"It's not you or this house, Mom. That's not what the problem is, so stop trying to take the blame. Stop trying to make this better—"

"I'm sorry, I'll stop—" I was interrupted by Rose's landline ringing. Piper called in an SOS from the shop. Apparently, she was overrun with customers.

I hung up the phone and turned to the boys. "Piper needs my help at the cafe. Come with me? We can pick up a pizza on the way and you can hang out in the loft and take a break from this conversation. Sound good?"

"I could eat," Nick answered through a mouthful of chocolate.

"Yeah. That's cool." Finn crossed to the front door and headed outside without a backward glance.

Nick clarified. "He's just pissed at Dad. Not you."

"I know, Nicky." Of the two of them, Nick appeared

more sensitive. But Finn also felt things deeply; he was just prone to hiding his emotions under a layer of anger. It was only a matter of time before the sadness leaked out alongside it.

With a sigh, I stood, swiping my keys from the coffee table to lock up behind us.

* * *

The afternoon hours weren't usually busy at the shop. My jaw dropped as I led the boys through the back entrance and heard the bustle of customers out front. "Violet?" Piper shouted after popping her head through the doorway. "I'm so sorry to bug you today of all days. But I'm swamped!" Dare I hope that my shop was full because people were craving afternoon coffee and not because of the rapidly spreading gossip about Tom and Bethany and their naked morning rendezvous in my bedroom?

I knew better.

"This damn town is nosy," Finn grumbled behind me.

"Want us to go out front and work? You can stay back here," Nick offered.

"No, go on up to the loft and eat your pizza. I got this. It's just like Grandpa always says, it's best to face your troubles head on."

"Yeah, but Dad is our trouble too—"

"No, he's not. He's your father and I still have hope that one day you'll be able to get your relationship with him back on track."

"Yeah, right," Finn chortled. "You let us know if you need us to come down." He turned and stomped up the stairs.

"I will." I watched as Nick followed him up. After tying

55

an apron around my waist, I headed out front to face my audience. I was no fool. They were here for a show..

"Coming, Piper," I called as I washed my hands. One deep inhale and sharp exhale later and I was through the swinging doors and down the tiny hallway that led behind the counter.

"Vi, I feel terrible. Are you sure you can handle this?" Piper leaned in and whispered.

"I'll be fine. I'm already halfway back into denial, exactly where I like to be. Let's not talk about it right now. I'm the one who is sorry. You've been here alone, and it's too much." I grinned at her and made my way to the order area to help the next customer.

"Don't apologize. You've had a horrible day. And later—maybe not today, but soon—I have a bottle of wine and some homemade French onion dip with your name on it. Add a bag of Ruffles and *Magic Mike* and we'll get you all sorted out." She grinned back and continued squirting caramel into the macchiato she was creating.

I nodded to her over my shoulder. "Bribing me to spill my guts, are you?"

"Of course I am. You know the rules."

"Indeed, I do." I answered her with a half-hearted wink as I took my place behind the counter to deal with today's unexpected tide of coffee seekers.

"You're cool as a cucumber today, boss." Piper's sarcastic remark came as I passed her on the way to the refrigerator to refill the cream.

"Like ice," I agreed with a laugh. Piper had been my best friend since we met in kindergarten. Back then she was a brunette with a bob; currently she was a bleached blonde, working a top-knot and victory curls. Piper was fond of the rockabilly look. Her attire always outshone my casual skinny jeans and coffee quote T-shirts. Today she was gloriously outfitted in a 50's style purple plaid button-down dress, matching apron, heels, and full face of makeup. I hadn't bothered to change out of my yoga pants from this morning before rushing down here.

"There have been a lot of questions about you today. Like, *a lot*. Sweetbriar is buzzing, as you probably guessed. I've spent the day repeating the following phrases, 'Mind your business,' 'She's totally fine,' and 'Yes, I've heard the news.'"

"Yeah, I never thought I'd be the focus of the town gossip mill. An old married lady like me."

"Old. Yeah, okay. Thirty-seven is not old, Violet, especially when you look like you do. And you're about to be single. Prepare yourself. That's all I'm saying, girl. The sheer number of men asking about you today was unreal. Prepare—"

"I'll ask my dad to bring me some pepper spray." I was only half-joking.

We were interrupted by a haze of rosewater perfume and an extreme amount of rage-filled energy palpitating from the order area. "Sugar, I heard what happened. Are you okay?"

I looked down, way down, to find one of my favorite customers standing there with my grandmother. They were tiny, both in their eighties, and their matching pissed off little old lady expressions were terrifying. "I will be. What are we drinking today, Mrs. Brock? And you, Gram?"

"Oh, just a cappuccino and a blueberry scone, for each of us. And sugar-pie, once and for all, will you please call me Rachel? Mrs. Brock was my mother-in-law. I'd add the obligatory, 'god rest her soul,' but we all know that's not where that bitchy old biddy is resting."

"Coming right up," I answered. "I promise to try, Mrs.—er, Rachel." She snorted and rolled her eyes at me.

Gram beckoned me closer. "We know all about what happened this morning." With a dainty little hand, she patted her pocketbook. "I have two knitting needles ready to go straight into whatever body part of his you request, and Rachel makes her own soap; no one will question why she has lye around her house." She leaned in and her voice dropped to barely a whisper. "You just say the word, dollface, and we'll take care of business. All through time freakin' men have been thinking they can do whatever they want and getting away with it. We are well into a new millennium, sugar, and that shit don't fly anymore. Not with us. You've got to empower yourself, Violet, and take charge. We're here to help you. Just say the word and we'll do this thing." She stood straight and nodded sharply, emphasizing her point.

"You two freak me out, Gram. Still, I appreciate the offer, though I don't want either one of you doing time on my account."

Mrs. Brock—Rachel—snorted. "Underestimated as usual. We're old, not helpless, honey." She stormed off to the table in the corner with a huff, then stood at the edge, glaring at the teenage boys sitting there until they got up and moved.

"Her husband was a lousy cheat too," Gram informed me in a hushed whisper. "The day that old bastard died she threw the biggest party this town has ever seen. If you want, I could throw you a little shindig? I'll make a pitcher of my famous margaritas," she offered.

"I'm good for now. Last time I had one of your margaritas I forgot who I was for an hour. I can't keep up with you,

Gram. But we'll have dinner soon." I tried not to, but a small laugh escaped.

"Did your momma talk to you? About taking her place organizing the gala with Jake?" She pushed, "I think you should do it. It will take your mind off things. The best way to get over one man is to get under another, if you know what I mean." She winked at me.

"No, she didn't mention it. But, at this point in my life, I'll do anything for a distraction." Was it the distraction, or the idea of spending all that time with—and possibly getting *under*—Jake? Swiftly, I shut that stream of thought down to head back into denial. It was safer in denial, like putting all my parts that required love and attention into stasis. Feelings can't get hurt if no one is messing with them.

"Okay, honey. I'll be over there. You let us know." She patted her bag with raised eyebrows, took their tray, and sauntered off to join Mrs. Brock at their commandeered table.

"They are goals," Piper commented from the other side of the counter.

"Absolutely," I agreed.

"That'll be us one day. Plotting murder and mayhem from our little rocking chairs. Maybe you should take them up on their offer?" she suggested with a loud giggle.

"You're crazy!" I shook my head in amusement.

Customers came and went. Sympathetic smiles were given, commiseration from a heretofore unknown sisterhood of wounded hearts was offered, and I felt a bit better about my lot in life. If I could manage to keep it all at the surface level of my thoughts—the inquisitive expressions on almost everyone's faces, the sympathy in their voices, and pretty much everything else that was going on in my shop today—maybe I would be fine.

Yeah, right.

I inhaled a deep breath of air and grabbed a cup to prepare my next order. One of the best parts of this town was also the worst: people cared. Some just wanted the dirt, but others wanted to offer genuine help. I wondered if finding my husband boning his secretary qualified me for the sympathy casserole phone tree? Would there be a plethora of covered baking dishes on Rose's porch when I got back? I had no doubt that news of where I was staying had already traveled throughout town. If people knew what had gone on in my bedroom, someone had to have seen Trevor, his truck, and the boxes exiting Rose's place and spread that around too.

"Next! Can I help you?" I asked as I turned around. "Oh! Jake. What'll it be?" I tried to cover my happy surprise with a small smile instead of the huge beam that threatened to spill out of my face. I was thrilled, nay, overjoyed to see him, to the point that it was almost inappropriate, especially considering the gossip mavens currently in residence inside my shop.

"The usual."

"Well, now you don't *usually* drink coffee this time of day. Are you checking up on me?" I questioned as I tugged him to the side.

"Of course I am," he whispered. "You had a rough morning and—"

"I'm sorry, I don't want to talk about that now," I murmured. "I'm going to focus on helping Piper. The boys are upstairs in the loft if you want to go back and say hi, and maybe check on them for me?"

"I'll head back right now."

"They have a pizza. How about a Coke?" I offered as I filled a cup with ice and soda.

"Yes, please." He took it and headed past me on the other side of the counter toward the swinging doors. I watched him move, frozen in place.

"Vi, look alert," Piper leaned in and whispered. "Don't feed the gossip meter, girl."

"Huh? Oh, yeah."

Customers came and went over the next couple hours. Piper and I kept up with the steady flow as the tip jar filled up and they left without the juicy tidbits they had come in searching for.

"Closing time," Piper announced when the clock hit four. The last customer had long since left and we had finished washing the dishes and cleaning behind the counter.

"Finally." I lifted the hinged counter, headed out front and plopped into an overstuffed purple chair in the corner to sprawl. "This has been the longest day ever."

"Do you want to talk now?" she asked as she sat at the table next to me.

"Not really. I feel like you probably got the gist of it all day long, right?"

"Yeah, but are you okay?"

"I will be. We'll be moving into Rose's place early. Matter of fact, our stuff is probably there now, courtesy of my siblings."

"Okay, my mother is expecting me. I'm going to head home. If you need me, call. I don't care what time it is."

"I will. Promise." Smiling, she got up, turned the window sign to closed, and locked the front door behind herself as she left.

I employed a cleaning service to sweep, mop, and sanitize the tables, chairs, and bathroom after the shop closed. As I sat here, I considered the fact that I might have to let that luxury go. I would probably need that money for bills or for the boys. I ran my hands into my hair, covering my eyes as I contemplated the chores I could do myself here to save a few bucks. I doubted I could continue to afford taking the first few weeks of the school year off to volunteer for Rose with her kindergarten class, either. I realized this divorce would end up being more complicated than just dumping my wayward husband.

"Time to go home yet?" Nick popped out from the swinging doors followed by Finn. Jake had left about an hour after he got here; he must have been on his lunch break. Now it was just me and the boys in the shop.

"Yeah, it's time. Should we pick up something for dinner on the way? Or swing by the grocery store? I'm not sure what Rose has in the fridge, if anything."

"Jake said he'd bring dinner by."

"Oh yeah, he mentioned something about that this morning." I smiled. I couldn't help it. The thought of seeing him was . . . well, I didn't even know how to describe what I was feeling anymore. But the thought of seeing him later tonight was like a light in the dark. One I hadn't expected to find, but was grateful to have.

Chapter 7
Jake

"I'm not a coffee addict. I'm just a little over-attached to it."

Even though I'd seen with my own eyes what a selfish prick Tom had become over the last few years, I had still held out hope that he would be there for his boys. Today proved that he wouldn't, and I was disappointed, to say the least. Finn and Nick were hurting. They tried to hide it, but I had known them far too long to let it slide. It had all come out over pizza and Coke this afternoon on my lunch break. They told me how Tom had been treating Violet—dismissive, disrespectful, rude. How he had been neglecting them in favor of work, which most likely was not about work at all, considering he was cheating with his secretary.

I wish I had known.

I wish they or Violet had confided in me.

When you grow up with someone, like Tom and I had, you can't help but give the benefit of the doubt. I had been caught up in giving it over and over until here I was, stuck in this untenable situation. I felt like a fool, halfway in love with my best friend's wife and wishing I could do something to take away the pain he had caused his family, while knowing deep down there was nothing I could do other than let the pieces fall apart the way he had intended.

I had been stuck on the sidelines when I had wanted to be in the middle of it. When it felt as if I *should* have been the one in the middle of it. Regret burned through me like acid filling my veins because I had seen her first all those years ago. And I had let her go. He did not appreciate all the wonderful things about her that made me love her in silence and I was left wondering if he had ever learned to see beyond her beautiful facade to the more spectacular inside. Hell, at this point I had to question if she even saw it within herself.

I had spotted Violet on the first day of my junior year of college standing in the cafeteria, beautiful and shy, talking to her friend. I watched her for a moment as she laughed and tossed her shiny brown hair over her shoulder, smiling at Piper and lighting up the entire cafeteria. I wanted her immediately; back then I was used to getting what I wanted, so I didn't hesitate to start my approach. But Tom beat me to it. He got to her first. So I stood there and I held back like a good friend would. I watched her blush as he approached her. I watched her smile at him and touch his arm and flirt back as he charmed her, all while I stood there and did nothing.

Through the years I watched as she became his wife, the mother to his children, then a business owner. She moved further and further out of my reach, even as she became one of the best friends I'd ever had in my life. My heart had splintered into pieces as time moved on. Some I'd kept hidden, while others I gave to her and her boys to keep.

This became my normal. My feelings were manageable, and I lived my life, semi-happily existing around the one huge missing piece while I tried to fill my heart with new ones.

I no longer felt that way.

A glance at the clock above my desk told me dinner time was approaching. I'd told both her and the boys I'd get them fed tonight. It was a promise I intended to keep. They needed someone on their side. Violet had a great family, extensive and loving, but they needed more than that. Brothers and sisters and mothers and fathers were not the same kind of support I could offer. They needed what they had lost, and I intended to—

What? Step in?

With a shake of my head, I shoved my chair back and stalked to my door to leave. Harper had gone home so there was no one at the outside desk to witness my juvenile behavior as I stomped out of my office suite and contemplated where to pick up dinner.

I found myself in line at Imperial Palace, a favorite of everyone, bitterly laughing to myself as I realized I already knew what to order without even having to ask. How pathetic was I? I'd attached myself to the perimeter of Violet's family enough to know their preferred dishes from the local Chinese food restaurant.

I mulled this over on the way to her house. *Jesus. I should either get my own life under control or move all the way into hers.* The thought of doing so sent a jolt of heat down my spine. With a twist of the wheel, I pulled in next to Violet's Range Rover and tried to pull myself together at the same time. Playing it cool was the only way. Anything else would be pushing too hard, too fast, too soon.

"Jake! Hey, man," Nick yelled from the other side of the back yard fence. "Aunt Rose had Uncle Luke grab all the good patio furniture. Dad's going to be so pissed when his favorite hammock is gone."

I chuckled. "Your Aunt Rose is something else," I mused.

"Yeah, she's—she really helped my mom out today. She's the best. They all are. We got home and our room was all set up for us and everything." His eyes grew glassy in the early evening dusk as he turned toward the back porch entrance. "Let's go inside."

"Yep," I answered, unsure yet of what to say.

Finn was at the fridge, filling a glass with ice. "Imperial Dragon? Sweet! Mom is in the living room trying to figure out Aunt Rose's remote controls. Her electronics obsession is almost as huge as Dad's is. Her TV is epic, and we get to keep it!"

"That's great. Should I gather plates?"

Nick piped in. "Nah, Rose's coffee table is stocked. I think I saw chopsticks in there when I was digging around for the chocolate earlier."

"Then let's get to it. Grab me a drink while you're in there, Finn?"

"You got it, Jake. Thanks for coming. Seriously."

"Where else would I be, guys?" The boys exchanged a glance, the meaning of which I did not know. I left them in the kitchen and crossed through the open doorway into the living room. This house was old and boxy, having been built in the forties when open plan design was not a thing.

"Jake! You came." Violet greeted me with a smile. She eyed the bags in my hand and that smile turned big. "Tell me you brought some lemon chicken and egg rolls."

"You know I did." I sat next to her and we were soon joined by the boys, who passed drinks around as Violet opened a drawer in the huge square coffee table and dug out paper plates, chopsticks, and napkins.

"My sister . . ." Violet said, shaking her head. "Once she plants herself on a soft surface, she does not like to get up. I'm seeing the merits of it tonight." I passed her the chicken with a smile and laughed as the boys rapidly filled their plates, then stood up as if to leave.

"Where are you going?" Violet asked.

"Can we eat in our room and finish setting it up?" Nick asked.

"Oh, sure, go ahead. But just for tonight, yeah? You know how I feel about you guys having food in the bedroom."

"Yeah, we know." Finn raised his eyebrows meaningfully at me as he left the room. I shrugged, not knowing how he expected me to respond. Or what he wanted me to do, other than cheer up his mom—which was my intention.

Once the boys were ensconced in their room, door closed, I turned my attention to Violet. I'd noticed they had closed the hallway door as well, leaving Violet and me alone in the spacious, yet cozy living room. This house was built like a large rectangle; each room was separated by a doorway, with a front and back porch popping out on either side. It would be easy to just shut off each part of the house and have all the privacy you needed, which was a good thing considering how small it was. Though who knew how thin the walls were? Would the boys be able to hear us?

"How are you doing? Are you feeling okay?"

"I'm okay. I think." Her eyes met mine as she reached for the container of fried rice. "Honestly? After the day I've had, I'm glad to be feeling kind of numb."

"Are you tired? I could go and let you get some rest." I

offered to leave even though doing so was the last thing I wanted to do.

"No," she quickly answered. "Even though the boys are here, I don't want to be alone yet. That doesn't even make any sense, does it?"

"It does. They're kids and you need someone to take care of you tonight." Her cheeks heated as she glanced at me through her eyelashes.

"I can take care of myself. I've been doing it for years. I feel—"

"Lonely? Is that it?"

"Yeah. It doesn't make sense with the number of siblings I have, not to mention my nosy mother, but I have felt alone for a long time. You know what the craziest thing about today is?"

"Tell me."

"Leaving Tom made me feel less alone." Her cheeks colored even more as her eyes darted from mine.

"I get that. Being in a failing relationship is draining."

"Yeah," she whispered. "And Tom and I have been failing for years."

"God, Violet, I wish . . ."

She froze, eyes burning into mine. "What do you wish? Tell me."

I wish I had made a play all those years ago. "Never mind. How's your dad's ankle?"

Her shoulders dropped and her weary expression dimmed half a shade darker before she shook it off and powered forward. "Oh, he'll be fine. My mother is determined to make him take it easy. Speaking of that, my grandmother mentioned something about me taking over gala planning duties for my mother. Are you okay with that? I mean, you don't have to worry, it won't be my first big event in town."

"I'm not worried. I thought it was a great idea." Beneath my beard, I felt my own face start to flush. This was both what I'd wanted and feared. The idea of working closely with Violet was heady and tempting. "We'll need to set a schedule that works for both of us—"

"How about over dinner a couple times a week? Since we both work during the day."

"That will be perfect. Tuesday and Thursday nights?"

"Excellent. I have my book club at the shop almost every Wednesday."

"I know." She smiled and took another bite of chicken. It seemed as if she was searching for something to say. "Uh, I'm lucky they packed everything for me. All I have to do is a bit of unpacking in my room. For such a shitty morning, this day didn't turn out half bad. Except for the gossip sesh at my shop, that is."

"Gossip sesh?" I chuckled, then stole a bite of Violet's lemon chicken with a wink.

"Yeah, the usual suspects showed up to take my measure and see if I'm doing okay. You know how it is in this town." Her tone was breezy, but I could tell she was bothered by it.

"I know exactly how this town is. You promise to let me know if anyone gets too intrusive and I'll put a stop to it. You don't owe an explanation to anyone."

"Thanks," she whispered.

"Of course. I got your back, Vi. Always."

"I believe it." Her smile was tentative. Even though she said she was okay, I knew there had to be a lot of hurt simmering beneath the surface.

"You don't have to put on a brave face for me, Violet. I hope you know that."

"I know it. I do, it's just—I feel like I've experienced every mood that exists today, and I want to settle on one before I go to bed."

"Maybe you should just let go and feel whatever you feel."

"An amused look crossed her face. "I'm not sure you want to be here for that, Jake." She laughed.

"Why wouldn't I?"

"I was pretty angry earlier at the house, with the whole tequila, throwing-my-glass-in-the-pool, crying-all-over-Rose thing. The crying didn't freak you out?"

"Very little freaks me out anymore."

"Seen it all, huh?" she teased.

"We're not college kids anymore. Emotions don't scare me, Violet."

"Well, emotions annoyed Tom, that's for sure." My eyes narrowed as I studied her face for the meaning hidden behind her words. "I really don't want to talk about him though. I'm sorry."

"No need to apologize. Not to me."

"Thanks."

"No need to thank me either. There's no place I'd rather be right now," I confessed.

"You're just . . . amazing. You've been here for me and the boys all day."

"I—"

"So, I, um, thank you." She tucked her chin into her chest as her face turned bright red.

"You're welcome, sweetheart."

"Oh . . ." Her face turned even more red. As I watched her struggle for words, I felt it in my heart. She was gorgeous sitting there with her face devoid of makeup, hair in a bun. Simply beautiful.

"Do you need any help unpacking?" I broke the charged silence between us with an innocuous question. Every other thing I wanted to say to her in this moment would be crossing a line that neither one of us was ready for.

"Sure. I have a few boxes to put up in the closet, and the rest is just my clothes. I'm keeping Rose's furniture."

"Let me clean this up," I insisted. "I'll meet you in your room to help you unpack."

"You're too good to me," she murmured.

"I want to help."

"I'll stop saying thank you and instead just tell you that this means a lot, Jake."

She stood, and I nodded as she left the room, once again overcome with the sense of regret that had plagued me earlier. I followed behind, wondering if being in her bedroom was a good idea. I already knew it wasn't. But I did not stop.

"I have a few boxes that need to go up on the top shelf of the closet. Do you mind? You're the tallest human I know. Actually, I guess Finny is the tallest now. Sorry." She giggled as she handed me a flower-covered hatbox.

"Hey, six-four isn't too shabby, is it? How tall is that little booger now, anyway?" Her eyes drifted over me as I placed the box on the shelf. "Hey, there's something in the way up here." I reached into the corner of the closet and tugged until it came loose and landed open on the floor. It was an old photo album, covered in fabric and full of my old modeling pictures.

"Ohhhh, my god." Violet said, snatching it up and slamming it closed. "Rose will literally *die* if she knows you saw this. Or if she knows I saw it, or that we know that it even exists. I mean it, you can't tell her. We have to stuff it back up there. Here, take it." I took it but didn't stuff it back into the corner. I couldn't help but flip through it. I had grown up poor. College and law school had been a far off, almost unreachable goal for a kid like me until I was discovered at age seventeen by a talent scout at a mall in Portland. Modeling had paid for my education and allowed me to travel all over the world.

"This takes me back." I chuckled. "I guess she had a bit of a crush, is that it?"

"*A bit?* You could say that. Rose and Lily, both. Every time you came over, they would have a minor freak out. You have to notice how people react to you, Jake. I mean, come on."

"Not so much lately. But when I was still modeling, yeah, I noticed. I was happy to be a hunk of meat as long as I could pay my tuition. Now when it happens it's kind of weird. Those days are long gone and luckily, I've managed to live them down. At least enough to be taken seriously about getting my charity off the ground."

"Well, you look almost the same. Just a bit of salt to add some flavor now." She reached up, tracing a finger along the silver hair at my temple. I leaned into her touch and she inhaled a sharp breath. It was irresistible and I wanted more, which meant I had to go. "Um, I have two more boxes for the garage, but I can have the boys take them out tomorrow," she murmured.

"Nah, I got it. Then I'd better head home. I have an early morning. Uh, you do too at the shop, right?"

"Yeah." Her words were nothing but breath. "I do." Her glistening eyes had me caught; I couldn't look away as I took the boxes from the end table by the bed.

"Are you sure you'll be okay?" I was reluctant to leave. I

knew she was more upset than she was letting on. But the idea of insisting that she let me stay felt intrusive. I backed out of the room, hesitating in the doorway. "I'll lock up after myself. Promise you'll call if you need to talk. Please, Vi?"

"I promise."

I should have forced myself to leave, but I couldn't stop myself from blurting what would inevitably be too much. "I think the world of you, Violet. Please don't let—don't let him steal your spirit, okay?"

Her gorgeous eyes filled with tears as she mouthed, "Thank you," and smiled.

Damn. She had blown straight back into my heart and now it was wide open in the palm of her hand.

Chapter 8
Violet

"Love yourself as much as you love coffee."

I knew I shouldn't open this box. But apparently, I was Pandora and unable to resist. Instead of the world's troubles unleashing themselves to run amok, it was a flood of memories of the boys. The smell of baby detergent hit me as I opened the box. Long lost memories—good ones—washed over me as I remembered the family I once had.

"Shit," I whispered.

Finn stuck his head in the door. "You okay, Mom?"

"Yes," I answered too quick, my voice cracking over the word. "I'll be fine. I've had a long day. I just need sleep. I know it's early, but why don't you and Nick go to bed, or relax in your room, okay?" I was emotionally exhausted, and my control was beginning to slip. I knew we weren't done talking this through, but I had the feeling I was about to break, and I needed to be alone when it happened.

"All right, but if you don't feel like being by yourself or whatever just knock on our door. Okay?"

"I will. Promise." He turned to go, but then spun back.

"Mom."

"Yeah, baby?"

"I'm sorry you stayed with Dad so long because of us."

"Oh, honey, no. I was trying to keep our family together for *all* of us. I'm your mother. It's my job to take care of you, to make sure you have what you need. I'm the one who is sorry I couldn't make it work."

"We both know it wasn't your fault, okay? I don't want to pretend he's something he's not anymore. It makes it hurt too much whenever he lets us down. Don't you remember Dr. Simon saying that last time?"

"I remember. Why don't you two put on a movie or do homework or something to take your mind off today. I'm going to do a bit more unpacking then hit the sack. I'll come tuck you in later."

He laughed. "Tuck us in?"

"Yeah. You're never too old for tuck-ins, and I think we should go back to that."

"Whatever makes you feel better," he muttered as he left.

I stared out into the hall as he entered his room and shut the door, wondering if there had been—even though I knew deep down there wasn't—anything I could have done to keep our family together. The box of baby keepsakes beckoned me from the edge of the bed, and I snatched it up again, dumping it all on the quilt. Two tiny hospital bracelets, a pair of blue knit hats, and the matching little outfits I had dressed them in for the trip home spilled out along with photo packets of the pictures I had ordered from the hospital's photographer. I picked up a pale blue blanket and lay back on the pillow, nudging everything else aside with my leg as I tucked my face into the soft flannel fabric and cried.

"Violet?" My mother's voice rang out from the living room. Of course. She had a key to the house. She had all our keys, and she always seemed to know when to use them.

"Hello," I answered lamely as I sat up.

"Oh, my sweet girl—"

"Don't. Please don't be nice to me right now." I managed to shove the words out through my closed throat. She grabbed the box, replaced the contents and set it aside. With a light push, she shut the door and sat next to me on the bed.

"Come here." With arms held out, she waved me over. "And don't tell me to leave. There is no way I'm going to let you be alone like this. I'm spending the night with you. My bag is in the living room."

"Like what? I'll be fine," I lied. My voice sounded strained even to my own ears, and I could feel my shoulders start to shake as I spoke.

"I've got you. Just get it out before it eats you up. You can't hide from feelings like this, Vi. They'll wait for you around every corner until you face them head-on." Her knowing eyes roved over my face as she gathered me close to her side.

"Okay, but don't tell anyone," I insisted as I collapsed against her. "Especially since I'm going to end up messing up your shirt real bad." I sniffled as tears started to pour out of my eyes.

"I won't say a word, darling."

A knock at the door had me bolting upright.

"Oh no, I don't want them to see me like this. I've spent the whole day fighting it," I confessed.

"Like what? Like a woman who had her life upended? They're practically grown men and they love you. They'll understand." She answered the knock for me. "Come in."

The door opened to Nick's concerned face, with Finn following close behind.

"We heard crying." Nick got a glimpse of me. "Oh, Mama."

Finn's face was made of stone. "I'll fucking kill him."

"No. You'll do no such thing! Please. This is why I didn't want you boys to see me like this. See? Mom, see?"

"You can't protect us forever!" Finn shouted. "And we—we know he's been hurting your feelings, saying asshole stuff to you, but we didn't know how to fix it. We didn't know what to do because it seemed like you didn't want us to know about it, and we didn't want to hurt you even more by saying something. Grandma, tell us what to do."

"You don't start with violence, even though it's a valid feeling. Okay? I mean, I've wanted to pop him across his mean mouth a bunch of times—but I refrained. Violence is not the way." she answered.

Finn blew out a sigh as the wind blew out of his sails, and he collapsed back on the chair in the corner. "I know, I'm just pissed. Sorry, Mom."

"It's okay," I murmured.

"I get the urge, Finn. I do," my mother interjected. "What he did was wrong on every single level a man can be wrong on, and I'm proud that you boys already know that. We're going to be here for your mom tonight. And I'm going to be here for all of you just like always. This has been a tricky situation, and I'm afraid even I didn't know how to handle it properly. And I'm an adult."

Nick sat on the edge of the bed. "It's okay to cry in front of us," he said with that sweet smile that used to cross his face as a little boy.

"Yeah," Finn added. "Especially since everything is out

in the open now. You shouldn't have tried to hide stuff from us. It was confusing."

"I'm so sorry," I murmured.

"I'm not mad at *you*," Finn insisted. "Dad hasn't been that great to me and Nick either. He pretty much forgot we exist, but I never say anything about it. Except when it's my turn with Dr. Simon." He shrugged.

"Poor Dr. Simon, juggling all of our feelings and unable to just force us to talk to each other and put them together." My lame attempt at a joke fell flat.

Nick's lips quirked up in a wry grin. "She told me every month I should talk to you about how I feel about the mean shit we heard Dad saying to you."

"Yeah, she told me that too," Finn confirmed.

"Well, crap. I guess I've been doing a horrible job of protecting you both." Mortified, I hid my face in my hands. "I didn't realize you'd heard so much."

"We heard a lot. Probably more than you know," Nick said, tucking himself into my other side and wrapping me up in a hug.

My mother waved Finn over with her free arm. "Come here, honey. This family needs a big hug." He joined us, sitting stiffly on the edge of the bed next to my mother until she pulled him into her side with a huge sigh. "Relax, Finny, and let me take care of you."

"Aren't we too old for this?" he questioned.

"Never. Everyone deserves to be taken care of and loved on when they need it. Don't you agree?" I had to give it to her. She had managed to wrap us all up in her arms and we were all in tears, letting it all hang out in the open, and she'd only been here for about five minutes. Meanwhile, I had been walking on eggshells, avoiding confrontation, and making a mess of everything for way too long. I was an utter failure as a mother. "Don't even think it, Violet." She interrupted my mental self-flagellation as if she knew what I was thinking. "You're a wonderful mother. You have two gorgeous sons. You've grown up, my darling, into a woman with a kind and loyal heart. You are a generous friend and sister. You're my beautiful daughter, I love you, and I'm so very proud of you. But it's time to let it go. You did your best and *he* was not enough for *you*."

"Do you read minds?" A startled laugh burst out through my tears.

"No, I just know you. And boys, I still have some hope that your father will come around for you two. He was a good dad when you were little and somewhere deep inside, that man has to be in there. But as far as your mother goes—it's over. We'll work on making peace with that together."

"Okay, Grandma," Nick answered.

"Yeah," Finn grunted then stood up. "I love you guys." He addressed us collectively and rushed out of the room.

I moved to follow him, but Nick stopped me. "Let him go. He'll get mad if you chase after him."

I heard his bedroom door shut, then settled back into my mother. "Okay, as long as he stays in the house."

"Is it okay if I go too? Just to watch TV or something?"

"Absolutely, honey."

"Love you, Mom. You too, Grandma." He kissed her cheek before shutting the door behind himself.

"I'm drowning, Mom," I admitted. "What do I do?"

"Are you sure you're drowning, darling? Is that how you feel? Really think about it."

"No. Actually, that's not how I feel. Not anymore." I shook my head. "I'm floating right beneath the surface of the water. I'm staring at the sun and the moon and the stars and for the first time in forever I have clear eyes to see them.

I have hope for more than just my boys. Like maybe I can be happy someday too. But isn't that selfish? Tom is their father and I had to leave him in order to feel this way—"

"He drove you away. *He* chose this. Growing together in a marriage is a choice. Is it a sacrifice? Sometimes, yes. But it can be a beautiful sacrifice if you both choose to create it that way."

"You're right. I know you are. I'm just so tired," I whispered as the rest of my energy suddenly seemed to leave my body along with the last of my tears. My tears were not about Tom; I knew that because I had been all cried out over him a long time ago. I was on the precipice of something big, my life was about to begin anew, and the possibilities were overwhelming. A mental image of Jake floated through my mind like a ripple on a pond before I shut my eyes against it.

"Get some sleep. I'll be here all night out on the couch. Rose is at the house to keep an eye on your father and his broken ankle."

"Oh crap! I can't believe I forgot about Dad—"

"Well, your day was pretty eventful. Get some rest, sweetheart."

"'Kay. Goodnight." I pulled my legs up and shoved them under the covers. She tucked me in and kissed my cheek.

"Don't worry, I'll tuck the boys in too," she said as she stood. "You're never too old for tuck-ins," I heard her murmur as she headed down the hall.

Chapter 9
Jake

"Forget love, fall in coffee."

Several weeks had passed since Tom's cheating scandal broke, but unfortunately, it was still one of the hot topics of Sweetbriar gossips. I sat waiting for Violet at the Riverview Grille hoping my choice of location for our first gala planning meet would not add fuel to the gossip fire. I had requested a semi-hidden table in the corner, but the privacy was getting to me. This waiting felt different than the subconscious and unending waiting I'd been doing over the years. Sparks of hope kept shooting up and down my spine to mess with my head. After a glance around the restaurant, doubts began to rise along with the sparks. Could I do this? Sit with her, eat with her, be with her here, when I knew that nothing stood in the way of someday making her mine?

Coming here was a mistake. This was supposed to be a business dinner to chat about the plans for my charity's gala. This place was far too romantic, this table was entirely too intimate and secluded, and she was going to get the wrong idea. I scrubbed a hand down my beard. My mind had been full of nothing but *wrong ideas* lately.

"Jake! There you are," she called, as she followed the host to our table. "Hi." She was stunning in the form-fitting, snowy white sweater dress and stiletto heeled boots she had worn to her coffee shop's Christmas party a few months back. I had been her de facto escort after Tom ditched her to work instead of attending her annual festivities. I had almost wrecked myself over her then and I was on the way to finishing the job today. I had always thought she was the most beautiful woman I'd ever seen in my life. I had always wanted her, only now there was an actual chance I could have her . . . and the thought of it was about to drive me to the brink.

"Hello, gorgeous." *Damn it.* As if in a trance, I stood, brushing off the host's attempt to pull out her chair so I could do it myself. "I got her, thanks. We'll take iced tea, right, Vi?" I was off to a winning and possessive start already.

"Yes, with lemon," she added with an adorable little smirk. As if she could somehow read the almost desperate thoughts running through my mind and found them amusing or cute. Tom was out of the picture; did I expect the Riverview Grille's host to take his place? *My place?*

Rein yourself in, dumbass.

But it was as if I had somehow become unleashed. Tom had cheated himself out of the picture and out of her life. Since that moment, every thought in my head screamed at me to make Violet my woman. This was real, it wasn't sudden, we were always meant to be, and it was absolutely going to happen.

I inhaled a huge breath to calm myself down as I took my seat across from her. Hazel eyes twinkled in the moonlight streaming through the window as she smiled at me. We were being treated to a beautiful, albeit cold, clear Oregon evening outside with starlight sparkling on the river. Those big eyes darted from the view out the window, down my face and over my chest as I settled into my chair. I found myself becoming determined to make this business dinner end on a completely different note—nothing but personal. "How are the boys?" I asked.

Her eyes darted up to mine. "They're actually doing okay. I think Finn is coming down with something though. He's at home resting on the couch, watching TV. Either that or he's become more adept at faking me out—he missed school today." She laughed, then thanked our server as our iced teas were placed in front of us. "I already know what I want." Her lips shifted to one side in a grin. "I'll take my rain-checked Reuben, please."

I passed my unopened menu to our server. "I'll have the same." She gathered Violet's menu and turned to go put our orders in with a knowing nod. Chemistry buzzed at our table; it was undeniable. Her tongue darted out to catch an errant drop of iced tea and I almost groaned out loud. For the first time since I'd spotted her way back in college, I thought of kissing her. I allowed myself to picture it in the back corner of my mind where I hid all the other ungentle-manly and painful thoughts I'd had about her over the years. Only this time I let the image fly, smiling at her as the imaginary kiss reached its fruition.

"Do I even want to know what you're thinking about?" she murmured as her cheeks tinted pink.

"Probably not," I confessed. "Let's talk about the gala." My one-track mind was about to get lost in a fantasy and now was not the time. All the control I had built up over decades, all the feelings I had tied up in their intricate knots, were rapidly becoming undone as I gazed at her, sitting there across from me with no idea what I contemplated beneath the surface of my smile. The things I wanted to do with her, for her, *to* her . . .

She cleared her throat with a nervous little cough. "Good thinking. Um, do we need a theme? Do you have a place in mind? My mother said you two would usually meet twice a week when you were planning stuff. Will that work? Maybe we'll need more time together than you do with her?"

I chuckled. "Yes, to all of that. Your mother suggested 'An Evening Under the Stars' as the theme in order to keep it simple—"

"Ahh, to keep it cheap?" She laughed. "My mother is great at getting the most bang for her buck."

"Exactly," I confirmed. "She suggested the rooftop deck on the Sweetbriar Hotel as the location since we won't have to pay for the stars to be there—free décor—and they're already prepared for outdoor parties. They have space heaters, fire pits, a tent for rain cover, cabanas—everything we'll need."

She leaned across the table, placing her delicate, red-tipped fingers lightly on my forearm. I shivered, wishing I had removed my jacket when I got here and rolled up my shirtsleeves so I could feel her touch against my bare skin. "That sounds perfect. But I want to tell you something before we get started."

"You can tell me anything, Violet," I murmured.

Her eyes darted down to the table before she reclaimed my gaze through the lovely fan of her dark lashes. "I really admire you. Starting this charity, sharing your story . . . You're so brave. I mean, a long time ago, Tom told me a little bit about how you grew up. Um, I'm sorry, maybe I shouldn't bring this up, this isn't my business—"

"No apologies, Vi," I soothed. "My dad was an asshole. It's not some big tragic secret. He was a liar and a gambler who treated us all like shit, cheated on my mother constantly and flagrantly, and refused to grant her a divorce. We were too poor to afford an attorney to fight him. He'd pop in and out of our lives whenever he needed money or a place to crash, mess everything up, smack us around, and then leave again."

"That's terrible." Her hand slid down my arm to place her palm in mine.

I inhaled a sharp breath. "It was, until my older brother grew big enough to throw him out and keep him away. But it's over, and now I'm in the position to help others. So that's what I'm going to do. I just wish she were here to see it." My mother had died of cancer almost three years ago.

"I think you're wonderful," she reiterated.

"I'm no hero. But I thank you anyway. So, speaking of helping and throwing out exes, do you have legal representation? Tom isn't going to go off gently into the night, you know. He's not the type to give you a fair deal, and you're entitled to support, part of the house, and maybe even part of his business. You are a large reason for his success, Violet. He wouldn't have graduated college if not for you working to support him. I was there, remember? I know how hard you worked back then. You and the boys deserve more. I know his attorney. She's a real shark, and I don't want to see you get taken advantage of."

"My mother called her attorney. Everything is going okay so far. Tom is being pretty reasonable, I think." She stopped talking to knock on the table with her free hand, I grinned at her superstition. "I'm not in the market for a shark—they're usually expensive. As it is, I might have to take help from my mother to pay hers, which I hate." Her eyes lowered to the table as her hand slipped from mine to grab her napkin and place it in her lap, fussing with it while avoiding my eyes.

"I have a recommendation. You can be the first to use the center. The test case, if you will. I have my own shark. Tearing up bad husbands is his favorite thing to do."

"It's not you?" Her eyes raised to mine.

"No, I was in corporate law. I needed to make money fast so I could open this place. It's my brother. Ren is raring to go. I'll give him your number, yes?"

"I can't take help away from someone who might really need it," she protested.

"You're probably going to end up genuinely needing it to fight Tom, and we're going to give it to you. You'll be helping us out too. We're not open yet and he's getting restless."

"Okay, give him my number. We'll see what happens." We turned in unison as our server arrived with our Reubens.

Violet thanked her, then shifted her friendly smile my way. I grinned back as her eyes warmed on mine. "You're a good friend, Jake."

Ouch. The dreaded *F* word. I wanted more than just her friendship, but I recognized that she was obviously still not in the place to give it to me. She had turned me upside down over these last couple of weeks. The anticipation of tonight's meeting had been building up in my mind along with the usual subconscious expectations and foolish wishful thinking. It hurt. I covered it with a return smile. "I try," I answered.

Her head tilted to the side as she gazed at me. "I'm still

married," she whispered as she caught my eyes in the deep hazel trap of hers.

Startled, I sucked in a nervous breath. "What did you say?"

"I can't, uh—" she fidgeted in her chair while her hazel gaze drifted to the window and into the shimmering, starlit, black of the river beyond the glass. "Never mind."

"Talk to me," the words came out gruff, with an edge that I had not intended to reveal. She flinched and I reached out a hand to cover hers. My thumb rubbed unconsciously over her bared ring finger. Her wedding rings were gone. Why hadn't I noticed that before? "That came out harsh. I didn't mean it like that. You surprised me, Violet. Please tell me what you're thinking."

"I feel something when I'm with you and I want to acknowledge it, even if you don't feel it too." She raised her chin, earnest eyes blazing into mine.

I chuckled because I sure as hell felt it too. "Oh, I feel it. Don't you worry about that."

"Oh, okay," she breathed. "I thought maybe you did and honestly, I'm too old to play games. Not that I even know what games people play nowadays, anyway," she confessed.

I held her gaze and leaned back in my chair. "I don't play. Not when I know what I want."

"Oh! That's a good thing—" She looked away, her cheeks a lovely shade of rose. "Oh my god, is that Bethany at that table over there? *Gah!* Don't look," she hissed as I moved to turn around. "What if she sees us?"

"Who cares if she does? We're not doing anything wrong."

"It's just . . . how does this look?" she murmured as her eyes kept darting behind me, I assumed toward Bethany's table. "You and I are here. Alone together."

"How does this make you look bad? We're planning a gala together. This is business. Nobody knows about our feelings. Try to relax." Her face turned bright red as she studied the tabletop as if it held the meaning of life. "What? Am I missing something?" I asked.

"No, um . . . I'm not going to point it out if you didn't notice," she stumbled over her words as she plucked a non-existent piece of lint from her sleeve.

"Is this a trick question? I thought we weren't playing games?" I teased. Reaching forward, I tugged lightly on one of the dark curls draped over her shoulder.

"It's just, I wore—"

I leaned back in my chair again and allowed myself the reaction I had tried so hard to keep to myself when she arrived. "So, you *were* trying to get my attention with this hot as hell sweater dress? Is that what you're saying, beautiful?"

Her blush intensified. "Yes," she admitted on a breath.

"I noticed." Reaching out, I tipped her chin up with a fingertip. "Believe it. I've seen nothing but you since you got here."

"Oh god. Maybe I'm just not built for this. I'm nervous. She's right there with her little friends and I'm still married. I mean, technically. Uh . . ."

"Forget her. We're not doing anything wrong," I reiterated. "Let's eat. Violet, take a bite, baby. Please try to relax. Everything will be all right."

"Okay." She picked up her sandwich and took a bite.

"You have a little something right there." I gestured to the corner of her mouth.

"Well, get it, please," she hissed. "We're sitting in a fancy restaurant. I'm wearing this scandalous sweater dress. I'm with my husband's best friend only weeks after said husband cheated on me. Heaven forbid I have a little something on my lip too." She flopped her sandwich to her plate, shooing away my hand and picking up her napkin before I could get near her face. "What are we doing Jake?"

"Nothing," I answered. *Lie.* We were shamelessly flirting, most likely on our first date, and we both knew it.

She sighed, nodding with relief. "Okay, I'm fine, we're fine. This is fine."

"We haven't done anything. *Yet*, that is." I winked.

"Oh god."

"Maybe this will help." I pulled my laptop out of my briefcase along with a notebook and set them at the edge of the table. "Better?"

"Yes, thank you." She reached into her tote and added her tablet with a grin.

"It's official. Nothing but work going on over here." I covered her hand—now hidden from view by our stacked work materials—with mine, she turned hers to the side to interlock our fingers.

"Yeah . . . work." Her lips quirked into an adorable sideways smirk as she lifted her glass to sip her tea.

Chapter 10
Violet

"My coffee is strong and so am I."

Nothing but work, my ass. We were flirting our brains out and it would be obvious to anyone who caught a glimpse of us. My cheeks didn't turn this red for no reason. I was struggling to be smart about this, but the way he sprawled in that chair across from me was way too sexy. He was beaming out more hot sex appeal than all the rays from the sun put together. And damn it, each one had hit its mark on me. I was burning up and turning into a puddle of horny goop on my side of the table. It had been a long time since I'd had a man's undivided attention, and it was making me high. Every brush of his leg against mine made me turn giddy as hell and I would need at least an hour alone in my bathtub later tonight to get past this or I might literally die.

We finished our sandwiches, chatting about the gala and taking notes the entire time, letting the subject of whatever we were feeling fade away. How I managed to eat in front of him without drooling or choking on my own tongue was a question for the ages. The more I looked at him without the blinders of marriage over my eyes—I mean, full-on checking him out while contemplating what he looked like naked—the more flustered I grew. The crazy thing was I'd seen him without a shirt many times over the years and I had never felt like this. Back in the days before Tom's secret jerk-face came out, Jake had come to all our barbecues and swam in the pool, tossed the boys around in the water with Tom, sat in the chaise lounges, soaked in the sun, and even occasionally brought dates with him. Basically, I knew Jake had an incredible body under that suit, as would anyone with a working pair of eyeballs. But now I found myself unable to stop imagining what his body could do to mine—or what I wanted to do to him.

Spoiler alert: none of the things I was imagining involved clothes or anything that wasn't completely and totally X-rated. I should be ashamed of myself for objectifying him like this.

"I think we got it for today," he announced after his last sip of iced tea. "Are you interested in dessert? Coffee?" He chuckled. "What am I saying? No one makes coffee better than yours."

"Got that right." I laughed. "How about a rain check on dessert? I should really get back to Finn and check on him." Our server brought our check, and Jake paid. Should I have paid for my own dinner? I didn't know the rules about what constituted a date anymore. *Gah!* I had no idea how to act around him.

"Deal." He gathered his materials, stuffing them back into his briefcase. I did the same, and stood. I felt awkward, like I had on my first date back in high school, and on my second date, and I'll be honest, on every single date I'd ever had until after I got married. I was not one of those cool women who knew how to handle a man. I couldn't understand why I was stressing out. This was not a date, but for a large part of it, it had felt like one.

He circled around the table to help me with my chair—*date, date, date!*

Eyes followed our every movement as we walked through the restaurant, particularly Bethany's. This had been a bad idea. I could tell the Sweetbriar gossip meter was pinging like crazy. We should have met in his office, or my shop. I shouldn't have worn my second best sexy dress. For the love of god, I should be in my third best office ensemble. But I knew what I was doing when I got ready for tonight. I was trying to get him to look at me like he had at my Christmas party. I could swear I had seen longing in his expression that night. Longing and maybe a little bit of lust. I needed that, I wanted it, and on some level deep inside myself I could admit that I had always craved it from Jake. But while I was married it had manifested in innocent ways, like helping him decorate his duplex, teasing him about his serial monogamist ways, and trying to fix him up with Piper after her divorce. (Piper had laughed her ass off, told me I was in denial, and stated she would never, ever go there with him.)

He was my friend and he had always been a good one. Trying to tempt him like this was probably stupid. What would I do if I lost him? The possibility was too horrible to think about.

"I'll walk you to your car," he declared somewhat bossily as his hand slid possessively along my lower back to guide me to the exit. It wasn't an offer; it was a statement of intent. Of what, I was not sure. My skin tingled beneath the layer of my jacket and dress as if he were touching the bare skin of my back. This was impossible! I couldn't think straight around him anymore.

"Thank you," I murmured, even though I should refuse him. He didn't answer. I had parked at the edge of the lot, close to the dock that jutted out over the river. It was a beautiful spot and somewhat deserted now that dinnertime was almost over. The locks disengaged as I approached and he opened my door, placed his briefcase on my seat, and took my tote from my shoulder to set it alongside his stuff.

"This was the best date I've ever had, and it wasn't even a date," I blurted. Damn my big mouth and lack of cool-girl poise.

A slow grin crossed his face, one that I'd never seen from him before, and his eyes focused like laser beams on my mouth. I gulped.

Could I dare think about what I wanted for a change? Instead of my gaze always being ten steps into the future, could I look at what was standing right there in front of me? Could I reach for what I wanted? Should I even try?

"I had always hoped there would be a time for us," he whispered. "I can't seem to be around you lately without wanting more."

"I feel the same way, Jake." My voice came out on a thin wisp of air because he had stolen my breath away along with every rational thought in my head.

He inhaled my words and stepped closer, raising his hand to my face in a gentle caress. The brisk evening air had momentarily chased away the constant blush I'd worn all night, but heat rose in my cheeks once again. I leaned into his touch with a sigh.

Had I ever felt like this?

I couldn't seem to remember.

"What are you doing to me, Violet?" He took my hand and placed it over his racing heart, I ducked my head with a grin, thrilled that I was the cause of it.

"I don't know. Maybe you should show me." I stepped into him, closing the inches between us I slid my hands up his broad chest to wind my arms around him and tuck my face into his neck for a hug.

"Look at me, gorgeous." Tenderly, the hand at my cheek slid into my hair, tugging softly to tilt my head back as his other arm wrapped around my waist to pull me even closer. He nudged my forehead with his. Our eyes met and held. "I want to kiss you."

"Yes." My lips parted on my answer as my eyes drifted shut. I felt his breath on my cheek. The soft scratch of his beard tickled as his thumb slid along my jawline, holding my face steady in his big, warm palm. Anticipation sparked along my spine as I felt the soft press of his lips and the hard push of his body backing me up against the side of my SUV.

Our kiss grew deeper and his arm at my waist tightened as his hand gripped my hip, bunching my dress in his fist as he held me. This kiss told me who he was. I was protected in his arms, hidden from view, sheltered from the cold wind dancing along the river as he gave himself over to our kiss. Logic and reason and everything I had told myself about why I should not be doing this disappeared. Nothing remained except for this moment and how he made me feel. Instead, I focused on his mouth on mine and the way he held me so close, like I belonged pressed up against him. Like just maybe I was where I was always meant to be.

I gasped for air but didn't pull away. I was breathless, without speech, completely lost in his arms. I could tell he felt the same as we stood there staring at each other through half-closed eyes, until with a rough pull he drew me into his body to rest my cheek against his chest.

"No one has ever kissed me like that," he murmured into my hair.

"I have never, ever felt like this," I confessed. "Ever."

"Cheater! You judgmental bitch. You have a lot of nerve, Violet." I gasped at the harsh words. My heart leapt out of the moment with a hard startled beat as my stomach sank and the heat left my cheeks, leaving me cold.

Jake stepped back. Over his shoulder I saw Bethany and her friends. "Watch yourself, Bethany," he stated. "Violet is not the cheater in this scenario, and you know it."

"I do *not* know it," she screeched. "But I know what I just saw. And you know what you just did! Some friend you are, Jake. I'm telling Tom." She stormed off in a huff, followed by her friends.

Tears filled my eyes. "Oh my god. What have we done?"

"We haven't done anything wrong. You've filed for divorce. You're as good as single."

"What are the boys going to think? They'll find out about this. Nothing is secret in this town. I'm so stupid! You *know* how she's going to make this look."

"The boys will be fine," he insisted. He took my hands in his. "We'll be fine too."

"Technically, I'm still a married woman, Jake. And you're Tom's friend. The boys—"

"Will understand. They're practically grown men, Violet. They're not children anymore."

"Okay, maybe you're right and they will understand. But that doesn't mean we should do this *now*. We just can't. I still have to get through the divorce. I need to figure out how to run the shop with less money, and I have to take care of the boys. I mean, Finn is sick and I'm here. What is wrong with me? I should be home with him right now. I know better than to make selfish choices like this."

"Like what?" His voice was soft. "Like being with me tonight, kissing me? Those choices?"

"Yes. I can't do this. I can't treat them like Tom does, putting his needs above theirs. I should be at home."

"Where do you come into play, Violet?"

"What?"

"When do you get what you need? Who takes care of you?"

"Um—"

"You matter too."

"Uh—"

"You matter a lot to me, in fact." My heart burst at his words. I wanted to matter to him, I wanted more from him than I was willing to admit, even to myself.

"Oh, Jake. I don't want to hurt you and I don't want to lead you on. I just can't see how I can—" There was too much on my plate right now. It wouldn't be fair to add Jake to it. I'd end up treating him like Tom had treated me and the boys—minus the asshole behavior, of course. Tom never made time for us, and we had felt that pain years before his negativity and rude words toward me had entered the picture.

"I'm not asking for anything from you right now. I only want to plan the gala together and keep an open mind, with no pressure. Can we do that?"

"I think so. Yes, I can do that. Probably."

"Shh, don't overthink. Get in the car. It's cold." He reached inside and took his briefcase, helping me into the seat with a hand at my elbow. I forgot myself when I was with Jake. Things I used to feel before I had the boys rose to the surface to mute the call of my responsibilities. Things like how good it felt to be desired, to flirt, to dress up and feel beautiful. But I couldn't get lost in my own wishes. I had two boys who needed me, a new house to take care of on my own, and a business to run—not to mention a divorce to get through.

Chapter 11
Violet

"Life happens. Coffee helps."

"**B**oys, I'm home." I opened the front door expecting to find them lounging on the couch, watching TV. Instead, I was greeted by Nick as he headed into the kitchen.

"Hey, Mom. Finn is asleep and I think he has a fever. He's all gross and sweaty. I'm going to make him take some more ibuprofen soon. The bottle says every six hours."

His symptoms had grown worse while I was gone, and I felt terrible. He hadn't had a fever when I left. "I should have been here. I'm sorry Nick," I followed him into the kitchen, tossing my tote and jacket to the couch on the way.

"Why? I can manage to bring him a couple of pills, Mom."

"Yeah, I guess, but you shouldn't have to take care of him, that's my job."

He turned from the refrigerator with a grin, bottled water in hand. "We're almost adults. Should we expect you to follow us to college?" he teased.

"Maybe I will," I joked. "What am I going to do when you guys are gone?" The question made me sad. I had been a mother almost my entire adult life. My boys were my world. Every choice I had made had been with them at the forefront of my thoughts. I pulled a chair out from the table and sat with a heavy thud while contemplating my life and what it would be like when the boys had grown up and moved out. I did not like the thought.

Nick stopped in the doorway. "Are you okay?"

"Yeah, I'll take care of Finn. Did you happen to take his temperature?"

"No. The battery was dead in the thermometer, and I couldn't figure out how to use that old one you have in the cabinet."

"I'll show you how. You know, for when you're off in the wilds of college and have a fever." I stood and held my hand out for the water and pills. "Go and grab it, I'll take these to Finn."

I could tell right away he was worse the second I saw him. I sat at the edge of the bed and placed the back of my hand against his forehead.

His eyelids fluttered open. "Mom?"

"I'm sorry I wasn't here for you tonight, Finny."

"S'okay," he mumbled. "I'm fine, except now my throat hurts."

"Open." I aimed my cell phone flashlight into his mouth. One look told me he probably had strep throat and I definitely should have stayed home with him tonight. I felt like a garbage mother. What kind of person leaves their sick child unattended like this? Shame on me. "I'll make it up to you, honey."

"I'm fine." He swallowed and winced. "Quit apologizing all the time."

"I'm sor—I'll try. I promise." His throwaway comment struck something in me, and I froze. I had been apologizing in some form or another ever since I got pregnant. I was always trying to prove that I was good enough because I dropped out of college and got married young. Now that my marriage had failed and everyone knew it, my impulse to apologize had gone into overdrive. My quest to prove my worth was getting out of control as gossip swirled around me. I needed to keep the boys out of it, but I didn't know how.

"Here's the thermometer." Nick entered the bedroom, hand outstretched. "I think you should take mine too. I'm not feeling so great, and a bunch of kids at school were out sick today. Something is probably going around."

I cleared my throat with a grimace. "I'll call the doctor first thing in the morning."

* * *

I stared bleary eyed at the red Walgreens sign. The flickering letter *n* was hypnotizing in the early pre-dawn light as I sipped coffee from my travel mug and waited in the drive-through for Finn and Nick's antibiotics. I was right about the strep throat; both boys had it and they were currently at home in their beds, miserably sucking on ice cubes. They hadn't been this sick since they were little boys. Luckily, our family doctor had allowed me to send pictures of their grody red throats and diagnosed them without an office visit because Nick was also right—it was indeed going around town. My boys were almost grown, but they were still male. Therefore, strep-throat and a fever had become equal to a man-flu of the worst variety. In other words, I had been up all night distributing ice cubes, cool washcloths, and snuggles. Perhaps I had fed into it and spoiled them a bit too, but I was okay with that considering all the other stuff we had going on in our lives at present.

Should I call Tom? He had a right to know when the boys were this sick. I would absolutely want to know. I sighed and pulled out my cell, but the call went straight to voicemail. *Big surprise.* I rolled my eyes and left a message, then sent a text. Even though it had been weeks, we had yet to make plans regarding the boys and our attorneys had not gotten that far in our negotiations yet. Apparently, Tom was okay with me keeping the boys for now. As far as I was concerned, visits should be up to Finn and Nick, but the fact that Tom had yet to call them, even just to say hello, was disappointing. My eyes burned hot as I tried to keep my tears at bay. Neither one had said a word about their dad since we had moved out, but the surreptitious checking of their phones and whispered conversations that I'd caught and tried to get them to include me in told me they were hurting.

I jumped when the drive through window slid open and a bag brushed my hand on the rolled down window frame. "Hey, Violet. Here ya go. I hope they get well soon."

"Thanks." I drove off while trying to take a mental moment to remind myself that once the boys took their first dose, they would be well on the way to feeling better. Torturing myself with mom-guilt was useless, yet I couldn't seem to stop it. I both wanted Tom to call the boys and drop off the face of the earth at the same time. I wanted my divorce. Freedom was within my reach, and I could not wait to have him out of my life completely. But I had just left him a message about visiting the boys and I wanted him to be a good father which meant I would have to keep communicating with him on a parenting level. I was living with opposite ideals stuck in my heart and at a loss about how to process the complicated feelings. Which is why I cursed him seven ways to Sunday when I saw his freaking Porsche parked in my driveway. The selfish jerk couldn't even park along the curb so I could get into the garage. I decided to suck it up for the sake of the boys and attempt to be nice.

I snatched my purse and the prescription bag and stormed out of my SUV, slamming the door behind myself. My body language and actual language didn't have to match. He didn't deserve that much consideration. Plus, I was just too frickin' tired to maintain my entire personality. Something was bound to slip through the cracks.

One breath, two breaths, three deep breaths, four. Damn it. Not only was I still not calm, I was about to hyperventilate with anger. I hadn't seen him since the day of the bang heard around Sweetbriar. But the fact that he had been ignoring our boys pissed me off more. Hurt me? Whatever. Hurt my freaking boys? I may or may not murder you in your sleep with a dull, rusty spoon.

"Hi." My monotone greeting once I reached the porch said everything about how thrilled I was to see him cool, calm, and collected, all fancy-pants dressed for work, swinging on my gosh-damned porch swing. I wanted to take a *swing* at his stupid-ass face. He smiled at me and I flipped him off. *Oops.*

"Nice," he chuckled. "I guess I deserve that."

"You deserve way more. I assume you're here to check on the boys. If not, then you can leave right now."

"I was here to talk to you, actually. But I guess I can pop in and say hello. Do they get up for school this early?" He continued casually swinging, pushing with one foot. It aggravated me; I had no time for things like swinging on a damn porch swing, and here he was relaxing when I'd been up all night with our boys.

My head drew back on my neck and my jaw dropped a little bit. "Didn't you get my messages? I texted and I left you a voice mail. They're sick," I hissed, waving the Walgreens bag around. "Antibiotics. For strep throat. I've been up all night with them. But I guess this isn't unusual, is it? You never gave a crap about stuff like this before. I always handled it."

"What isn't unusual? What crap? Of course you handled stuff like this! You're their mother, for Christ's sake." He paused and took a deep breath. "I don't have time to fight with you, Violet. I'm here to offer you a deal. I want to buy your shop." He smiled as if he'd offered me a billion-dollar lottery ticket rather than insult me in the worst way possible.

He didn't know me at all.

"No," I managed to answer through a clenched jaw.

"I thought you might say that. But that's not all I'm willing to offer. Let's forget about the lawyers and the negotiations. I've let this go on too long." His eyes shifted to the side, then back to mine, and I braced myself for a lie, maybe two or three. I could always tell when he was lying. Shifty eyes were the number one clue.

"What the hell are you talking about?" I demanded. "I don't have time for this. I have sick boys to take care of. Your sons, in case you forgot."

"I know. And this is what I'm getting at, so hear me out. Please. I've treated you and the boys unfairly. I want you to move back into the house, and I'll move out. I want to buy the shop. I want to take care of you and Nick and Finn like I should have been doing this entire time. Telling you to leave like I did was terrible, and I'm sorry." The apology part of his statement was muttered under his breath.

Tom never apologized for anything or admitted it when he was wrong. If he'd shown up with a bunch of flowers and gifts for the boys and stuck to useless flattery, then maybe I would have believed he gave even half a shit about any of what he had just said. He was not the type to go back and correct a mistake he'd made. He always tried to make us forget about his bad behavior by offering meaningless words and gifts instead of sincerity or apologies.

"I don't know what game you're playing, Tom, but I don't want any part of it. We should stick to having our attorneys speak for us. And I'll never sell my shop. *Never.* So get that out of your head. Do you want to see the boys or not? They need their medicine."

He stood and glared at me. "I have to get to work."

With a shrug, I stepped off the walkway onto the lawn so he could leave. "Bye." I turned as a car pulled up behind mine to park at the curb.

Seconds later Jake stormed up the cobble stone path to stand at my side. He all but growled at Tom, "What's going on?"

Tom studied us as he walked down the steps. "It is true then? Bethany said some things about you two, but I didn't believe it. Are you fucking him, Violet? My best friend? You'd betray me like this?"

"Betray you?" I whispered. "Betray. You?" I muttered as his words sank into my brain to unravel every bit of control I had been holding onto. "*Betray you?*" I shrieked. Jake wrapped an arm around my waist to hold me back—from what, I did not know. Other than I wanted to hurt Tom badly, maybe smack that smug look off his face or scratch his judgmental eyes straight out of his stupid face. He had some freaking audacity to say that to me.

"Get the fuck out of here." Jake told him as I stood trembling at his side. His arm tightened, holding me up as every bit of my temper left my body and I deflated. My life with Tom—no, my *wasted* life with Tom—flashed through my mind and I sagged at Jake's side. All the sacrifices—my college education, my time, my love, my dignity—had all been wasted on a man who had never deserved it. All of it had been happily sacrificed to create the family I had thought we both wanted.

My life with Tom may have been a lie, but, damn it, I didn't have to live that way anymore. I had my boys, and they had always been the best thing to ever happen to me.

Tears flooded my eyes as I observed the anger on Jake's face, anger he was feeling on my behalf. I had people around me who cared. It was time to sever, once and for all, the hold Tom still had over me.

Enough.

I straightened. "I don't want to see you ever again. Don't come here—"

"What about the boys?" he sneered. "You can't keep me away from them."

"I never tried to! You haven't seen or called them in weeks! You weren't even here to see them today and they're sick! I called you, I left messages. Remember? And as of now? It's up to them if they want to see you or not. I'm not going to make them."

Tom stabbed a finger in the direction of the house. "Maybe I should go check on them now. Make sure they're okay," he pushed.

"Maybe you should get the hell out of here and I'll call

my attorney to set up a visitation schedule!" I shouted. My eyes drifted past my yard to see a few neighbors peek their heads out of their front doors. *Shit, shit, shit.*

"You mean your mother's attorney," he scoffed. "Be prepared to lose everything."

"Leave. Now." Jake let me go and advanced on Tom.

"I see. I get it now. How long has this been going on?" Tom poked a finger into Jake's chest. "How long have you been fucking my wife?" He shoved Jake's shoulder. Jake didn't budge, but somehow he grew bigger, like every muscle in his body had just flexed. And holy moly, there were a lot of them flexing. My eyes bugged out at the sight. This was not going to end well.

"She's not your wife anymore." He ground out the statement through his ticking jaw.

Tom scoffed. "You always wanted her, didn't you? You jealous piece of shit. You always wanted what I had."

Jake shook his head. "You're delusional. Shut your mouth and get out of here before this gets any uglier," he warned.

"Please. Stop this," I interjected. "The neighbors are watching. Just go to work, Tom. Think of the boys. Please."

"Shut up, Violet. You turned out to be nothing but a slut. We're not even divorced yet. What kind of mother am I leaving my sons with?" He'd lost his mind. Tom could get mean, but never like that. I stood there shocked and overwhelmed with incensed hurt at his outburst. Tears filled my eyes, but I managed to blink them back before they could fall and humiliate me even further.

"Go inside, sweetheart," Jake said without looking at me. Instead, his eyes remained fixed on Tom with a malevolent glare. "I'll handle this."

Tom snorted. "Yeah, go inside, *sweetheart*. Let your new fuck-buddy handle this."

"But—"

Jake's eyes sliced to mine. "Go inside and give the boys their medicine. This won't take a minute."

I nodded and darted up the porch steps, stopping at the door to pull my phone from my pocket as my mind whirled through ideas of who I should call for help. I settled on Cade. My little brother was a police officer who could break this up. I trusted him to do it quietly, without arresting Jake or allowing this scene to get any more out of hand. Lord knew I had no hope of breaking it up on my own. It went straight to voicemail. I left a message and spun back around, hoping I could think of a way to stop them.

"First. You will never speak to her like that again. *Ever.*" My jaw, which was already partially dropped, hung open as I watched Jake advance on Tom. My goodness, he was scary. His voice was pitched low with barely suppressed rage to end his statement on a growled "ever" as he shoved Tom back step after stumbling step toward the driveway with a huge palm planted in the center of his chest.

"Fuck you!" Tom straightened and stepped to the side, regaining his balance to shout, "This is *my* family, not yours! And I'm not leaving. Not until I see my boys." He dug in his heels, hands on his hips.

Jake grabbed an arm and spun him quickly around to frog-march him the rest of the way to his car. "Second. You will not see those boys until they *ask* to see you." He opened Tom's door and shoved him inside with a hand to the top of his head. "Start the car, Tom. We're done here. If you get out, the problems we already have will get worse. Do you understand me?" The car started as Jake turned his back and stalked in my direction. Tom revved his engine before backing out of my driveway and speeding off down the street.

The scary expression on Jake's face got more frightening when he caught sight of the tears in my eyes. His frown turned to a glare when one fell down my cheek and his face turned to stone when I called out, "I'm so sorry!"

"Do not apologize to me. Don't even think about it. I have always been one hit away from defending you, *always*. I was happy to remove that motherfucker from your presence. No, I was god-damned *thrilled* to finally have the opportunity. And I'll do it again and again and again until eternity if I have to. So do not apologize to me, Violet, baby. Don't you do it."

"My god, I think I just fell in love with you a little bit. Stop it," I blurted.

Shit, what did I just say?

A small sideways grin cracked the hard stone of his expression. "I won't stop it," he murmured as the grin moved across his face, softening his features as he allowed that glorious smile of his to shine on me. His soft blue eyes crinkled adorably at the corners as they met mine, and I drifted down to the porch swing behind me in a weak-kneed swoon.

I cleared my throat. "Well, thank you for defending my honor. I may be in shock right now, but I still need to tend to my boys." I stood and hugged his neck, adding a kiss to his cheek for good measure.

His soft smile turned tender as he looked at me. And as if he could tell I was overwhelmed and hanging on by a thread, he placed a sweet kiss to my forehead and took a step back to turn toward his car. "About that. I brought some of my homemade chicken soup—my mother's recipe—

for you and the boys. It's in the car. I'll go get it. Put it in the fridge and heat it up when you need it."

Every time I wondered if he could get better, he did.

Damn it.

I was in huge trouble.

Chapter 12
Jake

"*Everything is better with coffee.*"

I slipped out of my jacket as I opened my front door, sheepishly giving it a deep inhale before I hung it on the hook. Between the kiss at the Sweetbriar Grille and holding her back from attacking Tom a few mornings back, her scent still lingered on the fabric. The clean, floral perfume she often wore was all I could smell. Or maybe I was just caught somewhere between desire and wishful thinking and my imagination had run out of control. Either way, I wondered what it would be like to catch that scent throughout the day, every day, from her body, rather than the diminishing hint of what remained on my clothing. Or better yet, sleep with it filling my lungs every night. What would it be like to breathe her in and not ever have to let her go?

Besides my olfactory confusion, I also wondered what Tom was up to. After weeks of not hearing from him at all, he showed up to visit Violet out of the blue? He had been content to leave her and the boys to fend for themselves all that time, then he suddenly developed a conscience? I didn't buy it, and it had me worried for Vi and the boys. He was up to something. I'd known Tom since we were kids; he was *always* up to something. He was ambitious and forever working the angles. There was nothing wrong with ambition, but not when it took over your life at the expense of your family.

Over the years he had moved his real estate business up to the highest heights one could get in Sweetbriar, then moved on to conquer the surrounding small towns and vacation areas of Mt. Hood. Now he had offices all over Portland and the suburbs around it, and was raking in money hand over fist.

"Hi! We're home, hi!" I smiled and braced for impact. My great-niece, Bella, had arrived. I checked my watch; she was fresh out of kindergarten for the day and either bursting with news or wanting a snack.

"Bella! I said knock first," Harper shouted. "Incoming five-year-old love bomb, Uncle Jake!" I was not about to chastise her for barging in. I had a no knock policy for my girls, and she knew it.

"Bella boo!" I swept her into my arms. Maybe I *should* encourage her to call me grandpa or pop or whatever Harper had teased me about the other day. Between her own deadbeat father and my sister and brother-in-law cutting Harper out of their lives, she had neither. I was as close as she'd ever get to a grandparent, and I was family.

"How's Violet?" Harper didn't waste even a second before diving into what had been her constant greeting for me over the last month or so. Her question was followed by her smiling face popping into the doorway.

"As far as I know, she's fine. She texted to cancel our gala meeting tonight. The boys are still sick, but doing much better. I was about to start another pot of Nana's soup to take over. Would you two like to eat here tonight? I'll make plenty for us too." I kissed the top of Bella's head and set her down.

"Yes! Make Nana's cookies too." After a glance at her mother she added, "Please." A toothless grin followed. My mother had passed away almost three years ago. Making her recipes for myself and the girls always brought up good memories for all of us.

I smiled down at her as she followed me into the kitchen. "As long as you're my helper."

"Deal. Mommy, can I stay here and help?"

"If it's okay with you," Harper addressed me. "I'll help too, and we can make a plan."

"A plan?" I questioned as I took a pitcher of tea from the fridge. "I think I know what you're getting at and I prefer a more organic approach. So no, no plans."

After filling glasses with ice and lemon slices, she sat on a barstool on the other side of the counter. "No plans to handle Tom's BS? Organic? Are you crazy?"

"I thought you were going to talk about Violet. So, what exactly are you talking about? And how is it that you seem to always know what's going on around town lately?"

"Go wash your hands in the bathroom, Bella," she instructed. We watched her skip off to the hallway, then Harper faced me with a grin. "Secretaries and personal assistants in this town talk, and I mean a *lot*. There are zero secrets. You would not believe the things I hear when I head into town to pick up our lunch or coffee from Violet's, which, by the way, is a major gossip hot spot. Heck, Uncle Jake, I was at the dry cleaner picking up your suits today when I heard the news I'm about to tell you. There is like, an entire sub-network of information swirling around out there. You're lucky you have me because I'm loyal only to you and not addicted to thrill of trading the best stories. So, anyway, Tom wants to buy Violet's shop."

I sighed. "I already knew that."

"Okay, but do you know why?" My eyes snapped to hers. Her grin was smug as she sipped her tea.

"I do not."

"So, this is supposed to be a huge secret." She rolled her eyes. "But I'm going to frame the big secret within a medium secret to make it more fun." I nodded at her to go on with it. Secrets and gossip were not my thing. "Tom made a huge mistake when he hired Bethany and you know, had the affair with her and all that." She paused and shuddered dramatically. "That girl has had a huge mouth, ever since our high school days together. She's going to end up ruining him with her loose lips, especially since he both dumped *and* fired her yesterday."

"Holy fuck."

Bella gasped from the other side of the kitchen. "Mommy, Uncle Jake said a baaaad word. The worst one. Can I tell you what he said?"

"Should I give him a time out?" Harper asked with a laugh. "And no, you can't say it, silly girl. Get a juice box and go to the living room while we finish talking, okay?"

"Okay. You're in big trouble now Uncle Jake!"

Once Bella was in the other room Harper continued. "The big secret is boring, but major. Tom heard that some hotshot, out-of-state real estate developer—dang it, I forgot his name—wants to buy the strip of property Violet's shop is on and turn it into a downtown Sweetbriar experience"— she made air quotes around the word—"like Aspen or Vail or whatever. Basically, he wants to add some upscale businesses to Sweetbriar since it's so close to the big ski resorts up the mountain, starting with Violet's building. The problem is, all five businesses are individually owned, not rented. So they have to be bought one by one." She took a sip of her tea before continuing. "Unfortunately, Tom has managed to get his hands on two of them. If he owns the whole thing, he can sell it and make a killing."

"Unless Violet or any of the others refuse to sell to him. Then he gets stuck with retail space he doesn't need and has to sell, possibly at a loss." I finished for her.

"Yep. According to Bethany, he can make more money selling the property as one entity, rather than five individual pieces of a strip mall or whatever."

"Damn it. Violet doesn't need this now."

"Right? She has enough going on." She sipped her tea with a smile. "How's that going, by the way?" I raised an eyebrow but didn't answer. "Fine, keep your secrets. I'll just have to be content with hearing everything second-hand."

I chuckled. "Discretion is a good thing. Don't you think?"

"Dude, someone should talk to Tom about that."

"Someone should talk to him about a lot of things."

"Speaking of Tom things, there's another story going around the gossip mill too. You sure taught that crap-bag a lesson the other day, didn't you?"

I shrugged. "Don't tell me the specifics of what is going around. I don't want to know."

"Nothing bad. Only good things, combined with the usual stuff about your feelings about Violet, blah, blah, blah, et cetera. You know."

"Yeah, I know."

"This would be about the time you should find someone new to date. You know, to throw off the gossip hounds. Am I wrong?" she teased.

I gave her a look. "This is not dad talk, is it?" I teased back.

"Meh, who knows? I never ever really talked to my dad. You know, before they kicked me out of the house."

It had been years and her laugh and expression told me she was joking, but I felt bad anyway. "I'm sorry, Harper. I didn't mean it that way."

"I know you didn't and it's okay. Bella and I have you and our life is better for it."

"Mine is too. What would I do without my girls?" Be lonely as hell, that's what I'd be doing. I still had my older brother to talk to, but he was constantly busy and seemed reluctant to get too close to anyone—including me.

My cell interrupted the conversation. "It's Finn. I should probably take this." I held up a finger and stepped into the living room. After hanging up, I pocketed my phone and snagged my jacket from the hook. "Harper, bad news. Violet is sick and Finn didn't want to call Dahlia. She has her hands full with Ben's broken ankle. I'm going to pick up her meds and help out."

"Take this." She was at the counter filling a bag with containers of frozen soup. "And I won't tell you how I knew you'd need it. I also won't tell you to think about why those boys are calling you all the time lately, but maybe you should." She added crackers and a bottle of ginger ale.

I chuckled. "Do I want to know?"

"The usual Barrett family circle of gossip and match-making. Jude told me the boys have their eye on you for Violet. They want you to swoop in." My eyebrows raised as my heart warmed. I couldn't help but smile.

"That's nice," I admitted. I'd always loved Violet's boys.

"They love you, just like I do. You're like an uncle-slash-dad to them too, and you always have been. This shouldn't really be a surprise."

"I love you too. But I—"

"I know, I know, you don't want to talk about it. I understand. You might get what you've always wanted and it's scary."

I couldn't admit to her, or even to myself, exactly how scary it was, so I just took the bag with a nod. "Thanks. I have—"

"I know, more soup in the freezer. Oooh, and stuffed shells." She grinned and put the soup back to take out a foil-wrapped casserole dish. What could I say? Cooking my mother's recipes relaxed me. I didn't always have enough eaters, so my freezer was always full. "Take care of Violet and don't worry about me and Bella. We'll be totally fine."

"Call me if you need me." I took the bag and thanked her. "Bye, Bella boo." I ruffled her hair as I passed her on the way to the front door. "Tell your mommy there's cookie dough in the freezer, okay? I have to go help a sick friend but I'll see you tomorrow."

"Okay! Bye-bye, Uncle Jake."

Chapter 13
Jake

"Life begins after coffee."

After parking in the driveway, I found Finn wrapped in a bathrobe and slumped over on the porch swing when I walked up the front path to Violet's house. "It's cold out here. Aren't you still sick?" I asked as I approached, bags of food and medicine from the pharmacy in hand.

"Mom has a fever and has the chills. She's got the heater blasting in the living room. It's so hot in there, I can't stand it. I'm pretty much fine now, just tired. Nick is asleep in our room and I didn't want to leave them alone to pick up Mom's prescription. Thank you for this. Taking care of sick people is fucking exhausting."

"Not a problem. Let's get you back inside."

"Do you care if I go to bed? I can't stay awake anymore."

"Nope, I don't mind at all. Have you taken your antibiotics? Has Nick?"

He stood and threw open the front door. "Yeah, I've been setting the timer in the kitchen. I gave Mom some

Tylenol about an hour ago. She's still feverish but she won't get into bed and she didn't sleep at all last night. She keeps trying to get me to eat a can of soup. See?" I looked where he was pointing to find Violet dozed off on the couch, a can of Campbell's finest chicken noodle clutched tight to her chest and her cheeks flushed bright red with fever.

"I got this. Go on to bed."

"Thanks." He shuffled off down the hallway. His door shut with a thud and Violet shot up to sit on the edge of the couch. The can fell off her lap to roll somewhere beneath the coffee table.

"I'm awake," she gasped on a huge inhale. "Finny, I have soup for you. Let me take your temperature. Where'd you go? Where's the soup? I had a spoon somewhere." After unearthing a spoon from her robe pocket, her eyes drifted to the floor, followed by her body as she proceeded to look under the couch for the soup, crawling on all fours along the perimeter of the huge sectional. I tried to avoid checking out her spectacular heart-shaped ass as she crawled, but it was impossible, so I slammed my eyes shut to clear the image from my mind. She was sick and it made me feel like a jerk. From the moment I saw Tom kiss Bethany, visions of Violet started drifting out of the shadowy corners of my mind to gradually take over the forefront. She had become a constant and beautiful distraction from the minutiae of everyday life. I needed to kiss her again. I wanted her in the worst way, and it was driving me crazy.

"Hey, Vi," I greeted, trying to hide my longing for her behind a cool facade.

She sat up with a lurch to end up cross-legged with her back against the couch, after releasing a heavy sigh she answered, "Jake. I can't find the soup, and Finn needs it."

"I brought soup for all of you. Get into bed, get some rest, and I'll heat it up."

She rubbed her temples and scowled. "No, no, no, I can't. Mommies have to make the soup."

"Not when they're sick, they don't. Come on up here." I placed my bags on the coffee table and held out a hand to help her up.

"I always make the soup." Her eyes narrowed as she regarded my outstretched hand with suspicion and swatted it away. Sadly, I realized Tom was exactly the type of man who would expect his wife to take care of the kids no matter what.

"I picked up your medicine. Let's go in the kitchen and I'll give it to you." I changed tactics in an attempt to placate her strangely adorable hostility.

"Well, I'm not sick. I just needed a little nap is all. I'm perfectly fine to make the soup."

"But I came all this way to help you. Finn called me," I cajoled.

Her head tilted to the side. "You did? Aww, you came all this way just for us?" She held up her hands for me to take. "I knew I should have met you first. Instead of stupid Tom."

I took her hands and pulled her up with a shocked, "What?"

"I saw you standing by the Coke machine in the cafeteria." Her head tilted back, she plastered herself against me and rested her chin on my chest before continuing, "I told Piper, 'I'm gonna marry that boy.' I meant, you," she whispered as an aside. "You were so, so pretty—I'm sorry, but I didn't know you were smart too until much later. She told me I should wait until the second week of college before choosing a husband, and we laughed and laughed. Then

Tom asked me on a date, I said yes, and now here I am, in this house, all alone with my boys, stuck living a life like a bad country song with a lying, no-good, cheating husband, and a missing can of soup. Where did it go?"

It took a minute for her statement to sink in. "I don't know what to say. I wish I had approached you first too, Violet." Tears filled her eyes, and she patted my chest.

"Because you're pretty, smart, and *super nice too*!" she cried before wrapping her arms around my waist and snuggling even closer.

I chuckled and kissed her forehead. Her fever was high. "Come on, gorgeous. You need to take your antibiotics." I guided her to a kitchen chair, then filled a glass of water from the tap. I passed it to her with a pill. "Swallow it and wait right here," I instructed. I ran into the living room to grab my bags so I could stick the soup and ginger ale in the fridge.

"Okie dokey. I'm going to shut my eyes. Just for one tiny little minute," she mumbled. She took the pill, let her head crash onto an arm, and bellowed out an indelicate snore.

"Let's get you into bed." No answer. I gently shook her shoulder. Nothing. She was out like a light, reminding me of all the times Bella would crash on the couch in front of a Disney Princess movie. And just like I would do for Bella, I scooped Violet up, carried her to bed, and tucked her in.

"Tom ruined everything. It should have been you, Jake," she murmured before turning dramatically to her side and tucking her hands beneath her cheek.

Well, hell. Dreams come true had just spilled from her lips. I leaned forward to kiss her forehead. "Goodnight, sweetheart," I whispered as I gathered her hair and moved it over her shoulder, out of her face. I jumped when I heard footsteps approach the open doorway.

"I knew it. I've always known it, or at least I suspected it for a long time. You love her, don't you?" It was Nick.

"Your mom is one of the best friends I've ever had. Of course I love her." The words tumbled out of my mouth by rote. That was my usual answer for the question that had reared its head off and on over the years from well-meaning friends or nosy acquaintances.

He laughed and headed toward the kitchen. "I'm too sick to argue with you. But I'm onto you and I approve. So does Finn. Did you bring more soup? I have to sit down." I didn't know what to say after that bomb dropped, so I followed him to the kitchen to heat the soup and decided to think about it later. He had taken Violet's place at the table, matching her earlier position with his head on his arm.

"Why don't you get comfortable on the couch and I'll bring it to you," I offered.

He stood. "Thanks. I owe you. And because I respect you as a man, I'm not going to pull some ridiculous *Parent Trap* matchmaking bullshit on you. But I really do have to sit down. I still feel like shit."

"I appreciate that," I called to his back. "And you don't owe me I'm happy to help." I located a pot, transferred the frozen soup, then peeked into the living room to check on Nick, who—as I should have known he would—had fallen asleep on the couch. He was obviously too old to put to bed and too big to carry, so I covered him with the quilt that hung over the back of the club chair in the corner and sat on the other end of the sectional. So far, this evening has been both informative and a bit sad.

I flipped the TV on and mindlessly watched while I allowed my mind to flick through long-buried memories. It wasn't until after graduation that I'd realized exactly what I had let slip through my fingers when I had turned my back and let Tom approach her first. The regret of that moment that had always existed somewhere in the back of my mind, and over the last few months, it had surged forward to dominate most of my thoughts. I had to find a way to let it go, at least for the time being. It served no purpose and would only end up coloring my every interaction with Violet in a bittersweet darkness, the pain of which weighed heavier on my heart with each passing day. She made me feel again. I was unsure if I should fight the feelings or not. All I knew was it seemed impossible not to give into them as I slowly sank beneath her waves. I had hope, but she was still married. I wanted her but didn't want to push her too hard and lose her. She said she had feelings for me, but were they real? Or was I just a better option than Tom? I did not want to end up a pathetic rebound on her way to someone else.

Driving my hands into my hair, I sighed and stood. Sitting here dwelling on what I had no control over was foolish. Shoving the idea of what could have been out of my mind, I entered the kitchen to stir the soup, turning the heat to low so it could take its time heating up. Then I cleaned the kitchen from top to bottom, moved to the bathroom, and cleaned that too, making sure to sanitize the light switches and doorknobs throughout the house as I went.

"You're cleaning." Finn stood in the doorway of his bedroom watching as I wiped down the bathroom doorknob.

"I don't want you guys to get sick again."

"I should probably start helping out more. Mom does everything now that we don't have Mrs. Lance to clean anymore."

"That's probably a good idea. I grew up with a single mom. We all had to help out." Growing up there was no such thing as "woman's work" as far as my mother had been concerned. I had no qualms about any of what I was doing. It needed to be done, so I did it.

"My dad is such a dick. Not because I might have to clean the house, that's like—whatever, I don't mind. But he always just kind of dumped everything on her and left all the family stuff for her to do. That isn't right."

"No, it's not. I'm proud of you for recognizing that and wanting to help out now. You're a great kid, Finn." I paused, perusing him. He looked better. "Are you hungry?"

"Yeah, I'm starving. How long have I been out? It might be time for Mom's Tylenol—"

"Hey, guys," Violet stood in her doorway, hair mussed up and looking beautiful. The glassy-eyed, fevered look she had earlier was gone.

I placed the back of my fingers against her forehead. "I think your fever is gone, or at least it's a lot lower than it was when I got here."

"I feel a bit better. In fact, I'm starving. I'll take that as a good sign."

"It is a good sign," I lamely repeated. "Uh, there's soup heating up in the kitchen—"

"You can get back into bed, Mom. One of us will bring it to you," Finn interjected.

"Aren't you hungry, sweetie? You go on to bed or get comfy on the couch and I'll—"

"I'm fine and I want to help. You've been up all night, so go back to bed. Please." Finn's tone left no room for disagreement.

Violet laughed softly as we exchanged a look. "I guess I'll go back to bed."

"I'll bring you a tray. Let us take care of you, Vi. And don't worry about Nick, he's asleep on the couch. I figured he might feel weird if I carried him to bed," I joked.

Confusion suffused her features as her mouth formed an O of surprise. "Did you carry me to bed? What time is it anyway?" She looked around as if the time could be told by looking everywhere but at me.

"I'm sorry if I crossed a line by carrying you. You were asleep at the table and when I say asleep, I mean practically unconscious. I apolo—"

"No, please don't apologize. Thank you for helping me. I'm not upset about you carrying me to bed. It's, I um, just realized how much time must have passed. Like, I remember you getting here, but nothing else until now. I hope I didn't do anything too embarrassing. I don't make much sense when I have a fever." She smiled sheepishly and my heart sank. Her memory of the last few hours was gone; the words that had filled me with hope disappeared as if she had never spoke them aloud at all. I'd felt like I had gone two steps forward with her . . .

This step back hurt.

Chapter 14
Violet

"Love is in the air and it smells like coffee."

I hadn't seen Jake in over a week, and I missed him more than I should. The boys were healthy again and back to school. I had also recovered from strep throat and the fever of doom and returned to work, and while we weren't behind on the gala plans yet, a week with no meetings was not good. But he hadn't called to reschedule, and it worried me. It made me feel like I'd often felt with Tom—on edge and jumpy, like I'd inadvertently done something to upset him. The comparison made me uncomfortable enough to put off calling him myself to arrange our next meeting. Clearly, confrontation was not my strong suit. And besides the confrontation aspect, the fact that how I was feeling reminded me of how Tom often made me feel told me I had a long way to go before I was over the hurt of my marriage.

Maybe it *was* too early for me to consider starting something with Jake. Jake was nothing like Tom and I didn't want to end up projecting my doubts and hurt onto someone new; that wouldn't be fair to either one of us.

Gah! All I wanted was Tom out of my life, but it seemed the ghosts of the hurt he caused in my life would haunt me forever.

Maybe I needed time.

Or more space.

Or a cheeseburger, extra-large fries, and super-massive Coke, chased by a slice of chocolate cherry cheesecake from the Sweetbriar Inn as a tasty distraction from these negative and useless thoughts.

My rational brain knew Jake and Tom were polar opposites. It also knew that Tom held no real power over me. I could divorce him, ignore him, leave him in my proverbial dust if I chose. It was a free country, and *I* was the one in control of my life, not Tom. Not even Jake and the new and giddy way he made me feel were in charge.

Down with doubt and yay for rational thoughts, I decided as I swung my Range Rover into the Inn's parking lot with a grin. After an early therapeutic trash dinner with the boys, I would force myself to call Jake, get our gala meetings rescheduled, and exorcise a few of the butthead ghosts Tom had left me with. This was supposed to be the year of Violet and it was time I took my life by the reins and yanked them around, or whatever one was supposed to do with reins. I could do it; I could boss the hell out of my life.

School was out for the day and I'd left Holly to close the shop so I could be home for the boys. Even though they were better, I was still in overprotective mode and that meant I hovered and fretted and generally drove them crazy until I was assured they were okay.

I was at the coffee table distributing our early dinner onto paper plates when the boys arrived. "Yo," Nick greeted, tossing his backpack on the chair in the corner, then his coat.

Finn slapped the back of his shoulder. "Hey, remember what I told you?" He proceeded to hang up his coat and backpack very neatly on the hooks near the front door.

"Oh yeah." Nick gathered his things and followed suit as I sat there wondering what in the name of heck was going on.

"What's with the putting-your-stuff-away thing? You're not about to ask me for a dog, are you? You know I'm allergic—"

"No, we just want to be more helpful," Finn answered.

"Who are you and where are my real kids?" I joked.

"The same place our real mother went. What is all this delicious crap I see on the coffee table? Have you changed your mind and decided onion rings can count as vegetables?" Nick tossed back.

"Ha ha ha. Wash your hands before you sit down to eat. Give me hugs, then we can talk about your days over dinner."

Nick grinned. "There she is," he said as he crossed into the kitchen.

Finn hugged me as he passed me and headed toward the bathroom. "Be right back."

"We have news," Nick shouted after turning off the faucet. He entered the living room wiping his hands on his jeans. "It's about Dad," he added as he grabbed a Coke from the table.

I braced for impact. "Okay, what is it?"

"He wants us to spend the rest of the week at the house with him. He said he wants to apologize for not calling or coming by. He wants to make it up to us." My heart pounded in my ears as the irrational thought that I would lose my boys filled my mind. I tried to brush it aside; they were practically adults and more than capable of making their own choices. I set my burger down with a flop, no longer hungry since my stomach was too busy swirling with panic to allow me to eat.

"Um, do you want to? It's okay if you do . . ." I had to be the bigger person. Tom was their father, and they should have a relationship with him if that's what they wanted. I had no business standing in the way. Plus, after our divorce was settled, I may not even have a choice in the matter anyway. I should probably get used to being without them.

"No. We don't. But we talked about it and we think we should, just in case he means it. He was horrible to you. He like, forgot about us. But we still—it's complicated. We kind of don't know what to think about him. We were hoping if we talked to him, we could figure it out."

Finn sat on my other side and grabbed his container of onion rings. "And we also want to see what he's been up to lately. You heard, right?"

"Your father told me he wants to buy me out of my shop. Is that what you mean?"

Nick answered. "What? No. What would he want with your shop? That's weird."

"I don't know." I sighed. "Maybe he feels bad? And this is his way of trying to help me out?" The words sounded ridiculous, so I stopped speaking to shrug blankly.

Nick continued. "We heard that he broke up with Bethany and fired her. Bri just got back into town from her dad's house. She told me about it at lunch. Her mom heard all the yelling from the hallway. Bethany was pissed."

I didn't know what to say. "Oh my. Really? That's—"

"Crazy, right? He busts up our family over that girl, then dumps her ass a few weeks later. What the hell?" Finn shook his head then shoved a huge bite of burger into his face. Oddly, that brought my appetite back and I picked up my own burger.

"Language, Finn," I half-heartedly warned. They were almost seventeen years old; I was glad they still talked to me and let me into their lives, so I didn't push the language thing too hard.

"Sorry," he muttered. "So we're going to go. We'll see what he's been up to and then we'll report back to you."

"No. I mean, if you want to visit with him, that's your choice and I'm okay with it. But I won't have you spying on him. No lying, no sneaking around. I don't agree with that kind of thing and I won't support it."

Finn sighed; he was clearly frustrated with me. "But he lied. Obviously, he sneaks around. We can't let him get away with it—"

"Fine, we'll go just for a visit," Nick interrupted. "Right, Finn?"

"I guess so," he agreed with an eye roll.

"Okay then." I paused to take a sip of Coke and gather my thoughts. "Um, I'll miss you guys . . ." I turned away from the boys as my eyes filled with tears, but I managed to blink them back. I did not want them to feel guilty about spending time with their dad, no matter what their motivation was for wanting to see him. I knew Tom wouldn't treat them how he treated me. He never had before and at this point, I didn't think he would dare.

"We'll have our phones on. Promise," Nick said with a smile.

"Yeah, and we don't have to be there twenty-four hours a day. We're not little kids. And we can drive, Mom. We'll stop by the shop every morning before school," Finn added.

"Okay, you're right. I'm being emotional and silly, and I

know it. Let's finish dinner. I have cheesecake in the fridge." They exchanged a look. "What?"

"We should get to Dad's after we finish this. We were supposed to meet him before five." Nick's voice was sympathetic as he watched me carefully.

"Oh." I didn't know what to say. Rather, I had nothing good to say, so I stopped talking and sat there with a French fry held halfway to my mouth.

"Uh, we could wait until tomorrow to go?" he offered. Finn nodded in agreement.

"No, no. It's fine. I will be fine," I answered, a little too brightly. "More cheesecake for me, right?" I tried to laugh, then covered my lack of humor by stuffing the fry into my mouth. I didn't want to be one of those divorced parents who put their kids in the middle or made them feel guilty. If Tom was sincere about rebuilding his relationship with the boys, I wanted to support it. I owed it to Finn and Nick to give them a chance with their father. Plus, from what my mother's attorney had told me—I still hadn't returned Jake's brother's call—we would end up with equal custody anyway. I might as well not stand in the way of a visit right out of the gate. That wouldn't be a good look for me.

We finished eating in silence. I couldn't think of anything to say and they were too busy watching me, probably waiting for me to start crying or get emotional, so they kept quiet too.

* * *

The house was beyond quiet now, it was silent, and I couldn't stand it. Rain pitter-pattered on the roof above, but instead of relaxing me, it drove my heartrate up to a stressful pounding beat. I paced around the living room as my early years with the boys—the years when all I wanted was *just one* moment alone—flittered across my mind. Now I regretted those moments. Because this sucked, I was miserable, and I wanted my babies back. I could feel my mood deteriorate with each paced step, but I couldn't find my way out of this downward spiral of gloom.

On top of my moody gloom about the boys, my cellphone sat dead center on the coffee table taunting me over not being brave enough to call Jake. I was all alone and a big old chicken-shit to boot.

Gah! I rubbed my chest. I had to get out of this mood. I bit my lip and stared at the phone. With a curse, I picked it up, located Jake in my contacts, and hit dial before I could wuss out any further or contemplate what to say to him.

"Hello?" His deep voice filled my ear and I shivered. My mouth opened to speak, yet I couldn't seem to grab hold of a word. "Violet, are you okay?"

"Yes." I cleared my throat. Damn it. "I'm okay, uh—hi."

"Hi, gorgeous. What are you up to?" he drawled, and I had to sit down. Frick, his voice was doing all kinds of things to me.

I should have prepared myself better before I called. My Jake shields were down, and he was getting to me. "I'm not up to anything. Uh, we need to get our gala planning schedule back on track. I wanted to—"

"Come over. We'll get back on track tonight. I'd come to you, but I've opened a bottle of whisky. I shouldn't drive. I'm not drunk, but I've had a couple." He chuckled into the phone.

"You're at home?"

"I am. I've also started a fire. One more reason I can't leave." I slammed my eyes shut as I pictured him sprawled in his favorite chair by his fireplace. With a glass of whisky in his big hand, shirtsleeves rolled up his delicious forearms, and me, helplessly dangling like a fish on his line at the other end of the phone.

"I don't know if I should. I—"

"Right. You don't want the boys to get the wrong idea."

"Well, they aren't actually here. They're with Tom for the next few days."

"Are you okay with that?"

"I have to be, don't I?"

"You're entitled to feel however you feel. You don't have to pretend with me. I know it upsets you."

"How do you always know?"

"I pay attention, Violet." He sounded different. There was more coming through the line than just the sweet Jake I was used to. His voice was darker, with a gravel and grit that was all new. Was it the whisky? Or something else?

"You're so good to me, Jake. I don't deserve you."

"Don't you deserve to have a man in your life who will pay attention to you? I think it's the very least you deserve. You're worth the effort. A man should be willing to go to hell and back for you, Violet. He never deserved you."

"And you do?" A nervous laugh escaped, and somehow, I knew the more I questioned him, the more his answers would draw me in.

"Come over tonight and find out. My door is always open to you." The statement felt like a dare I wanted to take almost as much as I knew that I shouldn't.

"I'm not divorced yet, Jake. We shouldn't be doing this —" What I *should* do and what I *wanted* to do resided on opposite ends of the spectrum when it came to him. I had two teenage sons who needed a good example. They sure as hell wouldn't get it from Tom. I had to be the one to provide it. But they were with their father for the next few days, and they didn't need to know where I was or what I was doing.

"Your marriage vows don't exist anymore. You know that, right? Don't fight how you feel. Come over here and let me show you what you deserve." I would have *felt* his voice, deep, low, and rumbly, if I were pressed against his chest. His heart would beat against my cheek as he spoke, and his hands would be on my body. He wanted me; that's what came through the line. The filter he usually spoke to me through was gone. The sweetness, the congenial, platonic best friend quality had disappeared, and I was suddenly struck with the feeling that I hardly knew him at all.

But more importantly, I wanted to know this side of him. "You're not making this easy, you know," I breathed, still undecided.

"I'm not trying to." *Of course not*.

I huffed out a laugh. "Oh really? I'm glad you can be upfront about that."

"I earned that jab, so I'll let this go. I won't ask again because I think this should be completely your choice without any more pressure from me. Come to me, gorgeous, if you want. I'll be up late. And there will be zero hard feelings if you don't." He ended the call.

Damn. I set my cell next to me on the couch. After catching a glimpse of myself in the mirror by the front door, I headed into the bathroom to fix my hair. I decided to do whatever came naturally without thinking about it. I'd spent almost seventeen years thinking, planning, and doing what I was supposed to do. I was sick of it. I wanted something for myself. It was time to throw caution to the wind and go to Jake or end up watching a movie on TV. I would make peace with either place I ended up because it would be completely my choice.

I reached for a nude lipliner and some gloss, my mascara, and a rosy-hued blush. I made up my face, subtle and glowy, then I headed into my room to change clothes. I flipped through the hangers on my closet. Nothing was right. What I needed was soft and *accessible*, something deceptively casual yet sexy. I grabbed the pale pink cashmere lounge set Rose gave me for my birthday last year. I'd never worn it, because who lounges around the house in cashmere? Crazy people, that's who. Or as I now realized, ladies who wanted to do a little bit of casual seducing. I was out of my mind, but for once in my life that's right where I wanted to be.

I had gone from wanting to cry to wanting to *squee* with anticipation in a matter of one evening. I slipped into the soft cashmere, then headed to the living room. The couch beckoned, comfortable and safe. But my phone sitting in the middle of a cushion reminded me of how I felt talking to Jake. I snatched it up along with my purse and left.

Chapter 15
Jake

"All I need is for someone to love me like I love coffee."

I tossed my phone to the couch and headed to the kitchen for another drink. Two was usually my limit, but tonight, three felt necessary. Not enough to get drunk, but hopefully enough to pull me off the edge I had been walking on of late. Her fevered confessions still echoed in my head and it occurred to me this entire bottle of whisky would not be enough to quiet them. I poured the glass, shot it back, and prayed for silence. But a knock at my door was sounded instead. After placing my glass down, I darted across the house to answer it.

I swung it open and for a moment, all I could do was stare. "You're here." She was beautiful: long hair down and blowing in the wind, a few curls stuck to her face from her brief walk through the rain to my porch. I reached forward to brush them back.

She smiled at me, gazing up through her lashes. "You seem surprised."

I held the door for her with my arm outstretched. "I am. Get inside and let's get you warm."

She slipped out of her coat and pressed it against my chest as she crossed the threshold. I was still clad in slacks and a button-down shirt from work, and her other hand trailed across my forearm, bared by my rolled-up shirt-sleeves. Her eyes seemed to reflect what I felt: curiosity, attraction, and the feeling that we were about to take a step together into somewhere unknown. It gave me hope, and my heart, already racing with anticipation, thundered in my chest like the rainstorm outside—wild and out of control.

"I'm glad you're here. Come on." I hung her coat on the rack by the door, then took her hand. The remains of the fire still flickered in the fireplace, giving the room a dim golden glow. "Would you like a drink?"

"Yes, please. You make the best drinks." She sat on the couch. I knew she was fond of old-fashioned cocktails, so I made her a Manhattan.

"My gosh, you don't mess around," she said after taking a sip. "Delicious." Her eyes darted to the side as she placed the drink on the coffee table. I could tell something was bothering her. It was probably the boys.

I chuckled. "No, I do not. Thank you." I sat at the opposite end of the couch. "Are you sure you're okay? We can talk about it. Is it Tom and the boys?

"He's their father. I have to be okay with them going over there. I really don't have a choice. My attorney said we'll most likely end up with fifty-fifty custody anyway. I may as well get used to it. Plus, they wanted to go. I'm not going to stop them. I shouldn't try to stop them, right? What do you think?"

"I think you should feel what you feel and let it out. I also think you need to return Ren's call and let him help.

But, bottom line, I know the boys. And if it came down to it, Tom can't prevent them from walking out and going back to you whenever they want."

"I know they're practically grown but it still feels like I let two pieces of my heart go tonight." A brief hint of tears reflected in her eyes before she turned away to hide them from me.

"Come here, gorgeous." We met in the middle of the couch and she sank into my side. I swept her legs over mine and hugged her close. "Tell me what you want. Distraction or comfort?"

Surprised eyes met mine. "A little of both?"

I kissed her gently to get us back into the direction we were headed before I brought up the boys. "Okay?" I whispered against her lips.

"Mm hmm." The sound vibrated against my lips, tickling and tempting.

The fire flickered out, leaving us with only the faint twilight hour light sneaking in through my front window. I didn't need the light; I saw her perfectly because I had spent years memorizing her from afar. The tiny dimple on her chin, her deep-set hazel eyes, the few strands of silver at her left temple. I would know her in darkness. I would know her anywhere. My fingers traced over my memories, cupping her beautiful face in my palm, drawing her closer to deepen the kiss. "More," she whispered, wrapping her arms around my neck.

I wanted things to change between us almost as much as my fears and doubts needed them to stay the same. Could it be possible to have it all with her? Was I risking everything I cherished about our friendship by having her here and hoping for more? She was so soft in my arms. She felt essential and right and I never wanted to let her go. She gasped against my mouth and it hit me that I knew too much already. The way it felt to hold her close, the taste of her lips, the little moan she made in the back of her throat when I'd kissed her for the first time . . . It was as if each step forward were made on a crumbling path and once we took them, we couldn't turn around.

I kept her close to sweep her hair over her shoulder. The arched line of her neck beckoned me and I breathed her in, tracing the elegant length with my lips. Tonight her perfume would linger on more than my jacket. "You smell so good, you feel so soft . . . Stay with me tonight, Violet. We don't have to do anything more than this, I just want you close to me—"

"Yes, I'll stay." Hearing that word coming from her mouth—*yes*—was like falling into an out-of-body experience. Heat rose up my spine and I couldn't get close enough to her. She pulled my face up to hers with her palms at my cheeks and her fingertips slipping into my hair and took control with a deep, irresistible kiss. We stayed like that— pressed tight, hands everywhere, tongues dueling for dominance—up to the moment she moved her hands down my chest to tug at the buttons of my shirt until they were undone.

I leaned back into the corner of the couch, stretching my arms along the sides, not wanting to push her, curious to see how far she wanted to go. "You're so beautiful, Jake." She whispered the words as her lips traced down the center of my chest and her hands traced over my abs to reach for my belt buckle. My dick throbbed with the anticipation of her touch. "I've always thought so." She undid my pants and wrapped my hard cock in her soft palm before I came to my senses and took her hand in mine. Raising it to my lips, I kissed each finger before gently pushing her back into her corner of the couch. She panted, eyes blazing as she watched me expectantly.

We were moving too fast and too slow at the same time. I needed to get my bearings before I let this get too far, before I got too selfish to stop her, and took what I wanted instead of giving her what she needed. Tonight was supposed to be all about her, not my needs. About showing her what she deserved. I wanted to give her things I suspected she'd never had. I wanted her to need me, to be addicted to me, to love me, and never, ever leave me.

"Did I do something wrong?" she asked.

"Fuck no," I groaned before taking her mouth in a hard kiss. "I want to make you feel good." I let my hands slide up the warm skin of her sides as I raised her shirt over her head and let it fall to the floor. Her breasts were full, round, and lush, and peeking through the pale pink lace of her bra I saw the hardened rosy tips of her nipples. I darted my tongue out to taste one. She immediately arched against my lips and I smiled before sucking it fully into my mouth, lace and all.

"Oh, please," she moaned as she shoved the cup of the bra down for me.

"Anything you want." I sucked harder at her bared nipple, giving it a little nip with my teeth as she reached behind herself to unfasten the hooks. The weight of her other breast filled my palm as the bra loosened. I gave it a soft caress before moving to taste it, opening my mouth wide and letting the flat of my tongue trace up and down the stiffened peak of her nipple.

She bucked up against me, legs falling to the sides and wrapping around my waist as I covered her body with my own. I ground my dick against the heat between her legs, dying to strip her bare and sink inside of what I already knew would be the best thing I would ever feel in my life. But I refrained. I would get inside of her tonight if she let me, I decided. But not to take. I shifted to my side and nudged her over so her back was against the couch. Hooking the back of her knee with my hand, I slid it over my hip. "Can I touch you?"

"God, yes. Do whatever you want and don't stop." I slipped a hand in the front of her pants and down to find the lacy edge of her panties. Pushing them down her hips with my other hand, I cupped her in my palm, allowing my middle finger to trace around her slick opening. Touching her like this was something I'd never let my mind wander far enough to imagine, and it was everything and more. She was hot, wet perfection, and she was mine. I could smell her, the scent blending with the soft perfume she always wore, and it drove me wild. I'd never let myself think of having a moment like this with her and now I couldn't think of anything else. I kissed her, quick, deep, and dirty, loving how her lips reddened and her cheeks flushed when I pulled away briefly.

"I've wanted to kiss you like this for a long time." I whispered against her lips as I moved my fingers up to circle her clit. "That kiss by your car was nothing. Just a brief taste of what I need from you, and I still don't have it all, Violet. You're not ready for all I want from you, so I'm going to keep it to myself for now. I have to or my feelings will eat me alive." I gave her clit a soft little pinch before entering her with my fingers. She squirmed while pressing herself hard into my hand, squeezing my fingers as she began to ride them. She didn't answer me, not with words at least. Her hips writhed and she moaned as I fucked my fingers into her, pressing my palm against her clit as I took her mouth in another deep kiss.

She did this thing, a gasping moan before holding her breath, and each time she did it she squeezed my fingers further inside of her tight heat. As the rhythm of it quickened, I realized she was closer and closer to coming. I tore my mouth from hers with a groan. "Let it go, I want to watch." She dug her fingers into the tops of my shoulders, her eyes blazing into mine once before she slammed them shut and arched back into the corner of the couch with a loud, low moan.

"Please, please! Go faster," she gasped. I did as she asked, faster and deeper, seeking that spot that would push her over the edge while rotating the heel of my palm hard against her clit until she shuddered against me then relaxed back into the cushions.

"I've never—god, Jake." Her eyes opened and she smiled wickedly as she slid a hand down my bare chest.

"No, gorgeous. Tonight is for you. I told you I was going to show you what you deserve, didn't I?"

"Yeah, but—"

"Did you understand what I told you?"

"I thought I did." She answered on a breathy moan, still not yet recovered.

"When you *know*. When you need me as much as I need you, then I'll give you everything. I'll never take it back and I'll never let you go."

"I think I understand, and I don't want to hurt you—"

"There is nothing you can do about my feelings. They're mine to worry about. You'll end up in my bed, Violet, I believe that. But not when you're still hurting, not when you're scared of the future, and not until you're absolutely sure."

"I—

"Shh. Let's not talk anymore. Don't make promises you can't keep. I can wait."

"How do you always know what I need?"

"I pay attention."

"You're amazing. I get what you're saying. And I want to try—with you. You know I'll never go back to Tom, right?"

"I hope not. Even if I weren't in the picture."

"Good. But you need to know that I can't picture myself with anyone else. When I imagine moving on, you're all I can see. We might not be in the same place yet, but we're heading in the same direction, okay?"

"Okay," I whispered. That was good enough for me, for now. We slipped out of the rest of our clothes and I grabbed my remote to turn on a movie. She tugged the throw blanket from the back of the couch to cover us and we stayed here, tangled up together for the rest of the night.

Chapter 16
Violet

"Today's good mood is sponsored by coffee."

I woke early as always. Pre-dawn moonlight filtered in through the window as I lay sprawled half on top of Jake and half pressed into the back of his couch, warm and secure, and wrapped tightly in his big arms. I was in a new part of his life now and it fascinated me. I stretched lightly and he gripped my waist tight with one hand, then let it slide down to grab a palmful of my ass. "Good morning." His grin was too infectious to resist, not that I wanted to.

"Hey." I whispered, placing a kiss to his throat. We had forged a new path together last night. While I realized this was the same Jake I had always known, he felt different enough to be new, yet still familiar enough for me to feel safe. I had the feeling I would always be safe with him.

"You feel good here in my house," he murmured, dropping a kiss to my forehead.

"Yeah? I bet I can make you feel even better. Don't say a word." I slid quickly down his body to kneel on the floor, and before he could argue, I took him into my mouth. He was hard and huge within seconds as I sucked him to the back of my throat.

"Fuck, Violet." He groaned. "I won't argue with you now." I looked up to see him push himself to his elbows so he could watch me.

"I have to leave for the shop," I said as I kissed my way up the underside of his cock, lingering at the tip with my tongue and stroking him with my hand as I continued. "I have to open today."

"Yeah?" He grunted as he sat all the way up, spreading his knees wide and gathering my hair in his hand.

"Mm hmm," was all I could say. He inhaled deeply, and I watched his abs flex and release as I sucked harder. My eyes drifted up to his, and he returned my gaze, hot and intense, as his broad chest rose and fell with his panting breaths. I hummed again and he threw his head back and pounded the couch cushion with his fist.

"I'm gonna—" I nodded, but didn't move away as he came, shuddering out his release. I can't recall ever seeing anything as beautiful—aside from my babies—as Jake was in his orgasm. Sharp jawline tilted back, a small smile that was pained with his pleasure, and deep blue eyes boring into mine to pin me in place with possession and a depth of vulnerability that I didn't know could exist in a man. Tenderness washed over me as the path I hadn't known I could take all those years ago suddenly blazed into my mind with heartbreaking clarity as I gazed up at him.

"Get up here with me," he growled, tugging me up to wrap his arms around me, so tight I could barely breathe.

"Jake," I gasped. His hold loosened as he traced the bare skin of my spine with his fingertips and whispered a sweet thank you in my ear.

"Here." He lifted me, shifting so I sat next to him as he wrapped the blanket around my shoulders. "I'll be right back." He slipped his pants on and headed into the kitchen, returning with a bottle of water.

The vision I had of him the night before as we talked on the phone—sprawled in the chair in the corner with a whisky and his phone—crossed my mind as I stretched and took the bottled water from his hand. I sipped it, struggling to swallow it down through the sudden tightness in my throat. Overcome with emotion, I set it on a coaster next to my drink from last night. We'd gone from a simple phone call to this. Years had turned into minutes last night and I felt both exposed and at home—comfortable, like I belonged here, and vulnerable as if I could lose everything at any moment all at the same time.

He sat on the chair by the fireplace. His eyes searched mine. "It's going to be okay, Violet. I promise you. I know you have to get to work. We'll talk more tonight at dinner. Six o'clock, Sweetbriar Hotel."

My lips quirked to the side as I gathered the blanket tighter around myself. "You always know what to say," I murmured.

His head tilted to the side and he grinned as he pointed to his eyes then pointed at me. Yeah, he paid attention.

* * *

"Oh, barf!" Rose hollered at me from her usual tall table, dead center of the shop. My body swung to the side, changing to her direction.

"Shush, you. I don't know what in the world you're talking about." I slid into the chair across from her, holding the "hang on a minute" finger up toward the laughing Holly and Piper behind the counter. It was busy from the early morning rush, but they could handle it for a few more minutes while I dealt with my nosy Rosy Posy. The shoe was on the other foot for a change. It was weird.

"Sure, you don't." she snickered as she sipped her latte. "You looked pretty loved up, Miss Head-in-the-Clouds, floating here on the wings of your future wedding doves."

I chuckled. "How's married life treating you?"

"Ahh, deflection. I admire your strategery, though it's not going to work. Married life is perfection since my husband is the sexy, hot-cop man of my dreams. I have no complaints, and now that I'm getting it on the regular, the time I used to spend on fruitless dating and horny moping is over. In other words, I'm feelin' fine, so it's time to start mixing into everyone else's business again. Perhaps I'll start with you." Her eyebrows raised along with her cup as she mock toasted me.

"Uh, no thanks." I grinned and swiped one of her tiny scones.

"I was going to wait to grill you about Jake out of respect for your divorce, older sister status, and children, but you look intriguingly happy, so all bets are off. There's a spring in your step that only a session with a highly skilled dick can bring. Am I right?" she whispered.

My face had to be at least ten different shades of red. "Rose! People will hear," I hissed. "Whispering in here is useless. You should know that by now." People were on the lookout for lowered voices of any kind in my shop; a hand to the side of the mouth was not a deterrent to eavesdropping, and a red face acted like a beacon for juicy gossip. I needed to hide.

"Spill it—yes or no? I'll keep your secrets and ask no further questions if you tell me."

I inched closer to Rose. "Fine, yes. Not a home run, but yes. Bathing suit areas were involved. All of them," I confessed on another whispered hiss.

She burst out laughing. "Oh my god. 'Bathing suit areas.'" She snickered as she repeated my silly words. "Putting it that way is not an unbreakable code. But go you. Move on from that ass-face Tom in style."

"Whatever." I grabbed my tote bag. "I'm glad you're here anyway. I have something of yours. I found it in your closet the night I moved into the house. I've been carrying it around to give to you." I simultaneously cringed in sympathy and fought back laughter while at the same time selfishly happy to take the focus off myself.

"Oh yeah? What did you—" I held my tote open to show her the binder full of Jake's old modeling pictures. "Oh, shit. Don't you dare show that to anyone, Violet Marie Barrett. I couldn't take it with me for obvious reasons and I didn't want to throw it away, also for obvious reasons. I mean, look at it. It's too hot to get rid of." She chuckled, then covered her face with her hands.

"I would never show it to anyone, uh, deliberately. Rose, brace yourself." I paused for dramatic effect. "Jake saw it. It fell to the floor and popped open when he was putting boxes on the top shelf for me."

Her eyes got huge, and she shook her head. "No. That didn't happen . . ."

"It did. He flipped through and got all nostalgic." She closed her eyes and covered her ears.

"I don't accept that. Take it to your office and hide it somewhere. Let us never speak of this again."

"But—"

"Nuh-uh. Nope, no way. Hide it good for me, Vi."

"Okay, fine. I have to get to work anyway."

"'Kthanksbyeloveyou," she shouted over her shoulder as she made a mad dash to the front door.

"Love you too, weirdo," I shouted over my shoulder as I made my way toward my office. I passed Holly, saying, "I'll be out front in a minute."

She smiled. "We've got this. Take your time."

A rough hand grabbed my upper arm, shoving me into my office once I got through the swinging doors. I stumbled through the doorway, whirling around as it slammed shut behind me. "What the—"

"It's just me. We need to talk." Tom stood there, towering over me, and blocking the way out.

"Get out of my way. I have nothing to say to you." I tossed my tote onto my desk chair and reached around him for the doorknob.

He batted my hand aside. "We need to discuss something and it's going to be now. Where were you last night? Huh? The boys wanted to go home and I—"

"And you what?" I snapped back, hands on my hips. "What did you do? I'm not stupid enough to believe that if they wanted to go home, they invited you inside, Tom. So, what did you do? Spy through a window? Peek in the garage for my car? Neither is a good look for you since we're about to be divorced."

"Yeah, about that. I'm rethinking it."

I was aghast. "Don't be crazy. You can't rethink it. It's as good as done."

He gave a mirthless laugh. "I can do whatever the fuck I want in this town, and you know it. And what I want is to buy this shop."

"You already have my answer to that question, remember? It was no."

"And now you should have a better idea of where I

stand. Connect the dots—no shop, no divorce. And I'll also become extremely interested in custody of the boys. They went home to an empty house last night, Vi. Now, who's the one with the bad look?"

"Shut your mouth and get out of here." My eyes filled with tears. I brushed them aside with the back of my hand. "Give me your keys and go."

He tossed his copy of the shop keys on my desk with a smirk. "If you don't care about your own reputation or the boys', then think of Jake's. He's been trying to start up that charity of his for years. Trying to live down his modeling past, to get everyone to forget about his reputation as a serial dating playboy and the way he grew up—poor, with his trash father still running all over Portland, gambling and causing trouble. He has worked too hard to throw it all away on a whore like you," he sneered. "If you care about him at all, you'll think hard about what I'm telling you before you ruin his life."

My chest burned with panic, with rage. Like I was trapped in a maze with no way out, his words confused me, going against everything I had thought he wanted from me. "I can't believe this. I can't believe you! What happened to you?"

"I know what I want. And nothing will stand in my way of getting it. Not you. Not the boys. Not Bethany. All of you lack the ambition to understand what it takes to get ahead. I wanted a family to stand by my side. I tried with you, Violet. I did it all for you and the boys until I couldn't take it anymore."

"You may have started out doing it all for us. But what you ended up doing is something I can never forgive. We have kids together. One day we'll be grandparents together. Don't you care about that? Think of the boys." Desperation filled my every word. I'd been so close to being free of his bullshit, and now this?

"They made their choice when they left last night. I tried talking to them—"

"They're kids! I can't believe this—

"You need to listen to me—"

"No, I don't. Get out!" I shouted. He stomped out of my office and out the back, leaving a hole in the drywall as he threw the door open. I heard his Porsche peel out of the parking lot as I stood there trying to catch my breath.

The swinging doors to the front of the shop flew open. "We heard yelling," Holly shouted as she burst through, followed by Piper.

"I'm okay. Tom was here. He's gone now." It was a lie. I was not okay. I was nowhere near the vicinity of being okay, but no one needed to know. The fewer people who knew about this, the better.

"You're holding your arm. Did he hurt you?" she persisted.

After realizing I was indeed holding the arm Tom had grabbed, I let it go. "No. He just surprised me. I wasn't expecting him. He came through the back door."

"What did he say?" Piper chimed in. "Did he threaten you? Why were you yelling?"

"No, everything is fine, I promise. I don't want to talk about it. Please."

"Nuh-uh, I'm not playing around," Holly insisted. "What did you used to tell me back when I was in high school, Violet? Repeat it." Her eyes hit mine hard. "Pretend I am you right now and say it."

"I—I have to go. Can you two cover the shop for me please?"

"Real men don't put their hands on a woman, Violet.

No matter how upset they get. Don't cover up for him. Let us help you." Holly threw my words to her from long ago at my retreating back.

"I can't talk about this. Not now." I needed to think, to make a plan. And I had to be alone. I stormed out the back door feeling small again, and so, so foolish. Why had I ever thought I could get away from him?

Chapter 17
Jake

"Even a bad cup of coffee is better than no cup at all."

Sweetbriar was definitely a far cry from being a major city, but the lights of town still looked amazing from up here on the rooftop deck of the Sweetbriar Hotel, where I stood waiting for Violet to meet me. We were scheduled to tour the premises for the gala, but I'd also booked it for the night to surprise her with dinner. The hotel was four stories tall, made of brick, and overlooked the Sweetbriar River. The roof had a small enclosed fifth story facing the street, with a door that led down to the main part of the hotel and a bathroom, while the rear faced the river. It was open to the elements, but most of it was covered by an extended rooftop pergola. A row of cabanas lined one side, fronted by a few firepits meant for lounging with drinks and dessert or for private dining. It was perfect, and Dahlia was right: we would save a bunch of money on decorations. It would be beautiful up here without adding anything extra beyond candlelight on the tables and a few flowers placed here and there.

I turned to the deck's only entrance at the sound of footsteps and chatting coming up the stairs. "Thank you, and say hi to Nick when you get there." Violet called. She entered the main part of the deck with a smile. "That was Brianna, Nick's girlfriend. Isn't she sweet? And cute, too. I didn't know she worked here." Her smile melted away as she met my eyes. A jolt of apprehension blasted up my spine at the look on her face. The light in her eyes had dimmed.

What could it be now? "Yeah, I met her the night of your Christmas party. Nice girl. Are you okay? You look a bit frazzled. Busy day?"

"Yeah, you could say that." She hesitated at the edge of the deck.

Ignoring my apprehension, I held out my arms in a gesture of hope that we could pick up where we left off this morning. "Come here, beautiful."

"I—" She looked away, back toward the closed door that led back to the stairs. "I don't think I can stay. We shouldn't do this, at least not now."

I should have known better. Ice water drowned my heart as her words crept in to sink it. "Can we talk about whatever it is that snuck in to put that look on your face? Over dinner, maybe? Which happens to be set up on this table right over here." I grinned huge, deciding to ignore her trepidation for now. Maybe it was nothing and she was just hangry. Or maybe I could cheer her up and get her to talk to me. Violet was prone to cranky melancholy on an empty stomach or when she was over-tired or stressed out from a busy day.

She sighed, still unwilling to meet my eyes. "It's not you. It's me."

"Stab me through the heart with a classic break up line, why don't you?" A startled giggle escaped her. "Sit over here and eat with me, please. Maybe you're just tired because you've been running through my mind all day." I let my grin shift to the side as I stuffed my hands into my front pockets and lifted my shoulders up. That move had always worked for me in the past and I was not above trying it now.

I was gratified to see a blush rise over her cheeks. "Okay, sure. We can have dinner. But I don't want to hurt you. I don't feel like talking."

"You're killing me with the breakup lines, Vi. But you do look a little off today. Come over here and I'll turn you back on," I teased her with another cheesy pick-up.

"Oh my god. Jake, you are shameless tonight, aren't you?" She laughed as her blush deepened. "I just can't do this *right now*. I don't mean *not ever*." She threw her hands out to the sides in frustrated amusement and headed my way. Whatever was bothering her hadn't gone away, but at least I'd pushed it from the forefront of her mind. I could work with that.

"Then we definitely have things to discuss. Over dinner? Which is on the buffet table waiting for us to taste-test. Join me? Please? And for the record, I would never pressure you. What we did together last night and this morning has nothing to do with right now. I respect boundaries and will listen to you. I hope you know that."

Her eyes softened and she nodded. "I know. And I am hungry. But I don't want to talk."

"So you've said." She stepped into my arms for a

lingering yet friendly hug. It disappointed and relieved me at the same time. She seemed to need the comfort and I was more than willing to provide it. Out of respect, I didn't try to kiss her or hold her too close. And it took all my willpower to keep my face out of her neck in order to get a hit of that heady mix of Violet and perfume. When I felt the tension leave her body, I let go. She stepped back with a huge sigh.

"Let's see what we have," I offered, turning to lift the domed silver lid from one of the plates at the table.

"This is the fanciest lasagna I've ever seen. It smells wonderful." She slid into the seat with a grin. "I'm starving. I just realized I haven't eaten a single thing all day."

"I knew it. Hangry Violet is always—"

An eyebrow popped up as her eyes narrowed dangerously. "Always what?"

"Always just as lovely as regular Violet." I uncovered a basket filled with bread as an offering.

Her threatening eyebrow lowered, and I grinned as she took a piece. "Don't you forget it," she teased. "What else do we have over there?"

I set our plate covers on the side table and uncovered the one on the buffet. "Dessert. Tiramisu. Go ahead and start. I'll get the wine."

"Thank you, Jake." I grabbed a bottle of wine and two glasses then joined her at the table.

"It's so pretty up here," she mused. We were situated in the corner of the deck. The sun had just started to go down and the lights from the hotel were shimmering against the surface of the water.

"Do we give it gala approval? What do you think?"

"I think it's the best choice. Everything we've planned will work here—the auction, the giveaway, the presentation." She looked around while avoiding my eyes. "The space seems big enough. It's perfect.

"I agree. I'll put the deposit down when we finish with dinner. Now that's out of the way, what's going on with you? What happened this morning?"

She shook her head and shoved what remained of her garlic bread into her mouth to avoid answering.

"You'll feel better if we talk it out. Is it Tom?"

"Okay. Yeah, it's about Tom," she answered once she had swallowed. "What else would it be? He showed up at the shop this morning and ever since he left, Holly and the entire rest of my family has been all over my ass trying to find out what happened, so much so that I arranged for the boys to spend the night with my mother so I could shut my phone off, leave it at home, and ignore everything for a while so I could think. Please believe me when I say that I do not want to freaking talk about Tom. I need to weigh my options, and I need to figure shit out without having to explain it a thousand times. So can we eat this stupid delicious food and *not* talk about Tom?"

"Understood. We won't talk about him tonight. But will you please talk to Ren tomorrow? He told me you're not returning his calls."

"And I told you I was not comfortable having him take my case for free."

"But that's what we do! It is the basis for the center and the entire gala you are planning with me. And I would like to point out that you're working with me for free as a volunteer, so if it helps you sleep at night, consider Ren's legal work as payment for services rendered."

She stared at me, fork halfway to her mouth. I could almost see her brain working over what I'd just said. "You make some good points," she finally conceded.

"Of course I do." I chuckled.

"I'll think about talking to your brother."

"Good enough for tonight. Now, why are you trying to break it off with me?"

She shrugged, in a deceptively casual manner. "I'm not. I just feel like we should wait until my divorce is final. I can't have a boyfriend and a husband. It's just not right. It looks terrible for us both. If we start something now—like, officially—I will just drag you into my mess and it's not fair to you. Tom isn't letting this go and I—"

"What did he say to you this morning?"

Casual went out the window as she turned her face away with a mirthless laugh. "I can't bring myself to repeat any of it, okay? I can't even force myself to think about it. I tried all day to sort it out and I couldn't." Her fork clattered to her plate and she shoved it aside.

"Let me help you. Please."

"He has never been like that before, Jake. He really scared me. Damn it, I have to go. I have to get away from you before he finds out I was with you. What was I thinking coming here?" She jumped up from her seat, ran to the door and jiggled the knob. She spun around, eyes panicked. "This isn't funny. Let me out."

I rushed to her side to try the door for myself. "What are you talking about? Let me try." It was locked. "Did Brianna give you a key? Is she off for the night? Don't worry, we'll just call the front desk to unlock the door. Get your phone."

Her face turned pale. "I left my phone at home. Get yours."

"My phone died about an hour ago."

"Oh my god. Now what?"

"We don't panic, that's what. Come back to the table. We can't break a metal door down. We'll eat our dinner and wait. The kitchen staff will be up here to clean up the food, right?"

"Yeah, that makes sense."

I held out a hand. "Let's finish dinner and you can finish telling me about Tom. Then I'll explain all the reasons why I'm not giving up on us no matter what he has to say about it. If you don't want to be with me, that's an entirely different conversation." She looked away as she swayed closer to me and took my hand, clutching it tight and following me back to the table.

We sat and she gave me a recap of her horrible experience with Tom this morning. "It's a good thing we're locked up here or I—"

Startled eyes met mine. "You can't go after him. It's like he's waiting for it. He's one step ahead of me and he wants to ruin my life, Jake. If I don't give him the shop, he'll destroy everything I have. He'll try to take the boys away from me."

"He can't take your boys from you. There's no way he'll ever be granted sole custody. It won't happen. Those boys adore you and they're practically grown. And look, I'm not going to blow this. I've wanted you for too long. Are you going to say anything about us to anyone?" She shook her head. "Then who's going to find out? I sure as hell won't tell anyone. I have too much to lose—and yes, that would be *you*, Violet. I don't want to lose you."

"Keeping it a secret is a possibility, sure. But I don't know if I can hide the way I feel. There's a huge difference between living on the edge of a secret and—"

"We won't be on the edge, trust me. I've been on the edge—all these years, hiding how I feel about you and keeping it a secret? *That* was my edge. Ever since last night with you, I feel like I'm finally on solid ground, finally heading where I have always wanted to go, and I don't want to climb back up on that edge ever again. It's too hard to live that way."

"Oh, Jake. I feel the same. The last few years with Tom were a balancing act, always trying to keep the boys from finding out how bad it was and attempting to keep him happy and out of his horrible moods. And now I feel like I'm about to be stuck in that place again—"

"So we agree?"

"On what, exactly?"

"We keep this thing between us a secret. We figure out his angle, you work with Ren and get the divorce, and in the meantime, no one has to know about us."

"And the boys? How will I be able to keep this a secret from them?"

"We'll figure it out."

"We can try. But it might be too much. If it comes down to making a choice between being with you and saving you from Tom, I won't ask you to wait for me. I won't allow you to be in the path of whatever Tom is planning."

"Whether or not I wait for you is not your decision, it's mine. I won't let him hurt you. I'll do anything it takes to keep you out of his crosshairs."

"Whatever you say." The stubborn tilt of her jaw was probably a warning of things to come, but I didn't care. She was what I had always wanted, and I would never give up on her.

Chapter 18
Violet

"All you need is love and coffee."

The early evening glow had faded away. It had grown dark and cold, and there was no sign of the kitchen staff even though we'd long since finished with our dinner. "What are we supposed to do? Do you think Tom locked us up here?"

"I doubt it. He played a big hand today. It wouldn't make sense for him to have a go at you again so soon. He wants you to stew on what he said this morning. This has to be a simple accident."

My eyes got big. "Or maybe it's my mother, trying to play matchmaker. She has the boys for the night, Brianna works here, and this is something I would totally do. The dots are slowly starting to connect."

He chuckled. "Or it could be my brother, or Harper. Or hell, anyone in either one of our families who has even the slightest clue of what's happening between us and knew we would be here."

"Oh lord. Your family too? We're doomed." I laughed at

the irony, then frowned at my circumstances. "Doomed. You know who's frickin' doomed? I'm doomed."

"You're not doomed, Vi. Tom is a petty dick. He thinks his money gives him power. It doesn't. You know that, right?"

"In theory, yeah. But it felt like he had power this morning. It will feel like power when he ruins your reputation and tries to take the boys from me and forces me to sell my shop." I could feel my mood deteriorating, but I couldn't stop it.

"None of that is going to happen. Come with me." He stood up and held out a hand.

"Where? Are we scaling the wall and going home?"

"No, let's get comfortable in one of those cabanas. It's getting cold up here and it doesn't look like anyone is going to unlock that door anytime soon. We can take advantage of the situation and spend this time together."

It would be so easy to take his hand and let him take care of me. But what kind of woman would that make me? Jumping from man to man. From a husband to a boyfriend when I wasn't even divorced yet. It would make me a user; it would make me pathetic and weak, and I didn't want to be any of those things. "Jake, why do you want to be with me when you could do so much better?" I blurted. "I'm a still-married mess. My baggage has baggage. It will take me years to unpack all of it and be okay again."

Warm eyes met and held mine. "Give yourself some credit. You aren't a mess. You're stuck in a mess you didn't create. There's a huge difference between the two. Once we get you out of it and away from him for good, you'll understand what everyone else sees in you because you'll finally be able to see it too."

I took his hand and stood. "You're just too nice. That's all this is," I muttered as I followed him to a cabana.

"I am not nice. You're all that matters to me—you and the boys. I've said it before. When I know what I want, I do whatever it takes to get it. Come on." He drew the heavy curtain aside, allowing me to precede him into the cabana. It was lovely and cozy, and while it wasn't exactly warm, it kept the wind and the Oregon drizzle-rain from chilling us to the bone. A padded chaise lounge sat in the corner along with a tiny side table. "I'll gather the cushions from the other cabanas. We may as well get comfortable while we're here."

"Okay," I breathed out, feeling lost.

He came back with an armful of cushions. I pressed my lips together and watched as he made a pallet on top of the outdoor rug that covered the deck. Watching him, I got lost in a different way, a way that said, *even though I'm a mess, I'm falling in love with you and maybe I should tell you.* But I couldn't tell him; it wouldn't be fair. So I kept it locked up inside my heart where it would have to stay, at least for now.

After he finished, he sat and caught my eye, gesturing for me to join him. We didn't say anything to each other. He just watched me as I sank to my knees, then into his side to wrap my arms around his waist and snuggle my face into his chest.

"You're going to be okay, gorgeous. I promise," he whispered, then dropped a kiss to my forehead. "Wait a sec, I'll be right back." He pulled away and stood.

"Where are you going?"

"We can use the tablecloth as a blanket. I'll go get it. We should probably get some sleep."

"You think of everything," I murmured. He winked before slipping through the fabric in order to gather a makeshift blanket to keep me warm and comfortable. I stared at the fabric doorway of the cabana as it swished closed. Fair or not, I decided then and there to jump his bones so hard when he came back. This would probably be the only chance I would have to experience what it would feel like to be with someone who took care of me without expecting something in return, and I wanted to give him the same feeling. Even if it was only for one night. I had the fleeting thought that if my life wasn't such a mess, I could give him everything and never have to take it back.

Being stuck up here felt surreal, like we were in our own simple little world. Just a man, a woman, and a locked door —no messes, no complications, no consequences. I kicked off my boots and slipped out of my jacket. My fear-filled, chaotic thoughts drifted away as everything he had done to make me feel better tonight filled my mind instead.

"I found these tiny lanterns in the buffet table drawer, and these." He tossed a few outdoor throw pillows my way with a grin. I propped them against the wall and Jake passed me a lantern before he secured the cabana opening closed with careful knots. "Hopefully they work."

I flipped the switch, smiling when it lit up. "It works." Grinning up at him, I placed it on the side table as he hung the other from the hook on the ceiling. He grabbed the corners of the bunched up tablecloth in his arms, then flung his hands wide to let the it drift open to cover me. He then did the same with the buffet cover he had tucked under his arm.

"At least we won't be stuck freezing in the pitch dark." He shuddered.

My eyebrows raised. "You don't like the dark?"

"Be nice, don't tease," he chuckled. "No, I don't like the dark, okay?"

"I'm nothing but nice. Finn won't admit it, but he doesn't like the dark either. Come down here." I patted the space next to me and held the makeshift covers open so he could snuggle in. "I'll protect you."

"You don't have to tell me twice." He slipped out of his coat, spread it atop our pallet and did the same with mine. "It's trying to snow out there, but we'll be fine. I lit the firepits. It should help a little."

He stood above me, all broad shoulders, flat abs, and long legs, hot as could be. A small, hesitant smile spread across his face as any remaining uncertainty I held within my heart fled. We had nothing but this brief sliver of time to share freely and I refused to let it go to waste. I held up my arms for him and he sank to his knees next to me. "Come on, get warm with me," I murmured.

Taking my offer, he pulled me into his wide wall of a chest and settled us to lie back against the outdoor throw pillows he'd gathered. I melted against him, clinging tight to his solid frame. As he held me, the tension I'd been unwittingly carrying around all day left my body and I found myself clutching his shirt in my hands, desperate to get closer to the warmth and safety he provided without even trying.

"I got you," his whispered words at my temple ruffled my hair and I shut my eyes against the onslaught of thoughts about Tom and this morning and all the reasons why I should roll away and leave him alone. But one thing kept me from putting a stop to this night: the feeling that he needed me, mess and all, just as much as I needed him.

I lifted my face to his, seeking his lips for a kiss.

His kisses were just as overwhelming as the ones he gave me last night and the night at my car, which meant it would always feel this good to be with him. Zingy and tingly and sincere and real. I wanted to be with him always, but I couldn't. Not yet.

I shivered as his hands drifted down my spine to trace beneath the hem of my shirt. "Can I?" His voice, low in my ear, followed by his tongue darting out to trace the shell, drove me wild.

"Yes," I whispered. His question granted me permission as well, and I bunched the fabric of his shirt in my palms to pull it over his head. With his eyes burning into mine, he removed my shirt and we tossed them to the chaise in the corner along with my quickly unhooked bra.

We were pressed close, skin to skin, my breasts flattened against him and tickled by the light dusting of his chest hair. He felt even better than he looked, and my goodness, he was beautiful. His lips on mine ignited something deep inside me and I knew that no matter what happened tomorrow, this moment would live in my heart forever.

Passion and an oddly gentle aggression surged between us as our hands covered every square inch of skin we had exposed to each other. But it wasn't good enough. My hands drifted down to the waistband of his jeans.

I needed more.

I wanted all of him.

"Can I?" I groaned against his lips.

"Fuck yes." The words rumbled from his chest, exciting me, spurring me on as I unbuttoned his jeans, lifted my skirt, and straddled his lap. "Wait, condom. In my wallet," he gasped.

I froze above him. "I'm on the pill, and you should know I've been tested, uh, since Tom, and I'm okay—"

His finger pressed to my mouth. "I have too. Condom?" I shrugged and he smiled. "Let's do this right. He lifted me off his lap to stand and slid my panties and skirt down my legs, kissing me once on the inside of my thigh before wiggling out of his jeans and boxer briefs. He tugged me down, turning me onto my back beneath him as I let my legs fall to the sides to give him room to move.

I knew if this didn't happen now, I would never have this chance again, and then I would never know what it felt like to belong to him—and, oh how I wanted to belong to him, more than anything. And I wanted him to be mine. "I want you, Jake. All of you. Please don't stop." He entered me in one deep thrust, all the way, giving me exactly what I asked for.

"You feel so good," he groaned. "Like sliding into a goddamned dream come true." He paused, deep inside, and leaned forward as if to kiss me but he didn't. "I'm too close." His voice was a pained rumble as he pulled out and rose to his knees between my legs.

He left me pulsing around nothing, so close to something I'd never felt before. "What's wrong? Did I do something—"

"Yeah, you're too sexy for your own good." He slid down my body, randomly placing kisses and little licks against my skin as he descended. Once he reached his destination, he lifted my calves over his shoulders. I looked down at him and when we locked eyes, he smiled against my clit. The only word to describe him, kneeling low, naked, and doing amazing things between my legs, was *hungry*. His eyes drifted closed with pleasure as he licked me in delicious circles with the tip of his tongue. My legs shook, and my brain shut down as I reached low to run my fingers into his hair.

"This might take too long," I warned. "I'm not used to coming like this—"

He laughed against my slick skin. "You can take as long

as you need. I don't fucking care. Relax and let me take care of you." He groaned before sucking me into his mouth with rhythmic little pulses. I did as he said, arching involuntarily as he added his fingers into the mix, entering me with one, then two. He looked up at me with hot, hooded eyes, "I've got you."

Pleasure like I'd never known flowed through me and to my surprise, I realized I was getting close. This wasn't a means to an end for him; he was enjoying this as much as I was. He groaned against my skin and I melted into the cushions. Shocked, I whispered, "You're going to make me come." My toes curled as I let my legs spread wide to the sides to dig my feet into the cushions beneath me.

With his hands at my ass, he tilted my hips up to his face. "You know what to do, beautiful, so let go and do it," he growled against my clit.

I shut my eyes and felt all the tension in my body start to flicker and flame between my legs. I was coming, and nothing was going to stop it. "Get inside me," I demanded. I wanted him to feel what he was doing to me.

He rose to his knees. "I've dreamed of this," he whispered as he entered me, bending forward to briefly place his forehead against my chest before lifting to kiss me and take my hands in his, interlocking our fingers above my head. This chemistry between us was undeniable as he moved inside me, cherishing me in a way I'd never felt before. He was slow at first. Careful. Patient. And so sweet as he took me, making sure I felt as good as he did as he went harder and deeper, with each thrust after grinding thrust driving me closer to the edge.

"Jake, oh my god," I cried out, tumbling over the side in an all-consuming wave of pleasure. I watched as he shuddered through his own release, mesmerized. He rolled us so I was sprawled half on his chest with our legs intertwined.

With a flick, he covered us, and I burrowed into his side. "Stay close. I'll keep you warm," he murmured into the top of my head.

"Mm hmm. I'm not going anywhere," I agreed. "Except for maybe the bathroom. I mean, someone has to protect you from the dark," I teased. I wasn't ready to discuss the full weight of what we had done; I had to keep it light. It was obvious in how he had treated me every step of the way that more than our bodies were involved, and it would be impossible for me to deny my feelings for him if he pressed the matter.

"I'm not going anywhere either. I hope you know that, Violet." His repetition held more meaning than my words, yet I was too overwhelmed to return the sentiment right now. "Get some sleep, baby. Someone will be around in the morning. I'm willing to bet on it."

"Well, I hope they bring breakfast." I felt his laughter rumble against my cheek. "Night, Jake."

"Goodnight, gorgeous."

Chapter 19
Violet

"Shit happens, coffee helps."

"Jake? Violet? Are you guys okay?" I awoke with a start, all warm and cozy and cuddled up next to Jake for the second day in a row. The level of comfort I felt in his arms forced me to consider that this might be how my life was always supposed to turn out. I shoved the thought out of my head as I gently shoved Jake's shoulder to wake him up.

"Jake, get up," I hissed frantically. "It sounds like Brianna is back."

"I am so sorry," she shouted. "I saw your cars in the parking lot. The door must have locked behind me last night. I had no idea it would do that. But there is a fire escape, you know." Footsteps clicked over the deck. Were they headed our way? *Gah!* I couldn't tell which way she was going. There was no light shining through the slight space in the cabana entrance, which meant it was very early.

"Uh, it's okay, sweetie! Just prop it open and we'll be

down in a jiffy!" I shouted. "Fire escape? What the heck?" I muttered under my breath. I had not seen a fire escape, and definitely no sign that led to one either. *Ugh.*

We needed time, especially considering we were both naked as the day we were born and wrapped up in nothing but a freaking tablecloth.

"Okay, the door is unlocked now. Take your time!" she called back to me. I sighed with relief when I realized she was filling a cart with our dishes from the night before and not about to bust two naked adults in a cabana who really should have gotten dressed before they crashed together like a pair of idiot teenagers.

I listened intently with my hand cupped to my ear as her footsteps faded and the door closed behind her.

Movement against my side made me jump and sit up, gathering the tablecloth to cover my boobs just like every girl after every sex scene on every TV show ever made. I looked down in time to see Jake stretch. My mouth dropped open as I gawked at him. This was a multi-sensory experience. A full-on, arms over his head, moaning, groaning, and yawning *hello to the world* that I felt in every part of my body. I was going to do something dumb. I could feel it in the air. Just like that one song, it was coming. *Oh lord.*

"Good morning, sexy." Gravelly and deep, I felt his voice on my skin like a caress. His shoulders were broad and his chest was wide and inviting. The tablecloth drifted down his body to hide the morning hard-on that I had spied tenting the fabric when I first glanced down at him, and I was mesmerized. The sleepy-eyed expression on his face was adorable in every sense of the word, and it took every brain cell I owned not to re-jump him. I was absolutely not about to run my fingers through that mussed-up bed head hair or sink into his outstretched, beckoning arms. Nuh-uh, not me.

I ignored my own good sense and nestled back into his cozy embrace.

"Morning, Jake. We should get up and do all the things. Get dressed and—" I was silenced by his lips on mine and his hands moving over and around all my good parts.

"We have a few minutes," he growled against my lips. "I want you."

"Okay, yeah. I mean, what's a few more minutes?" I panted as he quickly and skillfully worked me up until I was an unthinking, horny mass of sensations. When I woke up a few minutes ago, I'd had a ton of reasons why I was going to get up and go straight home, rise and shine and all that boring bullcrap. but I forgot about all things sensible when I felt him hard and insistent between my legs.

"Get on," he groaned, tugging me up to straddle his lap with his hands at my waist. Arguing in the morning was stressful and sex was way more fun, so I got on, sank down, and we compared and contrasted our morning quickie skills together. Incidentally, they turned out to be top notch given we managed to get each other off in a matter of minutes. "Imagine starting each day like this." He ran his lips over my neck before he licked it and took a little bite. *Gah!* He didn't have to suggest it, I could think of nothing else.

"I don't even know what to say. That was—"

"Amazing, perfect, and everything beautiful in the world. Just like you."

"I wish we could stay up here forever," I accidentally confessed.

His eyes lit up on mine and the smile that spread across his face was knowing. "It felt like we were in our own world, didn't it?"

"Yeah." I sighed and tucked my head into his neck for one last hit of his scent before reality set in. His big arms gave me a squeeze. I ran my fingers into his hair and leaned back to gaze at his gorgeous face. I wanted to have the memory of his soft, sweet, morning-after eyes melded into my mind forever.

"We'll get there again, Vi. It's just a matter of time."

"What changed your mind? You know, about not sleeping together until you determined I was ready." I laughed at the ridiculousness of the question.

He leaned forward and kissed my forehead before answering. "Last night felt like the end of the world and the beginning of time all at once."

I nodded because I understood. "Like it was the only thing to do, meant to happen . . ."

Fingertips drifted across my cheek to press to my lower lip. "It felt right. Then you said yes, and it was everything I've ever wanted come true—"

I pressed my mouth to his, I could hear no more, not yet. "It was wonderful, Jake. But it's getting light outside; we should probably get a move on before we get caught all nakie up here. We were lucky that Briana is not a snoopy person."

"You're probably right. So, Ren will be in touch today. Talk to him. Promise me."

"Okay, sure . . ." I turned away. I never could lie straight to someone's face. *Gah!*

"Promise," he insisted.

I tipped my head back to his to make sure he could see my eyes roll. "Fine, I promise I'll talk to him." Now I had to. I never broke a promise. Damn it.

He squeezed my ass and pushed me back on his lap. "We have to get dressed."

"Time for reality," I grumbled.

* * *

Hiring Holly to work at my shop was the best thing I'd done in a long time. She was behind the counter when I finally arrived at the shop, bustling around efficiently, helping customers, and generally being awesome. She had called in a few of my backup stay-at-home mom baristas to help her out without me having to suggest it. She was living her life in sharp contrast to how I had been living mine lately—I was constantly running late, unable to focus, and generally a stressed-out mess.

"Good Morning, Violet." Her greeting was accompanied by a teasing smile. "It might be time for a raise, don't you think?" She met me at the corner near the cash register to chat.

"Yeah, and time to make you assistant manager or give you an official title or something." I knew I needed help and there was no shame in asking for it. My shop was doing gangbusters business ever since the whole Tom and Bethany cheating extravaganza happened. Their illicit banging and the fact that I was in and out of this place at all kinds of irregular hours made for good gossip, and gossip was great for business. I should have figured.

"Holy crap, really? Can I be the Countess of Caffeination? No, no, the Princess of Percolation, the Cappuccino Contessa. I know, how about HBIC—Head Barista in Charge, the official coffee mini-boss of Violet's Café? Will that fit on my name tag?" I shot her a look. "Fine. Assistant manager works. How much is the raise?"

"I don't know, five bucks?"

Her mouth dropped open. "I freaking love you."

"I love you back. You've been picking up my slack ever since the day we will not speak of, and I appreciate you. I'm sorry it took me so long to acknowledge it."

"You've got a lot going on. No apologies necessary. Can we share your office?"

I barked out a laugh. "Don't push it, dude."

"Worth a try." She shrugged, then her eyes got really big. "Can I help you?" she said to whoever was behind me.

A deep, gravelly voice answered. "I'm here to talk to Violet."

Holly half-snorted. "Of course you are."

"You're a tough one to get ahold of, aren't you?" I spun around to find Jake's big bro staring down at me. Correction, Jake's ultra-hot, almost-dead-ringer big bro. Also, those Moretti boys sure didn't waste any time.

"Ren, hey," I greeted.

"Jake called. You're finally ready to talk to me?"

"Uh, yes, I'm ready. We can talk in my office. In fact, go on back through the swinging doors. My office is the second door on the left. I'll get us some coffee and breakfast."

"Sounds good to me." He headed to the back of the shop.

Holly stood at the cash register staring after Ren. "Damn. What is it with this town? They grow them big and tall up in these parts."

"Fine as hell, too." I mused as I gathered a few mixed berry and lemon scones and some clotted cream.

Holly slid two coffees my way. "You got that right. Break you off a piece of that gene pool, big sister. I approve."

"Thanks." I grabbed the tray but immediately put it down when I heard a ruckus coming from the front door. "What the heck is that?" A hostile older red head with big hair barged her way through the door waving an empty takeout cup over her head and heading toward Holly with what I could already tell would be a petty, free-stuff-seeking complaint. I knew the type. Every town had them. I hadn't yet met this one, however, and she had me curious.

"I need to speak to your manager. You! Blondie, behind the counter. Who's in charge here?"

"That would be me. Hello, I'm Violet. How may I assist you?" Generic kindness was usually the way to go with this level of disgruntled crazy. One quick look around the shop said that yes, everyone was indeed staring at the commotion. *Freaking great.*

She tossed her empty cup in Holly's direction. It bounced off her chest before I could get in front of her. Zero to insanity in one second? This was very suspicious. People always wanted something free rather than to unleash a temper tantrum right off the bat. "All right, please leave. I won't tolerate you abusing my employees."

She ignored me. "This is America. I have rights! That barista served me a latte with hair in it. And it isn't the first time she's messed something up, either. The quality started going downhill in this shop since you hired her and I'm afraid I had to one-star you online." She glared in my general direction with arms crossed, foot tapping, while pointedly avoiding my eyes. What a load of crap. I'd heard nothing but good things since Holly started.

"I, uh—if I messed something up, me or any of the other baristas would have been more than happy to fix your order." Holly answered the woman in a shaky voice. She leaned in to whisper in my ear, "Violet, I don't even remember ever serving her."

"We aim to please here," I added, "Would you like your money back? Or another drink?"

"No, nuh-uh." She stepped up to the counter, shoving

the next customer in line to the side to point in Holly's face. "I've been coming here since this place opened. I'm going to tell everyone I know about how rude you always are to me."

I shoved her arm away from Holly. "Hey now, that is not necessary. Back off and get out of here."

She burst into tears, turning to face the customer area of the shop. "You shoved my arm! Ow! Oh my god! Is this how you treat your loyal customers? I can't believe this." She stormed off in a huff. Holly and I exchanged shocked glances.

"Yo, Holly. Are you okay?" We spun toward the door to watch Liam walk through, followed by my little brother Cade.

A stricken Holly removed her apron and handed it to me. "I have to go, Violet. I'm so sorry."

"I know, honey. Don't you worry about a thing." She ran past the guys. "I can't leave the shop now. Cade? Can you go after her?" But I didn't have to ask, he was already out the door followed by a concerned Liam.

"That was . . . something." I puffed out a frustrated breath of air.

"That was weird, Violet. I've never seen her before. And don't you believe one word she said about your sister. Holly is wonderful."

One of my baristas chimed in. "Just look at this." She turned her phone screen toward me. It appeared like a lot of people had become dissatisfied with my shop lately. My Google rating had tanked down to a one-star, as well as my Yelp and Facebook page.

"Great. Damn it. I knew something was up with her."

"Someone is trying to make you look bad," Ren observed from over my shoulder. I startled and turned to look up at him. I hadn't even heard him approach.

I raised a sardonic eyebrow. "Gee, I wonder who it could be?"

"Your no-good ex," a customer shouted from the back of the shop, inciting yet another wave of loud whispering to move around the dining area.

"Something happened between Tom wanting to divorce you and move on with Bethany and now," Ren said low in my ear. "Whatever he wants with the shop is another issue entirely, and you'll need more than just my help to figure out what it is. I'll see what I can do."

"Thanks, Ren."

He resembled a hot, evil villain as he grinned down at me. "This is gonna be my pleasure."

I was glad he used whatever his powers were for good.

Chapter 20
Jake

"Without coffee, something is missing."

"I'm going to miss you, gorgeous," I stated on the phone, because this was the only way I would be speaking to Violet for the foreseeable future.

Ren was a bastard for suggesting to her that we stay apart. But nailing Tom's ass to the wall and keeping Violet and the boys protected was vital, so I promised to stay away no matter how much it would hurt.

"I know you're upset," Ren said once I got off the phone.

"How much longer?"

"You know I can't tell you anything we discuss. She's my client. I'm not the bad guy here."

"I know you're not. And I know you're probably right, it's just—"

"You love her. I get it."

"Fuck yes, I do. It's been years, Ren. To step away now? It feels impossible. I should be with her."

"Just keep your relationship with her quiet and let me

do my job. I deal with trash like Tom every day. It's just a matter of determining what his game is. Once I have that, then it's all over and you two get your lives back. I hate to be the one to point this out to you, but you need to keep your reputation intact. Lyla's Place is partially dependent on donations. A scandal is the last thing you need."

"I know it does," I reluctantly admitted. I didn't want to care about superficial things like my reputation in town, but the sad truth was, it mattered. "It will be okay—"

Our heads swiveled to the doorway as Harper burst through, arms full of take-out bags. "I have news. Here, help me with this." I helped her untangle the plastic bags from her wrists and distribute our lunch across the table.

"Please tell me your secretary sources are talking about Tom?"

"Oh yes. Ever since the whole Bethany thing, he's been the talk of the town. So far, he's managed to get his hands on two of the businesses in Violet's strip, two office suites in this building, and he's making moves to acquire the Sweetbriar Hotel." She was smug as she popped a straw into the top of her soda cup.

"What the hell?" Ren exclaimed.

"He's trying to move straight up Mr. Out of Town Hotshot's ass. Tom wants to be a partner with whoever it is. I bet he wants to be on the front line when that MFer takes a bulldozer to half of Sweetbriar. They want to change this town and make it upscale, like Vail or Aspen, or whatever," she continued.

"No one who lives here wants that," I reasoned. "And we have to take everything you heard with a grain of salt. It's all, what? Second, or even third hand information. Pure speculation. Also, he can't buy office suites in this building. They're only for rent. That information is outright false."

"Fine, okay, but get this—most of Violet's business neighbors are refusing to sell and it gets worse. The deli next to Violet's place had a mouse infestation—white mice, the cute kind you can buy at freaking Pet-Co. I mean, Bethany heard there was even a few poor little hamsters in the mix. Could he be more obvious? And Mr. Harris, the dry cleaner, had a small fire last night. He was so pissed when I talked to him this morning. And today, what is up with that ranting weirdo at Violet's? This is all very *Scooby-Doo*, isn't it?"

"Wait, who told you all of this? Bethany?"

"No, she doesn't talk to me anymore since I reamed her out about cheating with Tom. I heard it from my friend Elizabeth." Ren and I stared at her blankly and I shook my head. I did not know Elizabeth.

"Keep up, Uncle Jake. Elizabeth, from the Quickbriar Stop and Go, where I get the killer breakfast burritos for us every morning. Elizabeth is Becca's sister." I gave her another blank look and she rolled her eyes in annoyance. "Becca, my best friend since kindergarten! You are terrible with names. Also, I swear Levi—Jude's brother—is secretly in love with her, but that's another story."

I shook my head to get the useless parts of her statement out of my brain. Ren just sat there with his lips twitching as he tried not to laugh. "Okay, Elizabeth. Gotcha. Go on."

"Anyway, Bethany told Elizabeth who told one of the firefighters who was fighting the fire at the dry cleaner. He told Jude about the mice and the fire, and Jude told me last night. And when I was at the dry cleaner this morning picking up your suits, Mr. Harris confirmed that there was definitely a small fire in his back room. So, obviously, Tom is sabotaging the businesses to get them to sell to him."

Ren shook his head while trying not to laugh. "It's not

really that obvious since we also have to factor in an angry ex-mistress or anyone else who may have heard the rumor of an out of state real estate developer and wants in on it. We also have to think about coincidence and accidents. But I agree, at the basic *Scooby-Doo* level of mystery, some of the signs point to Tom. But is he really that stupid? We have an eye on Violet and the shop now, so no worries there—she's covered. To put your mind at ease, I've called the police, Jake, and they're looking into various things that I can't discuss with you."

"Can you imagine if our little Sweetbriar turns into one of those snooty ski towns? Yuck. And no thank you. Traffic is already bad enough from people who already vacay here every winter."

Ren was lost in thought. "Snooty ski towns, huh? Keep your ears open, Harper. It will all come out. Secrets don't last in a town like this. I'm leaving. I'll see you two later."

"Later, Uncle Ren."

"I should just beat the shit out him and be done with it. Just like when we were kids. There was nothing a quick fist fight couldn't solve."

Harper shook her head. "You're not kids anymore. Money and power ruin everything, don't they? He'd probably sue you or have you arrested or something."

"Yeah, you have a point. I'll let that idea go—at least for now."

Chapter 21
Violet

"I don't need an inspirational quote. I need coffee."

"Have you ever felt like you've seized the wrong day? We should have waited until I was rid of Tom for good before we started this up," I whispered into the phone. "I miss you." Middle of the night conversations were our thing now. Phone calls, yummy phone sex, and a few clandestine meetings to work on the gala together had gotten us through the last few weeks-ish. Missing him had caused me to lose all track of time.

Jake wanted to move forward, whatever Tom was up to be damned. But I refused to let Tom try to ruin Jake's reputation like he had tried to do with mine, so I insisted we keep our secret, like Ren advised, until the divorce was completely ironed out. Tom was being a pain in the ass about the boys and how to divide our assets. I wasn't asking for much, not even what Ren insisted I was entitled to. Yet Tom was determined to drag it out just the same. I was still getting the sporadic one-star ratings and bad reviews for the shop on social media. No more random shouty ladies had appeared, but video of the big-haired, older, red headed rage monster incident was online on several of the Sweetbriar neighborhood Facebook pages. "Helpful" customers would share the—heavily edited to make me look bad—clip with me on occasion. And so far, Ren hadn't been able to prove Tom had anything to do with any of it.

The boys spent the occasional weekend with Tom where nothing really happened. They said all they did was eat dinner together and watch various sports ball games on television. They said they were fine with spending time with him, and he was trying to be a good dad to them again, so I allowed it to continue, and didn't have Ren try to fight it.

"No, I don't feel that way. In fact, Ren said your divorce is almost as good as done, right? I want you to co-host the gala with me—don't answer now. Think about it."

"I'll think about it. I promise."

"Thank you. Get some sleep, gorgeous."

"'Night." We hung up and I thought about the gala. I'd already planned to attend with the boys. Acting as co-host would inevitably put my feelings for Jake in the spotlight, which was a scary thought. Tom was laying low, and I was almost totally free. I didn't want anything to get in the way of it, but I also didn't want to hurt Jake. I headed into the kitchen for some milk and crackers to settle my stomach. My nerves were out of control and I was nauseated beyond belief. In fact, all I could seem to keep down lately were crackers. *The stress must be getting to me.*

"Hey, Mom." Finn and Nick were at the table eating takeout. Immediately the smell hit me, and I gagged. It was fish and chips from the food cart in town, complete with malt vinegar.

"I'm glad you two are home before curfew, but that fishy smell is about to make me barf." I ran to the bathroom, choking on bile until I made it to the toilet where I promptly threw up.

First nauseated all the time and now getting sick? What the hell could—

Oh shit.

Oh no.

Was I?

Pregnant?

Holy crap and freakin' duh.

I wiped my mouth, then scrambled back to lean against the bathtub, searching in the pocket of my robe for my cell phone all while trying to remember when I last had my period at the same time.

"Rose," I hissed once she picked up. "Pick up a pregnancy test and meet me in my bathroom. Shit! Rosy Posy, for the love of god, hurry!"

I hung up.

I stood up.

I washed my hands and brushed my teeth, dismayed when I gagged on the toothbrush. This was all starting to feel very familiar.

I burst into tears and smiled down at my still relatively flat stomach. It would never be *flat* flat. I had grown two babies in there and I was about to grow at least one more. I was good with it.

Whoa.

I should have known.

The stomach flu I had last week was not the flu.

The signs were already in my kitchen. I had every cracker you could think of in there, from graham crackers to Saltines to Cheez Its and everything in between. I had been chugging milk like a crazy woman, and lately my dinner—when I actually had an appetite—always included steamed Brussels sprouts, covered in fresh cracked black pepper, and dipped in mayonnaise, a side dish that at any other time would disgust me. But when I was pregnant with the boys, I couldn't get enough of those slimy green little balls of stink.

About twenty minutes later a knock at the front door burst me out of my insane reverie in the bathroom. I rushed to throw it open, but Rose pushed her way in. "Come on," she said to me while she headed for the bathroom. "Boys, your mother is sick. Steer clear."

"Damn, stomach flu again?" Finn's words trailed behind us as we rushed down the hall together. "Do you need anything?"

"No, sweetie. I'm fine, thank you. I'm coming, Rose." I slammed the door behind myself. "Uh, you're not going to watch me pee on this thing," I stated.

"When was your last period? Did you miss one?"

"I don't remember, okay? I can't think right now. Why is period math so hard?"

"Uh, probably because it's math under extreme duress? The answer is either something you want more than anything, or the opposite."

"Quit being logical, dang it. I already know I'm pregnant, okay? I mean, I'm pretty sure I am. My boobs hurt. I threw up multiple times last week and again just now, and I'm generally not a vomiter. All I want to do is eat meat or crackers and lots of it. Plus, I feel very murdery, so no one better piss me off. I could snap at any moment, just like when I was pregnant with the boys."

"I was a kid back then. I was too young to be your confidant, remember? You were terrifying—crying, laughing, eating everything in sight, then throwing it all back up. I mean, ew. But then you'd let me feel your belly. You'd point out which part was which boy, and they'd kick my hand, and it was like magic, Violet. And now, you and Lily are going to be pregnant together, and I'm just about to burst with joy. I'm excited and I know it's too early and it might not be what you want at this exact moment in time, but I'm happy for you anyway because I remember before you got with Jake how much you told me you wanted to have another baby and I just—okay, I'll stop rambling! *Argh!*" She laughed, stepped into the bathtub, and drew the curtain closed. "Do it. I'll shut up and wait in here." After the rustling sounds stopped, a hand bearing a white stick shot out.

I took the stick, along with some of Rose's joy. "All right. Give me a minute." I mentally prepared, did the thing with the pee, then set the stick on the counter on a piece of toilet paper. "Get out here."

After washing my hands, I set the timer on my phone. I clutched her hand in mine and we sat at the edge of the tub to watch the immovable little stick on the counter like it was the Super Bowl and we gave a crap about football. The alarm going off caused us both to jump and laugh like loons when it buzzed and vibrated.

"I don't know what we're really hoping for right now, Vi." Rose's gentle smile was like a balm to my frayed nerves.

"I don't either. Well, I do, mostly. But I'll be okay no matter what happens because I have you here with me right now."

"Damn straight you do. Always, no matter what." She reached for the test. We both inhaled a huge breath and locked eyes as she flipped it over. "It says pregnant, Vi. You're gonna have a baby. A new niece or nephew, oh my gosh!" She clutched my hand, tears filled her eyes, and I threw my arms around her and held on.

"I want this." I sobbed against her shoulder.

She squeezed me tighter. "I freakin' know you do. I knew it the whole time."

"It's the worst timing in the world, but I don't care. I want this. So much. More than anything."

She pulled back; her huge, excited smile forced a giddy laugh out of me. "What do we do now? I know, let's both call in sick tomorrow and go shopping! Should we buy a crib? A car seat? Start decorating? Oh, oh, oh! Let's go to breakfast then out shopping for baby clothes! Or frick, we could online shop right now!"

I burst into laughter. "It's too early for all that. Way too early. And I think I want to go into that clinic in town and have a real, professional, medical test. I don't want to say anything to Jake until I know for absolute one hundred percent sure that I'm actually pregnant."

"This test looks like it's a sure thing though. You barfing your brains out and drinking your weight in milk says it's true too, right? And the sore boob thing? And do the damn math! When did you get your last period?"

"All right, yeah, I guess. I mean, it is, but I—"

"Shh, it's all good. Never mind, I think I get it. You don't have to explain anything to me. I'll go with you. We'll drop in before work, okay? Then after you know for sure you can tell him everything."

"Thank you. I—uh, I'm not worried that Jake will react badly or anything, I don't want to get him excited or however he's going to feel about this, just in case it turns out to be a mistake."

"Shh, it's going to be okay. He's going to be so happy; I know it."

"Thank you. I'll take the clinic test in the morning, then tell Jake when it's done."

"*Boom!* We have a plan. I'll bring the donuts and coffee."

My face fell. "Oh no, I can't have coffee. Caffeine is bad for the baby. I wish I knew when I drank my last cup that it would be the last. I would have cherished it more. Maybe took a selfie and mourned it properly."

"You're right, I didn't even think of that. Dude, how will you even live?"

"My decaf blend isn't totally bad. *Ugh!* The only thing good about no coffee and how shitty I'm about to feel for the next nine months is that I get a baby at the end of it."

"You're a nut, Vi, and I love you. I'll see you in the morning. Get some rest. I'll bring you some chocolate milk or have Trev make you a protein shake."

"You're the best. Love you too, Rosy Posy. Thank you for rushing to my rescue tonight."

"Duh. Always, Vi. See you bright and early." She rushed back out almost as fast as she'd rushed in, and I rushed into bed so I could stop my mind from whirring through all the reactions Jake could possibly have when I told him the news tomorrow.

Chapter 22
Jake

"*Coffee saves lives, yours mostly.*"

The Quickbriar Stop and Go was hopping in the pre-dawn hours. People really did flock here for the breakfast burritos. But I was here to talk to Elizabeth, Harper's source for most of the gossip she had shared with me about Tom and Bethany. I wanted to meet her in person. I felt like if I could get news closer than third hand and ask her to specifically keep an ear out for Tom information it might be useful. I also wanted to get a read on what kind of person Elizabeth was, since her gossip sources might help Ren put an end to Violet's marriage faster—as in, force him to sign off on everything now. And of course, I also wanted breakfast burritos.

As I stepped out of the store to go to my car and head into work, I saw Tom's Porsche parked at the pumps with no Tom in sight. Shouting coming from the direction of the women's clinic next door had me changing course before I could even think about it.

"I want the boys next weekend, Vi. Non-negotiable—"

"I don't have time for this, Tom! They've spent every weekend with you lately. I'm not stopping them from seeing you. I let them make their own choices when it comes to you, and I hope you would do the same for me." She tried to step around him, but he grabbed her arm to swing her back into place for more of his tirade.

"You're such a god-damned liar," he roared back at her. "What teenage boy would turn down a car? None that I've ever heard of."

"Car? I have no idea what you're even talking about. Let me go," she yelled as she struggled to get her arm free.

I immediately saw red, but I was not the only one. Violet was flanked by Rose and Holly. Rose immediately went to work, struggling to remove Tom's hand and whacking him on the side with her handbag. Finally, Violet escaped from his grip and twisted away, while Holly took a huge step forward and, with her hands to his chest, shoved Tom backward. "Don't come any closer, Tom," Holly grit out.

He ignored her and pushed her back. She stumbled but did not fall. "Fuck you, Holly. I'm tired of your entire insane family! Fucking up my house, messing with my security system, screwing with—"

"What the hell, Tom?" I didn't recognize my own voice as I charged into the middle of their confrontation. Grabbing his arm, I threw him against the brick wall behind him and held him there with a hand to his throat.

I admit, when it came to Violet, I had a caveman streak that was hard to hide. I had to fight the almost constant urge to throw her over my shoulder and take her away from anything that could hurt her. My basest motivations had always been to protect, provide for, love, and cherish her. It was easy to hide the caveman behind other thoughts and urges when I wasn't hanging onto the last thread of my temper as I was right now. By pushing her this hard, Tom had shoved me to the edge of my control.

"Oh god! We have to call Cade!" Violet shouted as Rose and Holly tugged her back toward the steps of the clinic and out of my way. "I'm okay, Jake. Look at me, I'm fine," she pleaded. "Please, let's just all get out of here." I looked back and what I saw was fear. What I saw was the woman I loved in tears. The cause of it was standing right there, daring to threaten her even as I stood between them.

"Hey buddy," Tom sneered.

"Shut your fucking mouth and listen—"

"No, *you* listen. I have some advice for you. Make sure to get a paternity test before you get too excited." He looked at Violet over my shoulder. "It hasn't been that long, right, baby—"

"You liar!" Violet screamed and lunged toward Tom.

Rose held her back. "No! Think of the baby—"

Baby.

My body wound tight with rage.

I had no thought left other than he needed to hurt like he had hurt her.

I drew back and punched him in his smirking face. I grabbed his collar and did it again, then I let him fall to the ground.

I spun to face Violet. "Baby?" My eyes met hers. A nod was my only response.

"Stay down there, dumbass." The words were directed at Tom. I spun to see Cade and Trevor rush out of an unmarked SUV.

"I'm pressing charges. Arrest him," Tom mumbled as he wiped at his bloody nose with his sleeve.

I couldn't catch a coherent thought; I was still too

worked up to think straight with the word *baby* pulsing through my body and filling my ears like an out-of-control heartbeat. The look I'd seen on Violet's stricken face flashed in my mind's eye like a beacon. I was blinded by rage and stuck where I stood.

"Are you sure about that?" Cade asked menacingly as he advanced toward Tom.

"He shoved me," Holly's cool voice cut through the tension and we all turned to listen. "He grabbed Violet's arm and jerked her around. We could barely get her free. And he shoved Jake first. If you arrest Jake, then arrest Tom too. Because me and Violet want to press charges. What about you, Jake? Are you going to press charges too?" The last accusation against Tom was a lie. She had told it to help me, and it cut through my anger. I refocused on my surroundings, nodded a thank you to Holly, and stepped out of Cade and Trevor's way with my hands held out to the side.

"Should we arrest you too, Tom? Those are some pretty serious accusations." Trevor reached for the handcuffs at his belt.

"No. No, I've changed my mind. It was all just a big misunderstanding. Right?"

"Sure," I confirmed. "A misunderstanding."

"Get up. Get the fuck out of here," Cade barked and stepped back from where he was looming over Tom who stumbled to his feet and bolted to his car, peeling out of the gas station parking lot in a showy circle.

"Like that stupid Porsche can restore his manhood. What a prick." Rose sneered.

"Are you—?" I addressed Violet. For some reason I was hesitant to approach her.

"Yes. I am."

My head jerked back on my neck in hurt surprise. "But you're here without me?"

"Let's, um—let's go get some breakfast burritos," Rose suggested. "They need to talk." Everyone stood there gaping. "Come on, damn it. I need a breakfast burrito and a cherry slushy. I'm stressing hard, Trevor. Feed me." That did it. Rose led the way to the Stop and Go, while Cade moved the SUV to their parking lot.

I led Violet to the bus stop bench on the sidewalk to talk. "Why didn't you call me? I would have come with you. Are you okay? I—" I was hurt. It killed me that she would go to a doctor and not include me. Tom's paternity accusation flew across my mind and I quickly rejected it. This baby was mine; I had no doubt about it. But why would she come here without me?

Panicked eyes met mine. "It's not what you're thinking. This was just a test to confirm. I peed in a cup, that's it. I wanted to know for sure before I told you."

"But you suspected?"

"Only last night. Rose came by with a test, then we came here this morning—"

"Without me." I couldn't get past it.

I had to let this go.

"I'm sorry. This isn't a big deal, I swear. It's not like there was an ultrasound, or like I found out if it's a boy or a girl. This is nothing, I promise." The tinge of desperation in her tone made me want to gather her close and comfort her, but my wounded feelings kept me still.

"It's not nothing. It's everything." This positive test was a turning point in my psyche. I had the desperate urge to do something, anything, to make her understand how much I loved her. Our baby was growing inside of her right now. I had to make her understand that I would do whatever it took, no matter what it cost me, to be there for her. I forced myself to move and pulled her into my side.

"That's not what I meant, Jake. Please try to understand—"

"Marry me," I burst out.

She stood, shaking herself out of my embrace and spinning around to face me. "I can't! I'm still married!" She sobbed. "I can't keep doing this to you. Oh my God, you could have been arrested today because of me. I'll ruin your life, Jake. I can't do it to you. I won't do it."

"I don't care, Violet. I love you."

"I can't. I'll destroy you, Jake. Can't you see that? It's obvious Tom is after something. He wants to ruin me, and he'll bring you down too if we keep fooling ourselves into thinking everything will be okay. We both know it's true. Look at what he did to my shop!" I opened my mouth to say something, but Violet interrupted before I got the chance. "You can't argue with me on this. We both know it was all him. He got all those people to one-star me. He sent that woman in to make a scene. It took forever to get Holly to come back to work. Who else would know who to aim the wacko at? Tom knows Holly is shy about stuff like that, and he knows I need her. He wants me to lose everything—"

"You'll never lose me," I protested.

"This isn't about me not trusting you or loving you. This is about your reputation. I won't wreck your life, what you've fought so hard to accomplish—"

"None of that means anything without you."

"I didn't say never. Just not while Tom is still a threat to everything you're trying to do. Can you understand that? I'm doing this for us, for our clean start."

"I don't understand. I'm sorry, but I don't. Give me these nine months to make you fall in love with me, Violet, please. I'm telling you right now that I don't care one bit about my reputation. It's worthless—"

"It isn't! Your mother's charity needs you! Rich people don't like scandal, Jake. You need donations and grants and I don't even know what else. But it's all dependent on you looking good to your donors."

I sat there absorbing her words. They were all true; as long as I was in charge, I did need to maintain a good reputation. The charity depended on it.

I also didn't care. I needed her beyond reason, I loved her beyond measure, and I would convince her of all of it . . . but I could see it wouldn't be now. She was not budging. She was also carrying my baby and I was upsetting her. Being worked up like this couldn't be good for her pregnancy, or her.

"Let's talk about this more later," I suggested. "This arguing can't be good for the baby. And I can see what it's doing to you."

Her eyes flashed with hurt. "Later. Okay. We're getting nowhere now anyway. I'm going to the shop. I feel like walking. Tell Rose and Holly, please?"

"I'll tell them."

"Good, okay, thank you. Bye, Jake." She all but ran from me. I watched her go, all the way down the street until she entered the front door of the shop. I had no idea how to get through to her, but I couldn't stop thinking I'd just made a mistake by letting her walk away.

Chapter 23
Violet

"Coffee and friends make the perfect blend."

"I'm here to work with you, Vi. Not just stand here as you run circles around me," Holly announced as I yet again nudged her aside to prepare an order. I needed to keep busy. The ache in my heart would bring me to my knees if I thought about it for even one second.

I wasn't looking for love when I decided to get a divorce. I wasn't looking for *anything,* except maybe some peace or the part of myself I'd needed to bury in order to stay with Tom and still be able to function. With Jake, I had rediscovered the part of my soul that fed off mutual respect and the freedom to be myself.

I'd rather be alone then go back to the way I used to be. But deep down inside, I was afraid that I'd pushed Jake too far away today and would end up alone forever instead of until I was rid of Tom. And would it even be possible to get rid of him? For someone who didn't want me anymore, he seemed determined to keep me in his orbit.

"Violet, come on. You can't work like this. You'll make yourself sick."

"I'm fine. I feel fine and I want to work while I feel good, okay?" I hissed, keeping my voice down so my customers wouldn't hear. "I've got this. Take a break, have a coffee and think of me," I teased through a smile that I knew was unconvincing.

"Okay, sure. What do I want to drink?"

I sighed, relieved that she had given in. "Hmm. A hazelnut latte—no, a caffè breve . . . no, a huge vanilla steamer. And some peach scones. Ooh! And a pickle."

"Gross at the pickle, Vi." She laughed as I finished the next five orders and slid them onto the counter—they didn't call me the Coffee Queen of Sweetbriar for nothin'—for her to ring up. "I will never understand how you can remember this many orders at a time."

"Call it a gift," I mumbled around a mouthful of scone. After those five orders, the line was clear, which meant I needed to be distracted another way, and food never failed to serve that purpose. I decided that I would try to make a pickle steamer at home; I didn't need the weird looks here in the shop. Instead, I filled a mug with steamed milk and vanilla syrup and chugged it down—sooo good. I filled a tray with a few (five) scones, a clean mug, and a half-gallon of milk, then made my way to my favorite corner table by the windows.

"I remember you always drank milk when you were pregnant with Finn and Nick," Holly mused as she followed me. "It's interesting how you crave it again. I wonder why."

"Who knows? Some people think cravings are what your body needs, like calcium from milk, or protein, like when I feel like taking a bite out of a cow or robbing a

Burger King. But that would never explain the pickle thing. Who really needs a pickle?"

"Every pregnant woman I've ever met," she joked. "I finished arranging the food for tonight's book club, by the way."

"Awesome. All I'm going to care about for the near future will be the food table. Whenever, wherever."

* * *

Every other Wednesday was book club night at my shop. I usually ran it, but it wasn't unheard of for me to give the floor to someone else if I had other plans or didn't feel well or whatever. I had informed Piper of my "condition," as she liked to call my pregnancy, when I was on a break earlier today, and she insisted on taking over tonight. All I had to do was show up, eat snacks, and let people fawn all over me —her words, not mine. After the day I had, I must admit, her plan sounded great. Food, friends, and fawning. The three Fs were just what I needed for a successfully distracting evening.

I hadn't called Jake and he hadn't called me. I guess this was us giving each other "space." We hadn't broken up, but it felt like a breakup. I mean, something was broken, and it felt like my heart . . . also my gag reflex and my abilities to hold down food or not almost burst into random tears at the slightest provocation. In other words, I was headed well into pregnant hot mess territory. I was also a mess for other reasons, but I refused to think about those tonight.

I swung my SUV into Piper's driveway and honked the horn. She peeped her head out her side window and held up a finger—not the mean one, the hold-on-a-second one. I turned my radio up and bopped along to the beat as I waited. The music forced my mood to swing to good and I decided to roll with it.

I was so into it, I jumped when Piper poked her head into the car, then got in. "Hey, girlie. How's the uterus?" She laughed.

"Great. I'm not that far along. I only have the invisible symptoms, so people are gonna think I'm nuts and not know why. Later on, it will all make sense." I steepled my fingers together, evil villain style and cackled out a laugh.

"Yep, you're just as weird pregnant as I remembered," she teased.

"You look different. What's with the almost everyday clothes, Piper?" She was in high-waisted jeans and a cropped purple sweater. Spiked heeled boots, a leather bomber jacket, and her newly sleek bobbed hair completed the look. I, however, was wearing my favorite Uggs with a pink tie-dyed Sherpa loungewear set, skating the line between trendy and slovenly comfort.

"Time for a new look," she answered. "Honestly, it was getting to be a chore to do the hair every day."

I adjusted my messy ponytail with a grimace. "Uh, totally."

"You're adorable. Chill." The lights of the early evening street lamps flooded the interior of my car as we headed to the shop.

"Thanks for being so—thank you for being my friend." I sniffled while wiping tears from my eyes.

"Are you okay?"

I waved my hand around as another mood captured me. "Yeah, it's just been an entire day. I don't know what to think about Jake. I'm afraid I ruined everything. But then I think maybe I should be alone for a while anyway."

"If you really think about it, you've been alone for years.

Being married doesn't make you *not* alone. If you want Jake, and he wants you, then get after it."

"Huh. I'll have to think about that. You may have a point." I pulled into a spot, shut the engine off and contemplated what she said.

"*May* have a point? I'm full of points, most of which are good ones."

"Very true. Let's go inside. I need to start eating my feelings."

"Good plan. I pulled together a last minute 'Pregnant Violet' theme. Better get prepared for all your faves. Don't worry, I didn't spill the beans. I just suggested dishes for the potluck table is all."

"I'm not worried. I know you can keep a secret." I got out and preceded her down the sidewalk.

"And listen. Between the two of us, Jake will love you forever. Trust me, you can't ruin anything when it comes to him."

"I have a lot of things to say about that statement. Like 'Oh really?' or 'I hope so,' and 'Why haven't you told me this before?' Also, 'What the heck are you even talking about?' and 'Nuh-uh.'"

Her lips quirked up in a smile. "Is that it?" I nodded. "Well, I have a lot of answers. Most of which are obvious if you think about it. But it's book club time, so we'll get into all of it later."

"Hey, Vi!" Most of the book clubbers—which consisted of most of my family, extended and immediate, my stay-at-home mom emergency baristas, plus a few loyal customers—greeted me in unison as I walked through the door.

"Hey, guys." The tables had been lined up in the center, like a long dining table full of food, wine, treats, and containers of flavored milk, which made me laugh. I started salivating at the sight. Of the food, not the people—that would be weird.

I took a seat between Rose and Lily who each wrapped an arm around me. "Don't make me cry," I hissed. "Be less nice to me."

"You got it, bitch," Lily replied, deadpan.

I smacked a kiss on her cheek with a laugh. "That's more like it."

"Wine me." Piper took the seat across from us and held out a glass. Rose filled it with a chuckle as my mother flitted behind me to stop and kiss the top of my head.

"How are you feeling, darling?" she whispered in my ear.

"I'm good for now. I'm ready to discuss whatever we were supposed to read. I forgot." I shrugged. This would be the only time I hadn't read it, or even remembered what it was.

Cade sat on the other side of Lily. "It's *Storm of Swords*. You finally chose it for me, and you forgot about it?"

"Oh gosh, I'm so sorry. I read it years ago, so I'll be good. Promise."

"It's okay. I forgive you in advance." He chuckled softly as he grabbed a tray of mini quiche. "I already know we're not going to talk about the book. It's been all baby talk in this place since I got here. I'm happy for you. You had a rough morning and word of it spread around fast." He leaned in to whisper in my ear. "The word is not good, Vi. Tom told a bunch of people that you're pregnant and the baby is his. I'm so sorry."

"Well, I was fine. Working took my mind off everything. But how can I be fine now, or ever again?" A hysterical laugh escaped me before I could control it. "Thank you, by the way. For not arresting Jake." I inhaled a shaky sigh. "I can't believe this. Tom has gone crazy, I swear—"

"No one wants Jake in trouble, Vi. And we're handling Tom, try not to worry."

"Handling Tom? What do you mean? Who's handling him?"

"It's nothing for you to worry about Vi. Just police stuff, right, Cade?" Chiming in was Asher, my big brother, who was seated across from me, next to Piper.. If he knew even a tenth of what was going on with Tom, then *he* would be the one "handling Tom," not the police or Ren. Which was yet another reason I had kept a lot of my marriage problems to myself over the years. Ash was protective, and I didn't want anyone to get into trouble on my account.

"Ash is right. It's nothing for you to worry about. You already know we're keeping in touch with Ren. Look! Shit, is that Bethany coming through the door?"

"It is, and I can't believe it. I mean, what next?" I turned back to Cade to whisper-hiss, "I—please don't arrest me after I punch her stupid face off. I really, really want to."

"Don't do it. Please," he whispered back. "Or at least let me get out of here first. I'll be scarred for life if I have to arrest my pregnant big sister."

"I'm here to talk to Violet," she announced to everyone in the shop. Of course, discretion was clearly not one of her dominant traits.

"Dude! Turn your ass around and get the hell out," Piper stood up and shouted. "What the hell are you thinking, showing your face here?"

"Don't arrest Piper either," I instructed.

"Don't worry Cade, you won't need to arrest me. I am

under control," Piper called out. "I've only had one glass of wine."

"How many times?" Rose asked through a laugh.

"Touché. I pre-gamed at home and it's starting to hit me."

Bethany took a few steps from the doorway further into the shop.

"Freeze right there. All we have to say to you, Bethany, is nope. Get out. We're not gonna buy whatever crap you're selling," Piper hollered.

"Look, I get it, Piper. You're protective—" Bethany started.

"Nuh-uh," Piper snapped. "Protective is if I go and key your car in the parking lot or TP your house. Maybe somebody would call it protective if I screamed in your face at the Stop and Go or quit holding my tongue and told everyone in town what kind of person you really are. But we're way past that. You hurt my friend and tried to make her feel humiliated in her own damn house. I'm beyond protective now." She cracked her knuckles and shifted her shoulders up and down; she clenched her fists and glared daggers at Bethany. She was ready for a fight, just like way back in high school.

Gah! I had to stop this. Cade couldn't possibly arrest everyone.

"I thought we were in Sweetbriar, Oregon, not the ninth circle of Jerry Springer Podunk hell." All heads spun to my mother as she stood up next to Piper and wrapped an arm around her waist. "You can't just throw punches at the dinner table, Piper, darling. Be a lady and throw a glass of wine in her face. Here, take mine."

Piper took the glass with an evil smile. "Thanks, Mama D," she replied.

"Piper, Mother." I stood up. "I have this. Please."

"You're the only one I'll shut up for, Vi," Piper yelled. "Do it, girl! I have your back."

Some people dream of moments like this. Gaining the upper hand, getting their power back, the chance to put the shoe on the other foot, or whatever. It crossed my mind to throw some red wine on her pretty white sweater, then manhandle her out of my shop to make her feel as small and pathetic as I had in my kitchen way back on that terrible morning when I caught her with Tom. But the bottom line was, I didn't care enough to do it. She was just a twenty-something-year-old dumbass who got seduced by my—though I was loath to admit it—good-looking, rich, influential almost ex-husband. All I wanted was to never see her again. I wanted her to leave me alone and stay away from my shop. Seeing her brought up a lot of hurt; not just the hurt Tom caused, but this entire situation with Jake today and the forced pause we had to put on our relationship.

"What do you want? You have five minutes."

Her nervous eyes darted around the shop. "I owe you an apology and I —"

I shook my head. "Look, Bethany, try again. I know you aren't here to offer up anything that isn't at least fifty percent self-serving. Otherwise you could have apologized to me any time over the last few weeks in private instead of waiting to put me on the spot in front of my book club. It's no secret where I spend my days, is it? Everyone knows where to find me."

She rolled her eyes and hitched a hand on her hip. "Fine, you're right. I'm no longer with Tom, so I really don't have anything to be sorry for anymore. I'm sick and tired of everyone hating me. Tom's business has been hurting since he left you and he's been trying to buy real estate all over town to flip it to some rich guy so he can catch up on bills or whatever. But everyone hates him and won't sell to him, mainly because everyone loves you."

"That's why he's trying to ruin her reputation," Cade deduced.

"Yeah," she answered. "And then he broke our engagement and fired me to make himself look better. I got dumped by him, just like you did, Violet. But everyone still won't talk to me. I can't get my nails done, I can't get an appointment anywhere in town for my hair and it isn't fair. So will you help me?"

I laughed. "What do you expect me to do?"

"Just . . . tell people you don't hate me. Please?"

I waved my hand around the room. "I don't hate Bethany," I announced grandly. No one responded, except for Piper with her indelicate snort-laugh.

"Uh, can you try again, I don't think that did any good—"

"I really don't hate you, Bethany. But that's all you're going to get out of me. Actions have consequences. Do better in the future and try being sincere, then maybe you won't have to drive out of town to get your hair done. Oh, and this is very important." I pointed a finger gun her way. "Don't become a cliché, Bethany. A sad little scorned woman. Goodbye." Was turnabout fair play, or was I being petty? For now, I was good with throwing her words back in her face. I could always be the bigger person later if I ever believed she was actually sorry.

"But—"

"She said, goodbye. That means get out," Rose reiterated.

"Fine." She turned around and left in a huff.

Hopefully, she would learn something and in the future her actions would back up her apology. Then, maybe I would be more magnanimous. Or not. Where in the rulebook of life did it require an ex-wife to forgive her husband's mistress? "Well, that freaking sucked. I need cake and some Kleenex. Tell me there's a cake around here somewhere." I burst into tears. "I need to call Jake."

"I know, sweet pea." My mother guided me back to my office. "Get her some cake, Cade," she bossed.

"Yup, coming." I turned to see him slicing into a huge chocolate cake. I knew cake wouldn't really make me feel better, but the fact that I was surrounded by my family and friends when I felt this down about myself and my choices did lift my spirits a bit.

I slid into my chair behind my desk to call Jake. It went straight to voicemail and my heart dropped. I tried again, same thing, but that time I left a message. "There's no answer, Mom. What should I do?"

"Let it go for tonight. Call him in the morning. But I bet he'll call you first."

"You're right. I should let him have some space. He was pretty upset with me."

"Upset with you? Or upset at the situation? Be careful about taking everything so personally, darling."

"I'll try. But it's so hard."

She sat on the edge of my desk and leaned forward to hug me. "I know it is. I believe that this will work out for you though. Try to be patient."

"I'm pretty sure he told me he loved me yesterday, Mom, and I didn't say it back. I'm going to send a text." I texted him three words. Three words that had been ingrained in my mind from the second he first kissed me.

Clear and obvious, they'd been stuffed deep in my subconscious. Until now, those words had quietly guided me through the disaster my life had become, and up to this morning, they'd kept me close to him.

I love you.

I got no response.

Chapter 24
Jake

"One day I realized that 'sadness' is just another word for 'not enough coffee'."

I'm not proud of it, but I spent yesterday drunk on my couch, consuming whisky like it was water. I couldn't think of a way to get through to her and the pain was unbearable. Yesterday morning I lost it all. Everything I'd ever wanted had slipped right out of my grasp like it never existed. She had me completely undone. I couldn't think. I couldn't breathe without her. The only way I could cope was to get numb. Without the whisky coursing through my system, I saw nothing but her, what we could have had, what we hopefully still *did* have and could maybe get back. We made a baby and I wanted my family—her, the boys, the baby—together. Whole. We needed each other.

I told her I loved her yesterday, and it hadn't penetrated the depth of fear that Tom had her stuck in. I don't think she even heard the words. Then, like an unthinking fool, I proposed, exposing everything she hated about our situation to the daylight without intending to. It may go down as the worst mistake I had ever made.

When I got home yesterday morning all I wanted to do was go back out and find her again. Or pick up my phone and call her over and over until I made her understand, made her listen, made her irrevocably mine in a way that no one could ever touch. But it would have driven her ever further away. I couldn't risk it, so I remained here at home, quiet and alone with nothing but the fear that I'd lost her to keep me company.

Now, here I stood, about to knock on her door as if I were knocking on the door that led to my future. In a way I was, because everything I wanted in the world was on the other side of it.

I rang the bell and jumped when, with violent force, the door swung open.

The Finn and Nick I saw standing on the other side were not the boys who I was used to seeing. These were two almost grown men acting as sentries for their mother and even though they were clearly angry with me, I could not be prouder of them.

Finn glared at me, but the hint of disappointment in his eyes gave me a sliver of hope that I could get through to him. "We don't know what's going on and we don't fucking care. She cried all night in her room with all the aunts. All three of them, man, and Grandma too. That's some serious shit. You're with her now, dating or whatever. We know that because we're not idiots. We hear things. You got her pregnant," he announced.

"Yeah, you hurt our entire family," Nick added. "Our mom *and* our baby sister or brother. Basically, we could kill you at any minute and it would be justifiable homicide. You hurt a pregnant lady's feelings. If that's not illegal, it should be. She's already a fucked-up mess, man. Everything lately makes her cry."

"I know it looks bad. Yesterday was terrible—"

"Why haven't you been answering your phone? Huh?" Finn poked a finger into my chest.

My mouth dropped open. "I—" I checked my pockets; I didn't have it. "Look, I was upset yesterday. I was a wreck. I thought I'd lost her for good. I spent most of the night drunk on my couch. Was that a smart thing to do? Obviously not—"

They exchanged a look.

"She called you last night," Finn finally said. "A lot."

"She texted you too," Nick added with a glare.

"I don't know where my phone ended up. I woke up, showered and came straight here."

Nick narrowed his eyes on me, and I inhaled a deep breath. This was utterly terrifying, and I wasn't even the slightest bit embarrassed that I was afraid of a sixteen-year-old kid. His opinion mattered. He held up a finger and pulled Finn aside to speak low in his ear.

"We decided to let you in. Don't blow this, Jake. You hurt her again and you're going to answer to us—"

Finn interrupted. "Nah, you decided. I'm still not sure."

It was time to lay it out. "Look, I've known you both since birth. Do you really think I'd put the relationship I have with you guys and your mother at risk? I'm more serious about this than I've been about anything in my life. I'm in love with her. I love both of you. I will not lose my baby. I will not lose you two, and I sure as fuck won't lose your mother. We're all going to be a family, whether you like it or not."

Nick grinned at me. "Let him in, Finn."

"Huh. Okay, yeah. I guess you can come in." He held the door open and stepped aside.

"Thank you." I was through the door, but I still had work to do. I looked hesitantly toward the hall. Was she really in there with Rose, Lily, Holly, *and* Dahlia?

"We were like level one, bro." Finn gave me a pitying look, sat on the sectional, and dug out the remote.

"Yeah, we're like low-level bosses, man. You've got some pissed off aunties in there. Good luck." Nick clapped me on the shoulder with a smirk.

"And Grandma." Finn snickered as he stuffed half an apple fritter into his mouth.

My hand went to the back of my neck. I should have brought flowers. Was it too late? I turned back to the hall and inhaled a deep breath.

"Hey. You've got this," Finn called out. I looked back at him. "She wouldn't have been that upset if she didn't like, have feelings for you and want to forgive you."

"You think so?" I grinned at him.

"Totally. It's like when we snuck out that one time go to Brianna's party," Nick added. "The worse the rage fit is, the more Mom loves you."

"Thanks, guys." I took the few steps down the hall and knocked on the closed door.

"Level two," Finn hollered.

I couldn't help but let out a small chuckle.

The smile faded when I looked down to see Lily and Rose standing side by side in the doorway, wearing matching pajamas, with matching tilted head glares, looking scarier than those creepy twins from *The Shining*. "Knock it off, you two," Dahlia scolded as she stood up from the edge of the bed. "Hello, honey. Come on inside." I tried to look over the top of Rose and Lily's heads but couldn't see Violet. Maybe she was still asleep?

"She called you," Rose announced, still blocking the door.

Lily raised her chin and poked me dead center in my chest. "A lot."

Dahlia's no-nonsense voice left no room for argument when she said, "Holly, drive them home." I glanced at her to see her rolling her eyes at me in commiseration. I don't know what I'd done to get her on my side, but I was thankful for it.

"We'll just go into the bathroom to change. Come on."

"I hope you have a good explanation for not answering your phone *all night long*," Lily hissed.

"I have no excuse other than I don't know where my phone is. I—"

"Lily, quit it." Holly held up a hand to stop me from finishing. "It's okay. You don't owe us an explanation, Jake. Only Violet." She shot me a sympathetic smile before addressing Lily again. "You weren't there. He was just as messed up as Violet was yesterday morning."

"I'm on the fence right now," Rose said. "But that doesn't really matter, because I'll always land on Violet's side. Lucky for you, I'm pretty sure you're on her side too, Jake. Fix this." She breezed around me down the hall toward the bathroom.

Lily followed, shooting me a tearful, apologetic smile on the way. "She was just so upset."

"It's okay. I'll make it right," I promised them.

"I know you will, sweetie." Dahlia patted my arm and followed her daughters down the hall. Leaving me alone with Violet.

"Hi," she murmured from her bed, where she sat with

her back against the headboard. "I'm a mess." She turned her face to the side, tucking her chin to her chest.

"You're gorgeous. Always," I answered, still lingering in the doorway. "Can I come in?"

She turned her head back to me, as if startled by my question. "Yes, of course."

"Thank you." This formality that had sprung up between us felt wrong.

"Please don't look at your phone when you find it. I, uh, called you quite a few times. I texted too. I went a little bit crazy." Her cheeks flushed pink, and I took a step closer.

"I'm so sorry. I spent the night with a bottle of whisky and my couch. I should know better, but I was hurting yesterday, Vi, so bad. I couldn't take the thought that I'd lost you."

"Oh god. What have we done to each other?"

"Nothing we can't make better."

"I feel restless, Jake, and unsettled. Like I can't go home anymore. But it's not the divorce or lack of divorce or whatever Tom is trying to pull. It's because I belong with you. You're my home and I want you to please let me back in."

"My door is always open to you. Always. I need you to believe it."

She held her arms open. "Come here."

I went. I sat on the edge of the bed and wrapped her in my arms.

"I've got you." I breathed as I kissed her upturned lips.

She pulled back. "I can stand on my own two feet. I've been doing it for years. But I want to stand with you now. I don't want to do this alone, Jake."

"You'll never be alone," I whispered as I placed my hand over hers on her stomach.

"We're still here," Finn shouted from the living room.

"And we can hear you," warned Nick. "So don't get all, you know, carried away."

Finn finished with, "We totally approve, we just don't want to hear it."

"Oh god." Violet shook her head. "This house is just too small."

"Get up, get dressed. I know where we can go. I have to show you something, anyway."

"Where are we going?"

Her smile lit up my heart. I had to kiss her one more time. "It's a surprise."

Chapter 25
Violet

"*Home is morning coffee in my favorite mug.*"

"Do I have to cover my eyes?" Jake drove through the mist up one of the winding mountain roads that led out of downtown Sweetbriar and into the foothills of Mt. Hood.

"No, you're gonna need to know how to get where we're going on your own," he answered.

"All right." I was growing more intrigued by the moment as I gazed out the window into the forest passing by. As we drove higher, the evergreens began to turn silvery white and the mist grew cold as tiny snowflakes began to swirl within it. I shivered.

He reached down with a flick to turn the heater up. "Better?" he asked, placing his hand on my thigh and giving it a gentle squeeze.

"Yes, thank you."

Jake turned down a winding, gravel-covered road and pulled to a stop in front of a lovely milled log cabin. Despite the frigid, early hour, the sun shone through the trees as we exited Jake's vehicle to head toward the partial wrap-around porch. My hand trailed along the railing as we went up the wooden stairs. "Is this your place?" I asked when we stopped at the front door.

"It is. Four bedrooms and two-and-a-half bathrooms on one acre of land. The Sweetbriar River flows across the back of the property, but the backyard is fenced in. I bought it about eight years ago to restore it."

"It's beautiful." I gazed across the covered porch, taking in the sturdy Adirondack furniture, the porch swing, and the almost floor to ceiling windows that dominated the front of the house.

"I hoped you would like it. Let's go inside."

Since leaving Tom, it had taken conscious effort to remember the difference between a house and a home. I had grown up in a home full of love, feeling safe and secure. But as each year spent with Tom passed, that feeling had dwindled little by little until it disappeared. I hung the school and family pictures on the walls, decorated the rooms, and made the boys feel as happy and comfortable as I could, but it never felt quite right.

My first step into this house felt like home, and I knew it had nothing to do with the walls that surrounded us. It was all him. Home was comfort, security, trust. *Jake* was my home. It was clearer now to me than ever.

"We could be a family here," I blurted.

"That's the idea, beautiful." He beamed down at me.

"The boys will love it."

He chuckled. "They already do. Where do you think we go whenever I take them fishing?"

"Right here?"

"Yeah, they already kind of have their own rooms."

"I always pictured something old and rustic whenever

they came home from one of your trips and talked about it. Kind of run down and crappy."

"It used to be. It was a disaster when I first bought it."

"That makes sense. Describing the ongoing renovation of this place would not be in their wheelhouse."

He chuckled. "True. Plus, we spent most of our time here outside at the river."

"Show me the rest."

"You got it." He led me over hard wood floors through a beautiful open downstairs living area and into a massive knotty pine kitchen. I could see us here, cooking together, laughing with the boys, a baby in the highchair . . . smiles on our faces.

I sighed. "What you've done is beautiful. I love it."

"Come upstairs." He held out a hand and I took it for him to lead me up, then down a hallway. The walls were covered with pictures; Jake fishing with my boys and some with Ren, picnics and boat rides with Harper and little Bella, and his mother. All smiles, all joy.

Home.

We stopped in an alcove at the back of the upstairs family room. In the center was a cut-glass set of doors leading to an upstairs deck that ran the length of the house. It was a cold morning—a light dusting of snow covered the grounds and little wisps of snowflakes still floated in the air —but he took me outside anyway, grabbing a quilt from a shelf on the way.

"Over here, gorgeous." He directed me to a seating area, flung the quilt out to cover a chair, then wrapped me in it as I sat.

I held up a hand. "I have to tell you something."

He sat in the chair across from me. "You can tell me anything."

"I'm sorry about yesterday morning. I should have called you the second I found out. I just—" I took in a deep breath, my lips flattened together in frustration. Why was it so hard to explain how I felt?

Understanding lit up his eyes. "No, I overreacted, and I didn't listen to you or give you a chance to explain."

"I pushed you away, and maybe part of why I pushed so hard was to see if you'd pull me closer. I know it was wrong but I—"

"I get it. It's part of why I beat myself up so hard yesterday when I got home. You needed someone to step up and fight for you. Instead, I let you leave."

"Yesterday was just ugly all around. Can you forgive me? Can we get back to where we were?" I felt my lower lip tremble. I bit it to regain control.

"Violet, baby, as far as I'm concerned, there's nothing to forgive." His eyes turned glossy as if he were fighting back tears. "And where we were? If you're asking about my heart, it's already yours. It's been yours. For years, Violet."

"I love you, Jake. You said it to me yesterday, but it didn't sink in until last night. You weren't the only one who didn't listen, and for that, I'm sorry too."

"It's okay. We're going to be okay." His chest rose and fell with a heavy sigh. "You know, sometimes I'd sit out here and think about all the times I wanted to kiss you and couldn't. All the times I wanted to just love you, Violet. But now, like a miracle, we're together and you're here with me. This time with you has been the fastest slow burn in history. I know so much about you already, and there's still a lot left to learn. But I'm here, and I'm yours, and I'll never let you go."

I leaned forward, resting my hand over his on his knee.

"And I'll never push you away again. I'll always come to you. I promise."

"God, how I love you." He gripped my hand in his, then raised it to kiss the back.

"I've never felt like this before. It's peaceful, Jake—" A sob stole the rest of my words and I couldn't continue.

"I know I messed this up yesterday, but that doesn't mean it wasn't coming from the heart." He sank to a knee in front of me. "Will you marry me, Violet?"

"Yes, I will marry you." He pulled a ring from his pocket; gold filagree and tiny diamonds surrounded a central diamond to form a lovely clover. It was stunning.

"This was my grandmother's ring. It's not the fanciest—"

I shoved my hand out of the warmth of the quilt so fast it made him let out a startled chuckle before he beamed at me. "It's perfect, Jake. Beautiful." My eyes shot to his, warm on mine and filled with love, as always. "It's family and history and love. It's you and me, and everything we're going to be together. I will be honored to wear it." He slipped it on my finger, where it fit like it was made for me. He stood and pulled me, quilt and all, to twirl me into his arms. We came to a stop at the deck rail where he tucked me tight against his chest and held me close. I let the rhythm of our heartbeats ground me while we watched the river below. My soul soared with happiness.

After a while he let me go, turning me to face him. "I'll make you happy," he stated.

"I know you will. And I will make you happy too. But—"

He took my hand, removed the ring, and placed it in the palm of my hand. "I know, Violet. And I can wait for everyone else to know it too."

"I hate this—"

"Don't." He placed a fingertip on my lips to quiet me. "What we have can't be taken away by anyone, ever. We both know that now, right?" I nodded through the tears that filled my eyes. "I'm strong enough to be here for you in silence, Vi, for as long as it has to be this way." The heartbreak in his expression belied his words, though I knew he meant them all.

"What did I ever do to deserve you?"

"Don't ask me that." His lips quirked up in that irresistible grin that I loved. "It will take me a lifetime to explain."

Our lips met. "Show me our bedroom?"

He scooped me into his arms without a word and carried me back into the warmth of his house to his bed.

Chapter 26
Violet

"'Be strong today,' I whispered to my coffee."

Shivering in the frigid air, I sat on my front porch sipping mediocre decaf coffee while I watched the neighborhood slowly wake up—cars exited driveways going to work, hands grabbed newspapers from porches, and joggers and walkers travelled up and down the street. All of them were living life, on the move, going somewhere. But not me. I was stuck here when I should be with Jake. When we should be busy announcing our engagement and planning our wedding.

Trapped on my porch, sun beams rippled through the trees to cast me in shadows, then take them away. Like I was living inside of a black and white kaleidoscope, dark with the lowest of lows, then bright with impossible hope. But I realized the only constant through the shifting of the light was I was not the one spinning the wheel. It turned based on Tom's whims.

Tonight was Jake's gala. We were not attending together, and I was not the co-host. My mother was going to do the honors for me. I finished my coffee and stood to pace the length of my porch. I was tired, but I did not need more sleep—I needed to wake up instead.

"Morning, Mom." Nick stepped onto the porch.

I turned to face him. "Why are you up so early on a Saturday? Are you guys planning to visit your dad today?"

"No." His tone jerked me completely out of my thoughts.

"Come here, baby." I held out my arms for a hug. Something was wrong. "Tell me."

"What?" He hugged me briefly before reentering the house. I followed behind, determined to fix whatever was weighing on his mind.

"What's bugging you?"

I got the classic, "Nothing," for an answer as he headed to the kitchen. I stopped between the living room and the kitchen.

Finn was sprawled on the couch, half asleep with the TV on. "It's Dad," he answered for Nick.

I remembered something. "Did he offer you boys another car?"

"Yup," Finn snapped out, while glaring at the TV.

I jumped as Nick slammed the refrigerator door, startled. "He's back to being a prick again."

"He was always a prick. He just tricked us for a while is all." Finn sat up, his eyes glinting with anger as he tossed the remote to the coffee table. "He never gave a shit about us."

"What do you mean?" I caught Finn's eye as I sat on the couch.

His expression closed up. "Nothing."

"I can't help if you don't tell me what's wrong."

His face twisted in a snarl. "It was fake. All of it. And you can't help us. There's nothing you can do about him.

He's back with Bethany. She moved in, and he wants us to move in too."

"Finny, I'm so sorry." I tried to understand why that would provoke such an extreme amount of hurt and anger. I got they were disappointed, but they'd never acted like this before. They were volatile and on the verge of tears.

"That's not all of it. Why does everyone think we're little kids, that we don't hear and understand what's going on? You do it too, Mom."

"Finn," Nick warned.

"Fine," he yelled back at Nick. "We know why you do it. To protect us. But it's still bullshit!"

"I don't know what to say. I'm sorry I make you feel like a child. I don't mean to. I realize you're growing up and I'll try harder to—"

He sighed. "It's okay. I didn't mean to yell. I'm not even really mad at you, it's just—" His face contorted before he covered it with his hands, shoulders shaking as he turned away from me.

I pulled him into my arms. It didn't matter if he was a teenage boy almost twice my size or all grown up and moved out. No matter how he saw himself, he would always be my baby boy to love. "Shh. I will make this okay. Whatever is going on, I will do my best to fix it." His shoulders shook as he cried, and I just stroked his hair and held him tight.

"Why can't he just be a dad?" he whispered. My heart broke as he wished for the only thing I could not control.

"We heard some things." Nick finally gave me a real answer as he sat on the opposite side of the sectional.

"Tell me."

"He only wants us to move in to make himself look

good. Divorcing you is bad for his business." His stricken voice pierced my heart.

"Oh, my boys. I—"

"Being a family man makes him look better. At least, that's what we heard his lawyer tell him. He offered us another car, so we'd each have our own. And a big allowance." His face crumpled. "He hinted around that he wanted us to make it seem like we were a close family before you left. He'd say stuff like, 'Remember when we went to Disneyland?' even though we were like, in fourth grade when that happened. Shit like that. Like we're too stupid to understand what an asshole he's been to you for the last few years. Like we were not smart enough to figure out what he wanted from us."

"Come here, sweetheart." I held my arm out and he let out a bemused chuckle. "What's so funny?"

"You are." His lips twitched with amusement, though his eyes were still glassy with tears. "This whole thing is kinda funny. I can barely see you over Finn because he's so big, and you want to try to hold me too. I love you, Mom."

"Well, I love you too. You're both still my babies, and I can try, can't I?" He grinned and got up to sit on my other side. I spread my arm wide to wrap him in it, then leaned in to smack a kiss on his cheek. "See, I've got you both. You're never too big to snuggle with your mother."

"I love you, Mom," Finn mumbled into my chest.

"I love you too, honey." I kissed the top of his head. We stayed that way, long enough for my arms and legs to get tingly and fall asleep from their weight. They really had grown up so much.

"I want you guys to stay with Grandpa instead of going to the gala with me, okay? I don't want you anywhere near your father tonight. I know for a fact he bought tickets."

"But what about you?"

"Asher and Cade will be my dates instead. I'll be just fine."

"Holy shit. Yeah, I'd say you'll be okay." Finn snickered.

"What about Jake?" Nick asked.

"I'm not going to hide things from you guys anymore. You want that, right?" Finn nodded while Nick said yes. "Okay then. Jake and I are in love, we're engaged, we're having a baby, and it's all a secret for now. Well, some of it is a secret."

"We knew about the baby and the love stuff. I'm glad you're engaged. We love Jake too."

I tilted my head back and met Nick's smiling eyes. "I know, and I'm so glad." Finn didn't say anything; he just leaned his head on my shoulder and hugged me again. "Eventually, we'll all live together in the cabin up the mountain—"

"Like a real family." Finn tilted his head back and smiled at me.

"Exactly, sweetheart. We'll make a new home together there."

* * *

The boys were in the living room blowing stuff up on a video game while I had moved to the bathroom to take a bath and stew in my anger at Tom, who I decided shall heretofore be referred to in my internal monologue and most likely directly to his face as Motherfucking Tom.

I'd thought it before, but now I really meant it. I needed a plan. I had to quit relying on others to fix my problems. Yeah, Ren was my attorney, and it wasn't a bad choice to let him do his thing. But I needed to stand up for myself too.

And I should have been doing whatever I could to get this divorce final and get Motherfucking Tom out of my life for good, instead of hiding out, keeping secrets, and avoiding confrontation.

While it may seem counterintuitive, after wrapping myself in my bathrobe, I found my cell and called my mother.

"Violet, darling, it's almost gala time," she singsonged into the phone.

"Yeah, about that. I realize that this is last minute, but I need a new look. One that will intimidate. I'm talking boobs, I'm talking booty, I'm talking the highest of high heels. Eye liner, lashes, and brows beyond my skill set. And red lips that say *don't fuck with me*. I need the kind of dress, Mother, that will strike fear into the hearts of my enemies. I've been weak; I've been too complacent. I've leaned too hard on you, Ren, Jake, and the family. I let you guys take care of me, defend me, protect me. I need to do it for myself. It's time I stood up to Motherfucking Tom. Can you help me with this one last thing?"

"Absolutely. I'm on it. Come to the house. Bring the boys." With a blink, I looked at my phone screen. She had hung up on me. Laughing to myself, I yelled for the boys to get ready to leave.

She was waiting for us on the covered brick porch. She waved excitedly once she spotted us down the long, winding brick driveway that led toward my childhood home. As we got closer, she started to hop up and down while my father laughed from a porch bench, his leg stretched out in front of him on an ottoman. I quickly parked and ran out. I hadn't seen my dad in a while. I'd missed him.

"Hey darlin' girl," he hollered. "It's been too long since you've been here."

"We'll be here for Sunday dinner tomorrow. You can count on it." I ran up the steps and into his arms.

"Good. It's about time. Hey boys! Pizza is on the way, and you can choose any movie you want tonight."

"Thanks, Grandpa." They hugged my mother before heading inside.

"I know they can take care of themselves, but we had a bunch of terrible revelations about Tom come out and I don't want them to be alone." Quickly, I ran through what the boys told me before we got here so my dad could be prepared in case either one of them got upset and didn't feel like talking about it.

"Tom turned out to be a no-good punk, didn't he? Shame, that is." Dad shook his head with disappointment "He was never one to listen to my advice."

"Yeah—"

"Well, you're onto better things, honey. And I'll be right here if the boys need anything. What are you planning tonight, Vi?" he asked.

"I'm going to, um, I don't quite know yet. Mom?"

"You're going to look like a beautiful nightmare and you're going to scare the shit out of him," she answered. I burst out laughing.

"Seriously—"

She steepled her fingers together, the action of someone used to being diabolical, rather than the sweet person she was. "Yes, darling, I am dead serious. Give him a piece of your mind and threaten to take him to the cleaners. He's a liar and a cheat, and we may be in a no-fault divorce state, but you can ruin his reputation in a thousand different ways. Think of the top three and brandish them like weapons. Plus, Ren is good at his job, he's mean as all hell, he can get you whatever you want in the divorce, and Tom knows it. He'll back off. Be strong."

"I'm going to do it. He's gotten away with too much."

"Cade and Ash will pick you up," Dad said. "Make sure they're near you when you talk to Tom. Please? I'd be there with you tonight if I could. I'm sorry I'm stuck here with this bum ankle. You know that, right?"

"Yes, Daddy. But you're going to be here at home taking care of the most important part of my life tonight. Think of it that way instead. Okay?"

His smile was reassuring. "I'll make sure they're okay." He used his crutches to make his way back inside, leaving me and my mother and alone on the porch.

"Are you ready, darling?"

"As I'll ever be, I guess."

"Everything is waiting upstairs. Hair, makeup, all of it. I'm so excited for you! You're going to let that jackass know you have your power back, and he can't mess with you anymore."

I inhaled a deep breath while my hand involuntarily slid into the pocket where Jake's grandmother's ring hid. "Power? I don't think I ever had any. I mean, it's been so long—"

"Oh, honey." She pursed her lips together and lifted my chin with a fingertip. "You listen to your mother right now. You have just made a huge, positive change for yourself and your boys. You've asked for and taken help from family and friends who love you when you needed it. And the most important thing is you are no longer willing to compromise yourself for him. Therefore, you have your power back. You've been fighting back quietly all along. The only difference is tonight you might get loud, right?"

"Yes, and I'm fairly certain I will definitely have to get loud. Thank you, Mom." I squared my shoulders with determination even as tears filled my eyes. *Motherfucking Tom! Gah!*

She took my hand and tugged me into the house. "Wait until you see the dress. And Becca is here to do your hair and makeup. Let me see your nails. Red! Perfect." Becca was Jude and Levi's age. Levi was particularly fond of her, or so I'd heard. Her family owned *the* salon in town—everyone went there. Well, everyone except for Bethany.

"Hey, Becca," I greeted as I stepped into my old bedroom where she had set up a mini beauty station. She was a beautiful brunette with brown hair so dark it was almost black and deep brown eyes. She and Levi were the best of friends as little kids, but I rarely saw her after they got into high school.

"My mission has been made clear by your mama." She mock saluted me with a huge smile. "Get prepared to reach knock-out status tonight, girl. He won't know what hit him."

I sat in the chair at my old vanity table. "Thanks, Becca. I appreciate you coming at the last minute."

"It's all good. I was already scheduled for your mother. I've been wanting to get my hands in your gorgeous hair for more than a trim for a long time."

"Aren't you going to the gala too?" I asked as she brushed through my hair. "The rest of your family is. It was so sweet of your mom to donate the spa day."

"She was happy to. And yes, I'll be there. Your mom said I could get ready here and ride with her."

"Um, aren't you going with Levi?" My matchmaker impulses had been buried. for what seemed like forever. It felt good to let them out again.

I saw her cheeks turn pink as she shook her head in the

mirror. "I'm going to meet up with Harper and Elizabeth. We're going to make it a girl's night."

"Oh, that sounds like fun." I made a mental note to arrange a lunch date with Rose. It seemed like our baby brothers needed our guidance when it came to love. Everybody in the family knew Jude had been a mess over Harper since high school. Levi had always kept his feelings to himself, but according to Rose, Becca would be his end game. I kind of agreed; they used to be adorable together as kids.

After a few minutes, her hands in my hair became too relaxing and I couldn't focus on matchmaking anymore. I fell into a peaceful state of calm as Becca styled my hair and applied my makeup. I heard my mother bustling about upstairs as she got ready, but it didn't distract me as I contemplated what would be the most effective way to communicate to Motherfucking Tom that I would no longer be kowtowing to his every whim.

"You're ready!" Becca handed me a hand mirror with a flourish.

I barely recognized myself. "Who even am I?" I whispered to Becca.

"Take some time with it," she encouraged. Her smile was huge as I studied my face. "This is my absolute favorite part of the job. You're gorgeous, Violet. I just exaggerated it."

"Holy crap, Becca. You are *very* good at what you do," I conceded as I tried unsuccessfully to stop gawking at myself.

Chapter 27
Jake

"I don't care what time it is. I need coffee now."

I did a double take, then a triple take, then I just flat out stared once I realized it absolutely was my Violet being escorted by Asher and Cade up the long black carpet that led to the entrance of the Sweetbriar Hotel where I stood greeting guests.

She was beyond beautiful tonight. My breath had left my body at the first sight of her long leg, clad in a high black heel, stepping out of the front seat of Cade's Bronco. Her hair flowed over her shoulder in shining waves and her dress was entirely made of deep purple, almost black sequins, or maybe shiny beads. I couldn't tell, mostly because it was skintight and cut almost down to her navel in a deep V, stealing my concentration from everything else but her gorgeous curves in the dangerous, absolute stunner of a dress. She turned to grab a little purse out of the car, and I saw the long, elegant line of her back, bared by another deep V cut. I took in a deep gasp, then quickly coughed to hide it.

I could not take my eyes off her. Gradually, I noticed that no one else could either. Each step she took caused the small crowd milling about outside to grow more hushed. A quick glance around caused my possessive hackles to rise. Asher slipped his arm around her waist protectively while his eyes darted around as if looking for someone. I could only assume he was looking for Tom.

"Why are you out here?" she hissed once they reached me. "Ren was supposed to be greeting the donors and guests, not you."

Asher gave me a chin lift and stepped away to give us some privacy as I cleared my throat. "Here's the thing—I don't care about anything but you. Ren and I switched places. He'll be the figurehead, and I'm behind the scenes from now on." I pointed to the easel holding the Lyla's Place Gala sign, which detailed what we were all about. Instead of my picture, Ren's face grinned from the corner of the framed sign. "Tom can run his mouth all he wants, because Ren is more than capable of deflecting all his bullshit with his sterling, albeit stern and threatening reputation. It should have been like this from the beginning." She shook her head in protest and started to speak but I kept going. "Please let me finish explaining. I'm going to be real honest with you, gorgeous, even though you probably know this already. I have a reputation with women as a serial monogamist, player type that I allowed to build up over the years to deflect the rumors of how I felt about you. Ren is a respectable widower."

"You dated a lot of women. So what? I wish stuff like this didn't matter so much." She grumbled under her breath, "People can be so judgy. And you worked so hard—"

I pulled her to the side of the wide expanse of the hotel's entrance, away from the open doors. "I'm still on the board. I'm still going to do everything I've done all along. The only difference is Ren is now the face. He'll give the speeches and greet the donors and be the one in front of the cameras. Those were my least favorite parts anyway."

"I can't ask you to do that for me," she insisted.

"You didn't ask. I *want* to do this. Besides, it's already done, and believe me when I tell you it's for my own selfish reasons. I can't live without you, I don't want to wait anymore, and I'm through with hiding how I feel. I love you, Violet."

Her eyes melted as she reached for my hand. "I love you, too, Jake."

"Good, because I'm going to take away every single thing that worried you, one by one, until it's just you and me left standing at the end, together. I don't want anything in the way of sliding my ring back on your finger and making you my wife."

"You look as beautiful as ever, Violet." Our collective heads turned to see a smirking Tom headed our way with Bethany on one arm and an older redhead on the other. Cade and Asher had also spotted them, and stepped closer to us.

Violet held out a hand, pausing us all. "I need to talk to you, Mo—Tom. Can you all give us a minute please?"

"Yeah, I don't think so." Bethany held out a hand and huffed. The redhead pulled her aside with a meaningful glare. She looked familiar, but I couldn't quite place her. Bethany sighed and they headed into the hotel with nary a backward glance.

"Sure, we can talk." Tom stepped toward Violet but stopped after he glanced over at Cade, as if looking for permission. "Is it about the boys?" Cade tilted his head, indicating Tom should follow Violet.

"Partly," Violet answered vaguely. "Come on." She grabbed him by the elbow and indicated he should go with her. I moved to follow, but she shook her head, pointing to the corner of the building. "I'll just be right over there. This will only take a minute."

Cade didn't look happy about it despite his implied permission. "We'll be right here, Vi." Cade said. "Holler if you need us." I wasn't okay with her being semi-alone with Tom either, but I got the impression this was important to her, so I didn't say anything.

Asher raked his derisive gaze over Tom, who visibly flinched. "I'll be right here too, Violet," he added with a small smile, but his eyes never left Tom as he spoke.

"What do you want, Vi? Bethany wants me to bid on the ski trip. It's kind of our thing now."

"Shut the fuck up," she snapped. "I'm going to do the talking." My jaw dropped, Asher grinned at Cade, and the three of us grew silent.

"So rude—"

"Listen to me. I'm sick of you and your games. For some reason, I tolerated your bullshit. but that ends *now*. Now that you've tried to pull the boys into it, it's done. Do you understand me?"

"Pull the boys in? You're talking crazy, as usual—"

"I said shut your mouth and listen."

"Fine. Talk," he ground out.

"Ren is inside with a revised set of demands. If you don't sign the divorce papers tomorrow—"

"Tomorrow is Sunday—"

"I really do not care. If Ren doesn't get a call *tomorrow* letting him know you've signed, I'm going to make your life very unpleasant."

"Be reasonable, Violet."

"Reasonable? Like you? Making demands, spreading lies about me, trying to ruin my shop with poor reviews and a viral video? You mean reasonable like that?"

"I had nothing to do with that!" he thundered. The three of us took a step to intervene.

"Shut your *fucking* mouth and listen to me!" We froze and exchanged glances. "I will make your life hell on earth if you don't give me what I want. Inside, right now, Ren has papers, Motherfucking Tom, and those papers outline what I'll take from you if you don't give me my divorce."

"Whatever, Vi." His tone was dismissive and we could hear him turn away from her and take a step. "I'll give my lawyer a call tomorrow, okay? Jesus Christ," he scoffed, and we knew he had no intention of doing as she asked. Again, we moved to intervene on her behalf.

"Don't walk away from me." His footsteps stopped. "I feel like I'm going to need the house to raise the boys in. Then half of it after they've grown. Do you think I could get half the house, Tom?" He didn't answer, and once again we remained where we were. Her tone wasn't just sharp, it was downright hostile and condescending and unlike anything I'd ever heard from her. "That's okay, you don't have to answer. Ren thinks I could. Sign the papers. *Tomorrow.* Or I'll take you for everything you have," she clipped. "I'll own you. I will ruin you, and I will fucking enjoy it. Did you know I'm entitled to your retirement fund? Ren does. He's been encouraging me to ask for a lot more. But do you know what I really want?"

No answer.

"Answer me, damn it!"

He sighed in annoyance. "What do you want, Violet?"

"I want to be free of you. That's all I've wanted since I left. But you wouldn't give me that, would you?"

No answer.

"I can be all kinds of unreasonable if you decide to keep dragging this out. Did you realize that me supporting you through your senior year of college and grad school means a lot to our judge? Ren does. He thinks I could get alimony, Tom, and a lot of it. I'm entitled to child support, too. In fact, Ren seems to think that you're such a piece of shit, if I asked for one of your balls, I could probably get it. Should I ask for one of your balls, Tom?"

Cade snorted and Asher cracked a smile. I grinned at them both as the three of us realized Violet was in control now, not Tom. "Answer her, asshole," Asher shouted.

"Fuck you, Asher," he shouted back. "No, I don't think you should ask for anything else. But what about the boys?"

"Our boys will see you if and *only* if they want to, and I promise that I won't stop them if they choose to see you. But you will not use them to improve your reputation. They are not tools to serve your needs. They are our children, Tom, and you will not make them feel bad about themselves in any way, ever again. If you do, all bets are off and life as you know it will be over."

"Fine. I'll sign the fucking divorce papers."

"When?" she demanded.

"Tomorrow, okay? God damn it, can I go find Bethany now?"

"Yeah, go find her. But make sure to ask her about the redhead, the one-star reviews, the mice, the fire, and whatever else she did when you find her, okay?"

"What the hell are you talking about? The redhead is her mother."

"Of course she is. I just realized that the redhead was the one who made the scene in my shop. There was no reason for it. You know how I run my business, so don't try to argue with me and say it was a real complaint."

"Yeah, whatever you say. I don't even know half of what you're talking about."

"Ask her, and from now on think about who you piss off and what they're capable of, genius. You scorned a spoiled brat, twenty-something girl like Bethany by cold dumping her, firing her, humiliating her, and leaving her with nowhere in town to get her hair and nails done. What's a girl like that going to do? Run her mouth and make you look bad? Yeah, probably. Try to ruin your business using your bad behavior and reputation for being an ass against you by attempting to frame you for a petty bunch of bullshit? Sure, why not. You're a selfish, narcissistic, idiot Motherfucking Tom. You want my free advice? Date an adult next, instead of someone just like you in the form of a bleached blonde bimbo."

We stepped back as he came storming around the corner followed by a satisfied looking Violet. "Cade, I think you should ask Bethany some questions," she announced.

"We're already on it. But good call, Nancy Drew," he chuckled.

"You mean, you figured it out already?" Violet complained. "I recognized Bethany's mother and made an educated guess of what she's capable of based on her unpleasant personality."

"Jude figured it out with Harper this morning. It's a long, ridiculous story that flowed through the Sweetbriar gossip network until all the pieces finally reached Harper. They put them together over breakfast, then called me. We can prove she bought mice and hamsters with credit card receipts, but not that she put them in the deli—yet. The dry cleaner fire is the worst offense and Trev is working to place her at the scene. Her mother is her alibi that night, by the way. The one star and video thing are jerk moves but not illegal, so there is nothing we can do about that. Sorry, Vi. If there's anything else, it hasn't come out yet."

"Except for the tiny fire, it's all so stupid," Violet said.

"Who's the rich prick trying to buy up the real estate in town?" Asher asked.

"I know this one," I answered. "Ren found out a few hours ago, and you are not going to like it. It's your cousin, Nicole, through a company she was hiding behind."

Violet gasped. "What? Why would she do that? She loves Sweetbriar."

"You'll have to call her and find out. All Ren discovered was her name. However, all deals have fallen through, except for the two units in your building, Vi. She owns those but there's no movement to purchase anything else, for now anyway."

"Let's not think about that. It's most likely moot since Nicole is not a prick. She probably had good reasons." Asher said. "I'm proud of you, Violet. You two will be fine, so I'm going to head inside and hit the buffet. Cade?"

"Yup, coming. I'm going to bid on that ski trip. Violet, you were great. Will we finally see you tomorrow at Mom's?"

She nodded. "Yep, we'll be there." He grinned at her and followed Asher.

"Tomorrow?" I asked. "Oh! The infamous Barrett family Sunday dinner at the homestead. Right?"

"That would be correct." Her lips shifted to the side in an adorable grin. "You now have a permanent invitation. And just so you know, my mother doesn't play around. She gets real pissy if we don't go."

"I accept that, and I can't wait. But that's not all I want

to make permanent," I said as I traced a finger from the tip of her chin, down the column of her throat, following the path between her lovely breasts to rest on my ring dangling from a gold chain.

"I've kept it close to me, Jake. I couldn't make myself put it away—"

"Turn around." Sparkling hazel eyes smiled at mine before she did as I asked. With a flick, I undid the chain and removed it, allowing the ring to slide into my palm.

She turned and offered me her hand along with a smile. I slid the ring home, then lifted her hand, sealing our future with a kiss. "I love you so much," she murmured.

"Forever, Violet. I love you too."

Chapter 28
Violet

"Coffee and love are best when they are hot."

"**O**h god." Hand over my mouth, I bolted out of bed and ran to Jake's bathroom to throw up. At least this time around it seemed like I would settle into "morning sickness" rather than the twenty-four hour a day constant sickness I'd had with the boys.

"Let me help you." Gentle hands pulled back my hair, securing it in a soft tie, and a cool washcloth was draped across the back of my neck. Tom had never done anything like this for me. Vomit and illness of any kind disgusted him. I started comparing Jake to Tom in my mind before I forced the thoughts back out again. Jake was a blessing to my life, and it didn't serve either one of us if I allowed the comparisons to continue.

I finished, flushed it away and sat back against the bathtub with a shuddering sigh. He passed me a glass of ice water, then placed a package of saltine crackers on the counter before kneeling in front of me. Of course, I burst right into tears.

"Thanks," I choked out through a sob.

"Anything you need. Would ginger ale be better next time? Or maybe a Sprite? Lily told me to get you ice water."

"You called her?"

"I texted. I couldn't just leave you alone in here, could I?"

"I—" My words disappeared as I cried harder.

"Come here, gorgeous." He stood, swept me into his arms and carried me outside to the upstairs deck of his house where he'd proposed to me. "Fresh air will do you good." He sat in a chair, tucking me sideways in his lap as I rested my head against his upper chest, and he lightly stroked my back.

The brisk morning air on my face cooled me down. I took a deep breath, and it settled my nerves and my stomach. A cup of coffee and Jake's cell phone rested on the table next to us, along with a haphazardly discarded quilt. I reached for the quilt, but he beat me to it, wrapping it around me and making sure it covered my feet. "You're amazing."

"I have our family to take care of, Vi. It's what I've always wanted." My heart burst into a thousand sunbeams at his words but I had less than a moment to revel in them before his cell rang.

He glanced at it. "It's Ren." With big eyes, I nodded at him to answer. Funny how my whole life could change with the swipe of his thumb.

I couldn't take it. I scrambled off his lap to pace the deck on the second ring. Jake spoke no words into the phone and his expression bore no clues . . . until a huge smile unfurled across his face and he placed the phone down. "You're free."

"He signed?" Tears flowed again, this time from relief and a happiness so profound I almost couldn't handle it.

"He signed a few minutes ago. It's as good as over, Violet."

"I want to get married by the river. Can we?"

"Absolutely. Anything you want."

Eyes blurry from tears, I stumbled into his arms. "Anything I want," I breathed. "I want to tell the boys."

"Let's get dressed and get them. I love them too, you know. They're part of this family we're making here, and I promise you, I will always treat them as if they were my own sons."

"I feel like I'm in a beautiful dream. How is this real?" I held him close, lost in the weightlessness that came with shedding feelings heavy with the burden of impossibility until just now.

He dropped his forehead to mine. "Because you're finally in my dream with me, Violet."

"We're coming true, Jake. It's finally our time."

"Finally." His hands drifted into my hair. He tipped my head back to touch his lips to mine in a brief kiss.

It wasn't enough. "Maybe we should go back to bed for a while before we tell—"

He didn't let me finish. Instead, he kissed the words out of me and carried me back to bed.

Chapter 29
Jake

"This house runs on love, laughter, and cups of strong coffee."

Stepping into the huge foyer of the Barrett house struck me with a sense of nostalgia. I'd been to a few of the Barrett family dinners during our college days, but none recently. Obviously there had been a lot of changes in the family since then. All the Barrett kids were adults, for one. Lily and Rose had stopped running away from me red-faced and giggling, for another. But the best part was that Violet was on my arm, about to become my wife, and carrying my baby. I had it all this time around.

"Hello my darlings!" Dahlia greeted. "Tell me something good."

"Tom signed the papers, Mom. I'm free."

"I can spot sparkle from a mile away. Get over here and show me that ring, honey." Violet's grandmother called out from a chair by the fireplace. Dahlia followed, and the women were gradually joined by Violet's sisters, leaving me the only man in a room full of Barrett women. It was like something out of a movie. Violet sat on the ottoman near her grandmother's chair, hand extended while they surrounded her and took turns hugging and kissing her flushed cheeks as they *oohed* and *ahhed* over my grandmother's ring on her finger.

"Yo, Jake! In here." Asher popped his head through an arched entrance. I followed him into the kitchen, which was not like out of a movie; it was like walking straight into the Food Network.

Cade sat at the kitchen table along with Violet's father, sipping iced tea, laughing, and working their way through a tray filled with various meats and cheeses. They greeted me with smiles and handshakes. Levi and Jude were on bar stools at the other end of the long island laughing at something they were watching on a tablet. And I could hear tiny footsteps running around upstairs as well as a few heavy ones, which meant Luke and Trevor must be up there with the kids.

"Is it like this every Sunday?" I marveled at tray after silver tray filled with appetizers and covered silver chafing dishes loaded with delicious smelling food.

"The family? Yeah. This crazy amount of food? Only on extra special Sundays. Like holidays and stuff," Nick answered. He stood next to Finn at the edge of the counter.

I opened my arms. "This *is* a special occasion. All right, bring it in, guys." They exchanged bemused smiles before stepping into my arms. It was time to show them what they meant to me. "I love you two, and I always have. You know that, right?"

"We know." As I had anticipated, Nick answered with words while Finn nodded and looked away.

"I'll always be here for you. Whenever you need me."

"You always have, Jake," Finn replied.

"It's time to get this party started," Ben, Violet's father, announced. "Fill your plates and head to the dining room." Using his crutches, he stood. "I couldn't be happier that you're here, Jake. Welcome to the family."

"Thank you, sir."

Gradually everyone funneled through the kitchen to take their seats in the dining room. The table was full and the chatter was happy as I gazed around at all the smiling faces.

"God damn it!" Was that Tom's voice?

Levi fumbled with his tablet, muting it quickly with a panicked expression on his face.

"Turn it off," Jude hissed.

"Was that Dad?" Finn asked, eyebrows down in a V of confusion.

"Uh—" Levi's eyes darted around the room. He reminded me of Bella when she was trying to avoid answering a question. His palm went to the back of his neck as he studied the table. "Would that upset you?" He muttered the question in Finn's direction.

"Hell no!" Finn exclaimed. "You're the one? I love you, Uncle Levi!"

He looked up with a sideways grin. "I love you too, kid. And, yeah, that was your dad's voice." He addressed Violet next. "I, uh . . . You know when we moved you out, Vi?"

"Yeah, I remember. What did you two do?" Her lips twitched as she tried not to laugh.

"So, okay, I downloaded your smart home app. I'm logged in, and every so often I—"

Nick burst out laughing. "You mess with stuff! You change the channels on the TV, and turn the lights off and on?" Levi nodded sheepishly. "You freaked the hell out of Bethany the last time we were there. She thinks the house is haunted. How did you manage to get control of the speakers?" Nick didn't stop for an answer. "Cheating songs would play randomly all the time. Epic, man. I thought it was Finn doing it, but I wasn't going to ask. Plausible deniability is essential when you—never mind."

"And what did the two of you do that requires *plausible deniability*, Finn? Nick?" Violet asked, her grin growing huge.

"*Pfft*. Nothing." Nick said.

"Did you lock the upper deck door of the hotel when Jake and I were up there?" She persisted.

"No," Nick addressed me. "Remember I told you I wasn't going to pull *Parent Trap* stuff on you?"

I chuckled. "Yup."

"I never said that. That one was me," Finn confessed. "With Brianna's help. Am I sorry?"

"No, you're not sorry at all. Don't worry about it for even one second."

"Nice!" He nodded at me.

"I almost feel bad," Cade chimed in. Trevor stared at his plate, shaking his head and laughing softly. "Tom has had quite a few"—he coughed—"dozen"—he coughed again—"traffic stops lately. In my defense though, he really should stop speeding."

"Well, hell," Asher chimed in.

"Not you too, Ash!" Violet burst out laughing.

"Yeah, me too. But I just threatened to beat his ass the old-fashioned way. A few times. Well, uh, every time I saw him in town." He shrugged.

"Oh gosh, Luke!" Lily burst out laughing.

"I, uh, may have done the same as Asher." Luke admitted.

Rose cleared her throat, while Holly sank down in her

seat to look out the window. "Next time something like this comes up, we should really coordinate."

"No! You two too?" Violet gasped.

"Yeah, Rose and I aren't proud of this—"

"Speak for yourself, Holly," Rose interrupted. "We regressed back to our youth and egged his Porsche. Bethany's Honda, too."

Violet covered her mouth, but a burst of laughter shot out anyway. "You guys!"

"Well, the fact that the little fucker is still alive proves that I didn't do a damn thing," Violet's grandmother announced, causing the room to burst into laughter.

"Remind me to never piss any of you off." I managed to speak through a voice filled with laughter.

"I love all of you, so much." Violet giggled. "Even though every single one of you is a nut."

Epilogue
Violet

"This morning, with her, having coffee."
-Johnny Cash

Weeks Later

Clad in a lacy, white, A-line dress and wearing purple rain boots on my feet, I stepped from the lower deck of Jake's—our—cabin onto the path that led down to the Sweetbriar River. Looping my arm through my mother's, the two of us made our way over river rock and gravel to where family and friends waited in two rows of folding chairs decorated with lavender ribbons and Baby's Breath. Dad's ankle was still in a cast, so she had agreed to give me away.

We paused at the head of the aisle as the music changed to Fleetwood Mac's "Songbird." "You look beautiful, my darling girl." Our eyes met and I hugged her close.

"Thanks, Mom. You do too," I whispered through the lump in my throat.

"Why do fathers get to be the ones to give their girls

away when it's the mothers who understand what they're giving them to? Marriage isn't always easy. As you know."

"I think you answered your own question with the word 'girls.' I'm not a girl this time, Mom."

Carefully, she brushed away my happy tears with her thumbs. "Your life will be filled with so much joy from now on. This is right. This is love. *This* is what you deserve."

"I know."

I wasn't even halfway down the aisle before Jake held his arms out to me, palms open, waiting for my hands to fill them. "*I love you*," he mouthed. The tears my mother had so carefully wiped away began again in earnest as my lower lip started to tremble. "Don't cry, gorgeous . . ." he murmured, even as his own smiling eyes filled with tears.

The world kept turning, evergreens shifted in the breeze, and our vows rushed by, so much like the river—white lace over immovable stone. But Jake and I remained still, in our moment of peace, eyes locked together as we gazed into our future.

Want more of Jake and Violet's happily ever after?
Scan the QR code for a bonus scene!

About the Author

Nora Everly is a lifelong bookworm. She started reading the good stuff once she grew tall enough to sneak the romance novels off the top of her mother's bookshelf and it has been non-stop ever since.
Once upon a time she was a substitute teacher and an educational assistant. Now she's a writer and stay at home mom to two small humans and one fat cat.
Nora lives in the Pacific Northwest with her family and her overactive imagination.

Find her at noraeverly.com

Also by Nora Everly

The Sweetbriar Mountain Series:

In My Heart

Heart Words

From the Heart

Heart to Heart

Change of Heart

Honeybrook Hollow:

Next to You

Make You Mine

By Your Side

Sweetbriar Short Stories:

Holiday Hearts

Conversation Hearts

Let It Snow

The Cozy Creek Collection:

Fall at Once

From Smartypants Romance:

Oh Brother!

Crime and Periodicals

Carpentry and Cocktails

Hotshot and Hospitality

Architecture and Artistry

Teachers' Lounge

Passing Notes

Star Crossed Lovers:

(*As Piper Everly, co-written with Piper Sheldon*):
<u>Midnight Clear</u>

Get exclusive sneak peeks of upcoming releases through Nora's
newsletter and Facebook group, The Everly Afters.